The Frisco Spiders

Warwick Payne

<u>The Frisco Spiders</u>

All characters portrayed in this book are fictitious, and any resemblance to persons living or dead is purely coincidental.

Original version produced between January and May 2002 as *The Understudies.*

Final version produced between September 2016 and September 2017, renamed as *The Frisco Spiders.*

ISBN-13:   978-1977679673

Published by Create Space, also available on Amazon Kindle

Dedication:

Dedicated to Rob Barnard, my best man, who inadvertently handed me the working title for this story when he registered our university five-a-side team under the name of The Understudies.

Since then, the same title has been used by a music band, so to avoid confusion, this tale is now known as *The Frisco Spiders*.

Acknowledgments:

Many thanks to friends and family for their continued support, especially my wife, Louise, and our wonderful daughter, Tabitha, who both generously let me off the hook from time to time to do a bit of scribbling.

By the same author:

The Portland Contract (2013)

Always Maxed Out (2015)

"Bugger."

It truly was the only word that did the situation justice. Gethin Thompson opened the shutter of the rural Sussex barn to establish what the commotion was outside. It was a fully armed police response unit equipped with assault weapons. Six vehicles and twenty officers had appeared from nowhere...and he was a wanted criminal on the run.

He didn't have long to dwell on his predicament. The first round from the bazooka sailed into the side of the flimsy wooden structure before he could blink. It destroyed half the barn, killing him instantly. Now only seven members of the gang remained.

The leader of the gang was Bryan Carlton. He'd known Gethin for twenty years, which triggered the mistake that cost his life. Usually so professional, he saw the red mist, grabbed two handguns and raced into the flaming wreckage of the collapsing side of the barn. He was nearly fifty, but his legs powered him forward, hurtling towards the scene of his death. Once he caught sight of the armed response unit, he started spraying bullets. None hit the mark, and before he took proper aim, one of the police officers returned fire with a semi-automatic.

Bryan didn't stand a chance. He was cut down in a blizzard of ammunition. His body sank to the ground. Then, for a brief moment, there was silence. It was broken by a muffled crack and a sound like a golf ball landing in heavy mud. The officer with the semi-automatic slumped forward. He was dead before hitting the ground. A single bullet was tucked neatly behind his left ear.

From the skylight in the roof of the barn, the rifle was drawn back, out of view. Behind the sniper scope was Claudia Carlton, daughter of the man laying dead some ten metres below. She'd also been seized with anger and reacted in the only way a skilled sharp-shooter could respond. As she laid the rifle at her side, her only other companion was her closest ally, Sophie Ashe. She said very little, but on this rare occasion, broke the silence.

"Did you get him?"

Claudia simply nodded and started curling into a ball with an expression of shell-shock. Revenge didn't taste sweet. Now she had to decide whether to go to pieces or pull herself together. What made her find the strength to keep fighting was that five other members of her gang were still alive. But for how long?

Claudia descended the ladder from the hay loft with Sophie following her every step. They were the only two females in the gang. The other members were Eddie, Ian, Marcus and Doug. All four were cowering behind an untidy heap of hay bales. Eddie was their electronics expert while Doug provided crowd control; Claudia realised that neither would be much help in the circumstances. Nor would Ian, their medic, who could do nothing for their fallen comrades. Only Marcus could make a difference. He was the getaway driver.

The gang worked for the Black Widows, the most powerful crime syndicate in Britain. They were expertly trained, which meant it wasn't a problem that the police had immobilised the Range Rover parked at the front of the barn, as the gang brought two getaway cars to each assignment. Hidden behind the barn was a Volvo estate. Marcus had the keys in his pocket.

Claudia led the remnants of the gang towards the rear doors. Only Sophie, who was never fazed by anything, remained calm as the rest of them fled the burning building. The air outside felt cool, despite it being a sultry evening in late May, such was the hellish heat in the barn. Marcus fired up the engine and the vehicle charged away, mowing through a field of barley.

On the opposite side of the barn, the police were oblivious to the Volvo. Its noisy departure was concealed by another round of bazooka fire into the tortured remains of the burning building. With only one road leading onto the farm, the armed officers had assumed they'd blocked the sole way out, but getaway drivers for the Black Widows treat roads as a luxury, not a necessity. Marcus was flying, rather than driving, as the estate car bounced through the rutted soil of the barley field until finding a dirt track that led into a nearby forest.

The third round of bazooka fire destroyed the rest of the barn. Had Claudia not pulled her accomplices out of the building, they would now be dead. Two of their number had been killed, but six had escaped, and once the police trawled through the wreckage of the barn it became clear the operation had failed. One of their officers had been killed, and three quarters of the gang they'd been chasing had escaped.

This is how it began.

*   *   *

Seven hours later, Claudia was on a dawn flight leaving London Heathrow. After fleeing the barn the surviving members of the gang drove to a warehouse in Slough. Run by Heathrow Baggage Company, air passengers could legitimately store goods in the front half, but that was just a mildly profitable cover for the activities in the rear. Hidden there was emergency luggage for all members of the Black Widows who might have to skip the country at short notice. Each suitcase had clothes and toiletries, and vitally, cash and a fresh passport. In most cases they'd already earned the money as the Black Widows paid slowly in lieu to prevent reckless spending. It also tied people to the organisation who could earn a lifetime's pay in ten years, which would keep flowing into their account over the decades so long as they weren't disloyal. That was Claudia's intention – to work for a decade and drift into respectable obscurity. It had not worked out that way.

As the Boeing 777 left the tarmac she studied her passport. To call it a fake wasn't doing it justice. It was equally good as an official one, chiefly because it came from the same place. While HM Passport Office prided itself on security, the Black Widows had contacts everywhere, who cooperated due to greed, fear, and usually both. All the same, the Heathrow Baggage Company had been overrun with operatives leaving the country in recent weeks, and for one simple reason. The organisation had been fatally undermined.

After collecting their luggage, the six surviving members of the gang headed to separate airports to begin the evacuation. Their final destination was the same, but each would travel alone to minimise the risks of being caught. There were rumours that police were turning a blind eye to minor members of the Black Widows fleeing Britain, and only arresting them if they dared to return, but Claudia couldn't be sure if that was true, and if she was junior enough to escape. She was certainly relieved to board the dawn flight at Heathrow Airport. She wasn't sure if the others would be so lucky.

Claudia's plane was the only one heading directly to the rendezvous point. The others were using smaller airports and would change flights in continental Europe. Being the first to arrive might sound like a privilege but she'd volunteered for the short straw. It was her job to find provisions and hotel rooms and collect her colleagues from the airport. More importantly, she'd be the first to face Homeland Security, as the gang was heading to America. Until then, she was stuck on a cramped flight for the next eleven hours, which was a major problem as it gave her time to think.

Claudia's thoughts inevitably turned to her father. He'd been the reason she'd joined the Black Widows in the first place. He'd raised her single-handed after her mother died when Claudia was just eleven. After that, putting food on the table was hard, at least until her father found a new employer. He was a mechanic by trade, and the Black Widows needed a steady supply of cars for its activities. Then he started taking part in the jobs himself, which put more money in his account. Only when Claudia was eighteen did her father admit what he actually did for a living. She could have disowned him, but was too close to him for that, and instead, went to university and – initially against her father's wishes – graduated into the 'family business'.

Now he was gone. The police gunman who shot him was also dead, but revenge left Claudia feeling hollow. It hadn't made things better, and it was the first time she'd actually killed someone. She'd never know if the policeman had a wife and children. It had simply been a split-second reaction on her part and now she had to live with the consequences. It could have caused her to break down, and if that didn't, losing her father was even more unbearable. Yet she couldn't afford to show her emotions in the confined space of the aircraft cabin. Any outburst would trigger a host of unwanted questions. She had to bottle up her feelings and hope they didn't overflow.

Having not slept overnight, Claudia should've rested on the flight but her brain was in overdrive. There was so many unanswered questions. How had the police infiltrated the gang? Would her colleagues escape the country? Would they meet again, and if so, who would lead the group? Perhaps the biggest question was what they'd do next; would the gang disband or start operating overseas? Claudia had answers to none of these questions, but knew she had to find them.

As the plane came into land, about the only decision she'd made was that something good had to come from her father's death. To simply walk away and pretend nothing had happened was an insult to his memory. She realised that shooting the police gunman wasn't vengeance but simply retaliation. Her revenge would be something far different, but as the aircraft slowed on the runway, she was uncertain what shape it would take. About the only thing she was sure about was where it would happen. She looked out of the window.

"Welcome to San Francisco," said the sign above the terminal.

The choice hadn't been a romantic or artistic one, but a business decision. The gang had contacts in the city who could help them, including an overseas operative of the Black Widows who was so talented at laundering money he was simply known as The Maid. However, arranging to meet him was far from Claudia's mind as she left the plane, as she was on collision course with Homeland Security.

Waiting for her passport to be examined took ages. She was disappointed that the security officer was a gruff middle-aged woman. She'd hoped for an unhappily married man who might take a shine to her appearance. Claudia knew she wasn't a catwalk model, but liked to look good and considered herself the glamorous element of the gang. All the same, with the events of the past twenty-four hours, she had to accept she probably looked wretched. She certainly felt that way. It was with relief, rather than jubilation, that she left the security area.

Two hours later she arrived at a dowdy motel on the city's outskirts. She'd taken three twin rooms for the gang and locked herself into the middle one. Nobody else was due to arrive at the airport until the next day. She dumped her bag on the nearest bed, the keys on the table and went into the bathroom. She'd been suppressing her emotions to the point where she could bear it no longer. She slumped to the floor, sitting next to the bath, and screwed her fists into her eyes. She then cried.

And she cried.

When she finally left the bathroom she was not the same woman who'd gone inside. The next day she'd meet the members of her team who'd also managed to escape. Then they would have to make a fresh start. There was no point going back. Her old life was dead to her.

*   *   *

The next day Claudia soon sickened of the featureless airport coffee lounge. She was over the raw grief of losing her father. Now she just felt bitter, and countless times more bitter than the sugarless espresso steaming under her bloodshot eyes. She was determined not to lose any more of her team who were due to arrive in San Francisco on separate flights. Doug should have been first but it was Sophie who appeared without a word at Claudia's table. Her eyes weren't bloodshot, but the usual cold and dead appearance under the simple strawberry blonde fringe. Claudia often wondered what those eyes had seen to make her so withdrawn, and every time she asked herself the question, she decided she was better off in the dark.

Sophie barely said a word, merely confirming her flight from Paris passed without incident. Ian also had a smooth trip and appeared soon after to break the silence. He was studying medicine, and a couple of years older than the others, who'd all recently been students at Sussex University on Brighton's outskirts. Ian considered himself more mature and sophisticated than his younger accomplices. He wouldn't be seen dead in trainers and arrived freshly groomed in a casual suit.

"How was Milan?" Claudia asked him.

"The coffee was better," he replied. Ian had the colouring to look Italian, and was learning the language. Claudia wouldn't have been surprised if he'd failed to arrive in California, but he clearly felt more comfortable putting the Atlantic Ocean between himself and the recent shoot out.

Eddie's appearance, by contrast, was best described as chic geek. His shiny metallic travel case, which resembled something out of a bad sci-fi movie, appeared in the coffee lounge and upstaged its owner. Eddie had spent much of the flight from Amsterdam agonising over whether to embrace Claudia when they were reunited. It was a badly kept secret that he was besotted with her, and an even worse kept one that it wasn't mutual. Her prickly body language when he arrived forced him to abandon his well-laid plan and he took a vacant chair, unsure whether to thank or rue his cowardice. As the group's electronics expert, he quietly retreated into his gadgets while waiting for the others to arrive.

The easy-going smile of Marcus appeared as the shadows started to lengthen. His flight from Barcelona had landed three hours earlier, but he was the first member of the gang to arouse Homeland Security's suspicion.

"That's not right," muttered Eddie. "Just because of your colouring and those dreadlocks."

"The name in my passport didn't help; Mohammed Marley," he said. "They didn't know whether to search me for weapons or weed."

"You should've chosen a better name," Ian advised.

"I did. I was meant to be Jenson Hamilton but somebody must've figured it was too flashy," said the getaway driver. Now they were just waiting for Dayfdd Lloyd Jones, better known to the gang as Doug Morgan. Yet he still hadn't appeared.

More time passed. Claudia was becoming concerned. In a way, she felt responsible for getting the rest of the gang safely out of Britain. But where was Doug? Had Homeland Security detained him, was he stuck in Europe changing flights, or arrested back home? The first two options were awkward, while the last was catastrophic. How much would he admit? Doug wasn't one of the former students but a small-time drug pusher recruited by Gethin, their recently deceased second-in-command. They'd worked together in the Welsh valleys, and decades ago probably would've mined coke instead of dealing its namesake. Gethin was the smarter of the two, and he'd been the first to die. Would more of them follow? It was certainly possible if Doug was spilling his guts in a detention suite.

As the sun began to set, the team reluctantly left their table with one of their number missing. They'd tried to phone his mobile without success. However, just when they'd given him up for lost, they sighted him near the terminal exit. Claudia was relieved to see him, then revolted when she detected the stench of stale beer. If he smelt that bad after a long-haul flight, she dreaded to think what he was like when he boarded the plane.

"I was in Germany, what did you expect? They know how to drink in those bierkellers, and I was happy to teach anyone who didn't," he boasted. Claudia now regretted sending him via Southampton and Munich, yet the Bavarian flight had arrived six hours earlier.

"They wouldn't let me board the bloody thing," he admitted. "I had to get a train to Frankfurt and try my luck there."

Claudia deduced his luck was obviously in, even if Frankfurt's wasn't. She rose to her feet, and the seated members of the team followed suit.

"So now what?" Ian asked.

"We collect our vehicle from the car park," she replied.

"What is it?" Marcus asked.

"I don't know. You haven't stolen it yet," she replied.

*   *   *

"America, where the car parks are paved with gold," said Claudia, leading her team into the airport parking lot. Countless rows of vehicles stood to attention but finding the right one wasn't easy. Marcus had been trained to steal just about anything but they needed something fast and reliable with six seats. Doug was the only member of the team who needed extra elbow room - to put it diplomatically - but that was offset by Sophie occupying no more space than a child.

"Let's just grab something and go," muttered Ian, looking uneasy.

"What's the rush?" Marcus replied, without a care in the world. Eddie then started admiring a BMW M4 until realising it was too small. The same applied to the 1960s GT beside it, which for some bizarre reason, had a tortoise for an emblem. However, it was another classic vehicle that was poised to take centre stage. Claudia wasn't a car expert but had an Achilles' heel for making a fashion statement and a weakness for retro Americana. She was gazing at a late 1950s sedan in two-tone baby pink and cream.

"That's the one," she announced, folding her arms with a satisfied grin.

"A bit conspicuous," warned Ian.

"The best disguises are always the most outrageous," she replied. Marcus, who'd been sniffing around a Range Rover, finally laid eyes on the car.

"You're joking," he scoffed, smiling in disbelief. "Do you know what that is?"

"Some kind of classic," said Claudia, who glanced at the radiator to establish its identity. "If I'm not mistaken, an Edsel."

She was too busy feeling smug to register the look on their getaway driver's face. She'd known him three years and never seen him frown, until now.

"It's a Ford Edsel," he clarified, "one of the worst cars ever made. It's a miracle it's still running."

Claudia then sidled over to Marcus and gently draped an arm around his tall shoulders, her standard manoeuvre when she wanted something from a man.

"But the question is, can you steal it?" She smiled.

"A six-year-old could, but why?"

Now Claudia batted her eyelids to seal the deal.

"Because I asked you to."

Five minutes later, after Eddie had ingeniously sabotaged the parking barrier, the Edsel left the airport. The bench seats were wide enough for three in the front and the back. Doug was wedged behind Marcus, and also disapproved of the vehicle.

"We look stupid," he complained bitterly. "Who owned this car? Frankenstein Barbie?"

"My favourite was Divorce Barbie," said Claudia. "She came with half of Ken's accessories."

"She's welcome to this heap of junk," grumbled Doug.

"Being serious, somebody must cherish this car to keep it running. They'll report it stolen as soon as their flight returns," said Ian.

"Agreed; we should dump it," said the getaway driver as they approached a quiet suburban crossroads, where he decided to underline his case. The tarmac was wet after a storm and the speedometer was registering thirty miles per hour. Without warning, Marcus pitched the hulking vehicle with its chrome-plated fins into an undignified skid past a convenience store. It swapped ends at low speed.

"Look, there's the convenience store again," he said, pointing through the window like a half-baked tour guide. Having expected the skid, he was the only occupant untroubled by the pirouette, except Sophie, who simply didn't care. Finally, once the car had stopped rotating, Marcus drove his dizzy accomplices to the motel. Once they arrived, it soon became clear that their mode of transport was the least of their concerns.

"What I can't understand," announced Doug, addressing the hastily-convened meeting in the central room of the three they'd booked, "is why you nearly left the airport without the boss."

Claudia noted he was pointing at himself.

"Who put you in charge?" Eddie asked, who found he could summon a lot of courage when Claudia was questioned. By chance, she'd been handed the room beside him at the Sussex University halls of residence, and while falling in love with the girl next door was usually a gradual process, in his case it was immediate. It finally drove him to the pitiful move of following her around, which led to him uncovering the dark secret of how she was servicing her student debts. He could have reported her, but instead asked to join her. It ensured he could be close to her, and guaranteed his silence. Recruits joined the Black Widows for a variety of reasons, but love wasn't usually one of them, especially unrequited.

"I'm the oldest here," Doug reminded the room. "You're a bunch of kids."

"I'm twenty-four," reminded Ian, "and age is no measure of experience."

"Experience?" He snorted. "Ever been inside?"

"No, because I'm not stupid enough to be caught," Ian retorted. Doug walked across to his seated opponent, towering over the medical student with his bulk.

"Ever sold drugs, instead of just snorting them?" He asked.

Ian's biggest flaw, which was known to the gang, was that he often raided the medicine cabinet at the start of his course, and gradually slipped into using stronger narcotics. He needed a reliable and safe supply, and the Black Widows were renowned as such. Their drugs weren't cheap, but they were good, and only fatal in excessive amounts. The Black Widows knew it didn't make business sense to kill their customers, especially when the useful ones could be coerced into joining the organisation to keep their secret safe. That's how Ian Haslett came to work for the Black Widows, and he'd been trying to escape ever since.

"I don't think we need a leader," he sighed. "Not if we're just lying low."

"We ain't here to hide. We're here to get rich," Doug replied.

"What do you reckon, Claudia?" Eddie inquired. She took a deep breath before replying.

"My father's dead," she said quietly, and it took every ounce of courage she possessed not to break down. "Something good must come from this."

"Such as getting out of crime," suggested Ian.

"Or making a bloody mint," countered Doug.

"Both," said Claudia, gazing around the room at her colleagues. "We should find a job that's big enough so we can leave this business."

"Such as?" Ian inquired, trying to hide his curiosity.

"I don't know," she conceded.

"She doesn't know," taunted Doug, "and she wants to be our leader."

"Give her a chance. We've only just got here," Eddie replied, before turning to Sophie, who he suspected would also side with Claudia. "What do you think?"

Her cold eyes scrutinised Doug, Ian, Marcus and finally Eddie.

"You're dumb, you're a coward, you only know cars and you're a geek," she diagnosed slowly in turn, before turning to Claudia. "There is no choice."

"So let's vote," she said, raising her hand. Eddie and Sophie gave their support. The other hands failed to rise. Doug nodded gratefully to Ian and Marcus.

"Now who wants a grown-up in charge?" He asked, raising his arm, but the men beside him were motionless.

"I'm not bothered who's in charge. I'm happy with either," Marcus shrugged casually.

"I don't think we need a leader," Ian added. For a moment, Doug was tempted to punch him in the face, but he summoned just enough self-discipline to walk away. He sank into an armchair, grumpily folding his arms.

Claudia was the leader, but knew she could only rely on half of the gang. The team was divided, they had no plan, and their money would soon run out. She rose to her feet reluctantly, then cleared her throat.

"Tomorrow I'll visit The Maid," she announced.

"I'll come too," Eddie declared. Claudia didn't refuse his offer; she needed all the support she could get. She then announced Sophie would source their firearms.

"What about us?" Ian inquired.

"Do what you like," Claudia yawned, as the jet-lag started to overwhelm her. On that note, she advised her colleagues to get some much-needed sleep.

"Might have known it was past your bedtime," muttered Doug, rising from his armchair and slinking off to the next room. Marcus followed, while Ian and Eddie headed the other way. For a moment, Claudia and Sophie were alone in the room, but then Marcus peered around the door.

"Just one question. Are we keeping the car?" He inquired.

"Definitely," Claudia replied, with a resolute smile.

"Bollocks," he sighed. "I should've voted for Doug."

As the rest of the gang slept, Marcus couldn't allow his head to touch the pillow until he'd resprayed the Edsel. It took a while and he also changed the registration plates. He was unsure if Claudia would like the new colour scheme, but frankly, he was past caring.

*   *   *

Despite her exhaustion the previous evening, Claudia woke early the next day. Dawn was breaking across San Francisco. She rose from the bed and moved a chair to the window. The view from the suburban motel was dominated by the city centre's iconic skyline. As she drew back the curtains, she turned the rear of the chair to face the window. She'd only slept in her briefs and slipped her legs either side of the seat, sitting on it backwards. She rested her arms on the rear of the chair and stared at the golden horizon. It looked full of promise, but also held great danger.

Claudia was thinking about her father. A tear formed in her eye, running down her left cheek and falling sorrowfully onto her folded arms. Three days ago he'd been alive. Now he was gone. It was not meant to be this way. Her father turned to the Black Widows to put food on the table. His plan was to spend five more years with them before retiring, but he'd fallen three years short.

Claudia's decision to join was influenced by her own financial problems, better known as a student loan. Her father had resisted, but finally conceded. At least he'd know where she was, and her talent with a rifle was irresistible. Just for light relief, her father took her to a shooting club aged twelve, but her accuracy was immediately apparent. Competitions followed, but she fell just short of international standard, which meant her impressive natural talent had no useful outlet...until she joined the Black Widows.

Her mind turned to her first job. It was relatively easy and involved smuggled cigarettes at Newhaven. The Sussex port was just ten miles from the university where she was studying. Four of the other seven members of the team were also there. Eight was the required number for fieldwork – the same as the legs on a Black Widow spider - and each team was named after its base. The unit drawn together under her father was known as the Falmer Spiders as the university campus was at Falmer on Brighton's northern fringe. The students were rookies and had to wait a long time after their training to receive their first assignment. When it came, Claudia wasn't afraid, but relieved.

The operation was designed to teach a group of smugglers a valuable lesson – not to cross the Black Widows. It wasn't uncommon for the organisation to demand a stipend from small gangs in return for protection. In this case, they brought tobacco from Eastern Europe to France and into Britain. They used the Dieppe to Newhaven ferry because it was the quietest, and least watched, route across the English Channel. However, the gang wasn't paying the full amount, which meant the overstretched customs services would soon be the least of their worries. The Falmer Spiders were instructed to dispense the inevitable punishment.

The assignment began at sunset. The team was assembled at Newhaven Fort on the west bank of the River Ouse. From their elevated position they could see the docks on the eastern side. They could also observe the arrival of the Dieppe ferry and the trucks rolling off the vessel. Claudia's father watched them come ashore until spotting the one carrying the tobacco.

The eight-strong team climbed into a pair of Land Rovers and motored down from the fort. They headed through narrow streets until reaching the one-way system and then cruised over the swing bridge. Finally they arrived in the docks, just round the corner from the secluded warehouse where the lorry was parked. The Black Widows knew the smugglers left the truck for several hours before unloading, that way, if the vehicle was followed, only the driver and the depot security guard would be caught. The smugglers only appeared once the coast was clear. Had the Falmer Spiders been ordered to kill them, the operation would have waited until the next day. Instead, as it was a first-time transgression, confiscating the cargo was deemed punishment enough. It had the added bonus of allowing the smugglers to continue their operation afterwards, albeit with a much higher stipend.

The team was now in position. All eight members would play a crucial role, and Claudia would fire the first shot. The truck was inside the building, which was surrounded by a steel fence. The security guard's office was beside the only exit, monitoring the high security barrier. It was too sturdy to ram and would have to be lowered, but first, they'd need to dispose of the guard. The first Land Rover was parked out of his view and it was Sophie that slipped out of the rear passenger door and crept silently up to the office, hiding beneath its window. She waited with her pistol. The gang had decided against smashing down the door – a better plan had emerged but it required total accuracy on Claudia's part. She left the Land Rover and took up position in the shadows. Her rifle pointed towards the office. Her right index finger squeezed the trigger.

The glass in the office window shattered instantly. Sophie wasn't bothered by the shards in her hair. In a heartbeat she rose with her tranquilliser pistol. The guard, still reeling from the blast, never saw the dart being fired and was soon unconscious. Sparing his life wasn't a sentimental act on Sophie's part, but an insurance policy if the operation failed, as the jail term for incapacitating a guard was a fraction of the sentence for murder. Claudia would have faced such a charge if she'd killed the guard, but her aim was true, and she broke the window without harming a fly.

Eddie sprinted to the office, climbing through the shattered window to override the barrier system. An electronics expert, it proved little match for him. The Land Rovers glided into the compound and the team approached the truck, the only other vehicle in the warehouse. The driver was asleep in his cab, having sealed the doors, but Marcus unlocked them within fifteen seconds. Sophie then discharged her second dart to ensure the driver's nap became the deepest sleep he'd ever experienced. He was carried to safety and Marcus climbed into the cab. Ian kept watch at the front gate while Gethin and Doug – the team's Welsh connection – verified the truck's cargo.

"Stupid pillock," Gethin complained, as Doug filled his pockets with cigarettes.

"Free smokes," he beamed. Gethin took his countryman by the scruff of the neck.

"I pulled a lot of strings to get you into this gang. Don't screw it up," he warned. Doug began to empty his pockets, but grudgingly. Meanwhile, Claudia's father directed the operation, calling Ian into the shed once Marcus had started the truck. Less than a minute later, the lorry left the depot in convoy with the Land Rovers. Five minutes later, they were cruising north on the A26 away from the coast. Ironically, they were heading towards the Cuilfail Tunnel at the nearby town of Lewes. A year later, that tunnel would witness the Falmer Spiders' finest hour. Claudia was just about to start reminiscing about it when she realised she wasn't alone.

Back in the motel room, without a word, Sophie had appeared at her shoulder. Unlike her colleague, she always slept fully clothed, even in summer. Claudia had never asked why; it was just part of the lengthy and often troubling list of things she didn't know about her closest ally.

"Couldn't sleep properly," Claudia muttered. "I haven't since dad was killed."

Sophie responded, as she so often did, with silence.

"A few years in the Black Widows would clear my debts and allow him to retire," Claudia continued. "It was never supposed to end like this."

"Who said it's over?" Sophie replied.

They both stared at the sun breaking over the skyline of San Francisco.

"Thing is, I didn't come here to make a fortune," Claudia revealed. "I just wanted the rest of the team to be safe."

"Don't mind me. I never look after anyone, because nobody's ever looked after me."

"I'll look after you," Claudia assured. "That's my job."

"Okay," Sophie conceded. "You're the boss."

*　　　*　　　*

The Maid had no office. He didn't need one. He operated from a secluded booth in one of San Francisco's trendiest nightspots. It was owned by another Brit, a young woman named Cat Trevelyan. She'd called her venue Always Maxed Out, supposedly inspired by the state of her credit card during leaner times. Nobody knew where her money came from, including The Maid. He kept out of her business and she returned the favour. In fact, the two rarely met, as he operated during the day, and she rarely surfaced until the crowds appeared after dark.

It was mid-morning when Claudia arrived with Eddie at her heels. They assumed the bench opposite The Maid whose paperwork was sprawled across the chrome-edged table. Claudia knew him by reputation but they'd never met. A simple but brilliant method allowed members of the Black Widows to make themselves known to each other. A ten-digit cipher was used, based on minutes, hours, days, months and years. By its very nature, it changed every sixty seconds but members of the Black Widows could easily work it out. The code was normally given while glancing at a phone, that way if they'd met the wrong person, it sounded like they were reciting a phone number. The Maid, on the other hand, recognised it instantly.

"More evacuees," he sighed, "there'll be no Black Widows left in Britain soon."

Six months earlier the organisation had suffered a catastrophic security breach. Police had come to learn the identities of nearly a third of its operatives, which should have been impossible. There was no such thing as a complete list of Black Widows' personnel. The organisation was split into eight sections and most operatives only knew a handful of people outside their own teams. Top commanders knew the identities of their lieutenants, but nothing further down. Even the section handling the payroll didn't have a complete list, with each accountant working a small part of the organisation.

However, one obscure accountant, now simply known as The Snitch, had other ideas. He compiled his own list, ferreting away every contact he came across during a seven-year period. He thought such a document could be useful, either to sell, or as a bargaining chip. It turned out to be the latter as The Snitch had a weakness for brothels and was picked up during a bust. To save his skin, he traded the list for immunity and a fresh identity. Detectives couldn't believe their luck and relocated him to a remote villa with every comfort imaginable. It was in rural Peru, to minimise the risk of the Black Widows locating him. However, they had to make an example of him and tracked him down inside three weeks. Unfortunately for The Snitch, it took him longer than that to die.

Further deaths then resulted from police trying to round up the operatives on his list. Black Widows rarely surrendered without casualties on both sides; the shoot-out involving the Falmer Spiders was a prime example. Police morale, having been sky-high after acquiring the list, sank lower each week as more officers were lost. Detectives were sick of breaking the worst possible news to grieving parents and spouses. The list had sparked nothing short of a war, and unacceptable levels of bloodshed. Something had to give.

The Maid, along with the Falmer Spiders, had been on the list, and escaped three months earlier. Judging by the paperwork on the table, he'd re-established himself with success.

Claudia introduced herself and recounted the story about the barn, then fell silent.

"Sorry to hear about your father," The Maid replied. He was a small man with a sympathetic face and tired eyes behind a pair of thin-rimmed glasses. His white hair was slicked back and his waistcoat gave him the appearance of a croupier at a casino that wasn't quite exclusive enough to attract the highest rollers.

23

"So, how can I help?" He asked, gently placing his hands together like a benevolent cleric. Money laundering was the first thing on Claudia's list, as there was no point committing crimes if they couldn't clean up the loot. The Maid blushed with embarrassment.

"I'm afraid in these unsettled times I'll need to ask twenty per cent," he sighed.

In plain English he wanted one fifth of the proceeds from their jobs. However, because he was a genius in transforming dirty money into currency as pure as the driven snow, it was a small price to pay. However, that didn't deter Claudia from haggling.

"As it's us, could you do fifteen?" She smiled, leaning over the table to ensure eye contact. She noted The Maid didn't break her stare, and discouragingly, didn't lower his gaze to admire her figure.

"Nice try, but I'm immune. Why else do you think I chose 'Frisco?" He smirked, before focusing his attention on Eddie and blowing a mischievous kiss. Eddie's eyes widened in alarm and he thrust a desperate arm around Claudia.

"We're together," he insisted, not with pride, but panic. The Maid studied the expression of bemused disgust on Claudia's face.

"I fancy the lady begs to differ," he smiled knowingly. Eddie's arm retreated in shame. "I tell you what. We'll say twenty per cent for transactions under ten million, and fifteen per cent above."

"Ten million?" Eddie gasped, turning pale.

"I don't want to spend the rest of my life doing this," The Maid replied. "A couple of decent windfalls and I can retire. Consider ten million an incentive. Now, what else do you require?"

Claudia said they needed reliable contacts for moving stolen goods. No sooner had she raised the subject but The Maid slipped a laminated card across the table.

"These nice gentleman will accept anything on this list. You'll notice drugs, art and jewellery are absent. The last two are a specialised market while the biggest mobs in town have sown up the narcotics trade. I wouldn't interfere with them if you savour being alive," he advised.

"Who are the main players?" Eddie asked.

"Mafia and Triads, and several smaller gangs. It's a tough city," warned The Maid, before removing his glasses and gazing into Claudia's eyes. "So be careful."

"On that subject we'll need weapons," she replied. Her team was unarmed as they couldn't risk flying with guns. Once again, The Maid anticipated the need and passed an address across the shiny table.

"Additionally, do you need visas?" He asked.

Eddie replied they were using three-month tourist visas. The Maid tutted and shook his head.

"They'll run out before you know, and emergency paperwork costs extra," he warned. Claudia immediately recognised the price for anyone counting the hours until possible deportation would be extortionate, such was the criminal underworld. However, she genuinely didn't know how long they'd be in America. Was this a permanent move, or just temporary until the heat was off? It was impossible to say, so she avoided the subject.

"One last thing. I need some documents for a car," she revealed.

"Stealing hot-rods already? You naughty girl," beamed The Maid, who asked for the details.

"Ford Edsel," she replied. The Maid looked up from his notebook in bewilderment.

"Are they making new ones?" He asked.

"It's original," Eddie clarified. The Maid's expression turned to confusion, then amusement and finally raucous laughter.

*   *   *

Ian left while Marcus was sleeping. He also left his luggage in their motel room, which he soon regretted. He'd been trying to leave the Black Widows ever since being coerced into their ranks. He'd given serious thought to vanishing when he changed planes in Italy, but a nagging sense of loyalty forced him onto the next flight. He couldn't desert his colleagues; they'd been through a lot, and for that reason, he hoped they'd see sense and disband the unit. If not, he'd feel less guilty about abandoning them and fleeing his criminal existence.

Beneath his handsome and groomed appearance and damaging drug habit, Ian was a good man. He wanted to cure the sick, but the Black Widows had other plans. Medics were essential for the organisation. Gunshot wounds couldn't be treated at the local infirmary without arousing suspicion, hence there was an underground network of field hospitals for wounded operatives. The medical side of the organisation was part of Section Three which also covered training and pensions. Ian was currently a member of Section Seven – field operations – but knew his card was marked for other duties. Most recruits served as field operatives before landing a specialist role, but the one earmarked for Ian was deeply unpleasant. Several years in shadowy field hospitals awaited, tending wounded criminals, along with the dead. When operatives were killed, the Black Widows tried to retrieve the bodies for two reasons. First, it stopped detectives asking questions if corpses vanished. Second, it meant casualties amongst the Black Widows were always under-reported, aiding morale and damaging that of the police. Then, after several years in the field hospitals, if he was lucky he'd be allowed to work in general practice in exchange for forging the occasional death certificate to make the whole wretched system work. It wasn't the life he wanted. He had to escape.

Before flying to San Francisco he'd carried out two pieces of research; first, where to obtain narcotics if required, and second, where he could find good Italian coffee. His search for the latter began at the Ghiradelli building, a former chocolate factory converted into retail near Fort Mason on the city's northern coast. He then strolled along Columbus Avenue to Stockton Street where a Sicilian café had been highly recommended online.

Ian took an outside table, ordered a macchiato, and watched the world go by. He'd already decided he was going to vanish, but had to decide when and how. It needed to be a clean break which allowed him, at some point, to finish his studies and become a doctor, free from the Black Widows. Returning to Britain was unlikely, but if he worked on his language skills, Italy was possible, at least once the dust settled. He certainly had no reason to hang around San Francisco.

And then he saw her. She was smart, elegant, olive-skinned and with hair as dark and rich as the finest espresso he'd ever tasted. She didn't see him, but he watched her cross the street and walk into the grand building opposite the café. It had only been a matter of seconds but he knew her image would burn long in his memory. He glanced at the sign above the door and took a silver fountain pen from his pocket. He wrote down the name of the building.

It was the Mezzogiorno Warehouse.

*   *   *

Meanwhile, in the corner booth at Always Maxed Out, Claudia and Eddie were draining their cups of tea while The Maid concluded his paperwork.

"Business looks brisk. How many Black Widows are in California?" Eddie inquired.

"Dozens," he replied. "Most are in Los Angeles but I oversee their affairs easily enough from 'Frisco. I prefer it here."

"The city or the venue?" Eddie asked.

"Both; our absent hostess runs a fine establishment. Where else can you find decent cider and Cornish pasties west of the

Scilly Isles? I also hear the music's superb, but I'm usually gone by then."

Claudia noted the poster above his head promoting a No Truth Told Here gig. Always Maxed Out specialised in upcoming British bands on maiden state-side tours. Now the Falmer Spiders were poised to make their own American debut.

"So if most exiles are in Los Angeles, who's left in San Francisco?" Eddie asked.

"There were four teams," The Maid revealed. "One moved across the bay to Oakland, the second is inactive, the third bungled a job and went into hiding and the fourth is relocating to Hawaii."

"So, it's just us?" Claudia asked, with a smile forming.

"It appears so," replied The Maid. "I guess that makes you the 'Frisco Spiders."

*　　　*　　　*

Within sixty minutes of The Maid providing details on where to obtain firearms, Sophie and Doug arrived at the specified address. It didn't look promising. It was a bleak warehouse on the city's outskirts with no public transport links. Doug had been forced to borrow the Edsel from a semi-conscious Marcus. The Welshman was mildly pacified by the new colour scheme of jet-black with white flashes, but the car still stuck out like a sore thumb which had been slammed in a door several times, painted green and gone viral on social media.

"Nice car," grunted the mound of hair and tattoos that opened the building's side door. Sophie provided the Black Widows' cipher, the mound nodded, and beckoned them inside. The building was on two levels. The ground floor seemed innocent enough and contained building supplies. It was only when a secret hatch to the basement was opened that the true business of the warehouse was exposed. It was an underground armoury where only recognised gangs and affiliates could acquire weapons. In

Britain, the Black Widows had twenty such arsenals hidden away, and due to local gun laws, operatives were only allowed to withdraw weaponry for specific jobs, which then had to be returned. As a result, the network was known as The Library Service, and woe betide any borrowers who returned their 'books' late.

The tattooed mound flicked several switches and lights gradually sparked into life across the basement. There was enough artillery to fight a war. He asked what they needed and Sophie, keeping her words to a minimum, reached into her pocket and produced a list.

"Two automatics, a tranquilliser gun and four-dozen darts," the mound recited. His brow then furrowed when he spotted a Smith & Wesson .44 Magnum on the list, and his jaw dropped when he read the final item, which was an Olympic-specification shotgun customised for field work. He turned to Sophie.

"Are you Claudia Carlton?"

Her reputation in the criminal underworld had preceded her. For safety's sake, Sophie was poised to dodge the question, but Doug steamed in, trying to look clever.

"She's our acting boss. We start them young these days. I'm in charge of the weaponry," he boasted, thrusting out his beer gut in pride.

"Then you'll know the .44 Magnum is the most powerful handgun we have," the mound replied. Doug looked baffled.

"It's for me," Sophie announced, without making eye contact. The mound regarded the pale and petite young woman beside him with amazement. She walked forwards, found the correct weapon and loaded the bullets.

"You know how to use that thing?" The mound asked warily. Before Sophie replied, Doug usurped the gun and waddled across to the test range, which was twenty yards long and surrounded by sandbags on all sides. Two unblemished targets awaited in the distance. He pulled the trigger and nothing happened.

"Safety catch," the mound sighed. Doug fumbled around for a few seconds then took aim again. The first chamber sparked and the firing range shook to the noise of a deafening boom. The kickback almost knocked the Welshman off his sturdy feet and the bullet missed by miles. Sophie shook her head, retrieved the gun, planted her feet firmly and placed her weight forwards. She took aim. The gun roared again and the left-hand target was ripped apart with a hole the size of a melon.

"Not bad," the mound conceded. "But impractical for someone your size."

Sophie's stare was cold at the best of times. Now it became icy.

"If I'm forced to blow someone away, I don't want them getting up afterwards to complain," she muttered.

The mound blushed, shuffled his feet awkwardly, and asked what automatics they'd require. Sophie walked alongside him, leaving Doug to stare at the daunting hole in the left-hand target.

"It's for show," Sophie replied. "So give him something scary-looking and don't teach him how to remove the safety."

Doug was still admiring the enormous hole in the shattered target.

"Can I have one of these guns?" He yelled.

"No," the other two chorused. The necessary money, paperwork and contact details were exchanged. The Frisco Spiders were armed. Now all they needed was a job.

*　　　*　　　*

The team gathered at Twin Peaks. As the name suggested, they were an awe-inspiring pair of hills nearly 300 metres high, right in the heart of San Francisco. They were a popular tourist spot, hence the group was surprised Claudia asked to meet there, as they weren't in California for fun. The scene was undeniably beautiful as the late afternoon sunshine melted into evening light and the shadows cast by the down-town skyscrapers lengthened effortlessly over the teeming streets below. Meanwhile, hordes of tourists were buzzing over the peaks like wasps on a ripe apple. Despite that, the group found a quiet spot on the northernmost hill, Eureka, where they could sit on the grass, enjoy the view, and their conversation wasn't audible to others.

"I still don't get what we're doing here," Doug complained.

"We're on tourists visas," Claudia reminded him, "and if somebody asked what you've done, what would you say?"

He looked stumped, as if fumbling for a smart reply that wasn't there.

"Exactly," she added, "and you can't say you arrived drunk, stole a car and bought guns."

"Yeah, it's been a good holiday so far," he smiled.

"I guess we need some stories as cover," Ian conceded, "and I've already been down-town."

"Buying coffee I hope," said Claudia, eyeing him accusingly. While his drug problems were known to the others, she tried to avoid raising it in front of the rest of the gang. The only member of the group yet to arrive was Eddie, who was making purchases of his own. Scammers keen to exploit the tourist trade brought suitcases bulging with fake watches and designer clothes to the viewpoint, and Eddie had taken full advantage...or more accurately, they'd taken advantage of him.

"I've got half a dozen T-shirts," he announced with pride, showing off his purchases. It didn't take long for the penny to drop.

"Guppi," recited Ian.

"That's a kind of fish, isn't it?" Marcus added.

"No, it's Gucci," Eddie insisted.

"Guppi," Ian replied, unfolding the misprinted garment in all its glory. Marcus started flicking through the other garments.

"Tommi Holefinger, Kalvin Clean, Pravda, and I guess this was meant to be Fcuk," he observed.

"They saw you coming," said Claudia, who was fashion conscious enough never to fall into such a trap. "However, it's a good holiday story. We went to Twin Peaks, and you got fleeced by T-shirt vendors."

"Brilliant," Ian sighed. "Now we just need to screw a few more things up and our cover will be perfect. Now here's an idea, what if we actually did what it says on our visas?"

"You mean go on holiday?" Marcus asked.

"Why not?" Ian argued, who reminded his colleagues they were no longer under direct orders from the Black Widows. "We could make a new life for ourselves."

"We can't stay more than three months," Claudia reminded him, "and I'm working to a tighter timetable."

"For what?" Ian asked.

"Our first job," she replied. Her announcement sent mutters rippling through the group. Ian frowned, Eddie smiled, Doug nodded, Marcus barely flinched and Sophie didn't react.

"Who are we working for?" Marcus inquired.

"Ourselves," Claudia smiled.

"And what's the target?" Ian inquired frostily. She didn't reply except for smiling and placing a finger across her mouth to call for silence. Eventually, when the suspense was too much to bear, at least for Eddie and Doug, she finally spoke.

"It'll be revealed at tomorrow's meeting," she grinned smugly.

It was a brave performance, as truth be told, she didn't have a clue where to start. She also had no idea that, before long, they would be involved in a job so audacious that it would become legendary amongst the criminal underworld for years to come. Even the wider public would come to hear of it, given how remarkable it was.

Claudia was aiming for something big. Something truly big. She just didn't know it yet.

*   *   *

The next day Claudia needed to think, which would be easier if she was relaxed. Nothing put her more at ease than a shopping trip, so after breakfast she travelled across the Golden Gate Bridge to the coastal retreat of Sausalito, which boasted several designer outlets. Sophie insisted on joining her; while she was quiet and withdrawn, she sometimes craved human company, even if she said nothing. In that respect, she was the ideal companion for Claudia, who needed to focus on devising a plan.

The two had met at Sussex University, which amongst its sports clubs, had a rifle and pistol shooting society. Claudia was obviously the star member, having narrowly missed Olympic qualification, but Sophie was a crack shot with a pistol. Nobody knew where she'd learned to handle one; her formative years were a mystery. Even after becoming friends, Claudia only knew that Sophie's mother, like her own, died young and they'd both been raised by their fathers. However, while Claudia was close to her dad, Sophie stayed on campus, implying she didn't want to go home, or there was no home to return to, and even more troubling, the existence she'd left behind clearly involved exposure to handguns.

On that note, Sophie travelled early to the secret armoury and checked out the Magnum and tranquilliser pistol. With America's more relaxed gun laws, she felt comfortable carrying them around. Indeed, comfort was the whole point, as she didn't intend to open fire, but had to get used to the weight of both guns, especially the Magnum. She wore a pair of shoulder holsters and, being left-handed, stored the tranquilliser pistol in the right one because it was more likely to be used. The firearms were concealed under a simple denim jacket, which she could wear in the sunshine without suspicion, thanks to San Francisco's mild oceanic climate. The garment was certainly less conspicuous than

33

the menacing leather trench coat Doug always insisted on wearing to look tough. It was also lucky that Sophie was flat-chested as it meant the pistols didn't stick out, but actually provided a bit of shape she otherwise lacked.

When they arrived in Sausalito the weather was perfect, but Claudia's mind was churning away like a thunderstorm. She needed a plan but her mind was elsewhere. Shopping trips usually left her without a care in the world, but now she felt the weight of it on her shoulders. It didn't help that she was suffering a bad-hair day. Even Claudia would admit she was vain; when she looked good she felt good. Even on the bad days she was still attractive, and knew it, but she wasn't quite Paris catwalk standard. She was superb with a shotgun, but not world class. As she browsed the boutiques, she came to realise she was good at many things but brilliant at nothing, or so it seemed. She was the girl not quite pretty enough for Chanel, and the aim not quite true enough for the Olympics. Now she had to establish if she was good enough to be a natural leader.

Claudia was also now an orphan, which in so many ways, added pressure. Her tourist visa would expire in twelve weeks but she was working to a stricter schedule. Sadly her father's death – where a Black Widows operative was killed without any close family to arrange the funeral – was not unique. The organisation had a network of undertakers who provided a modest yet dignified send-off, and Claudia knew such an arrangement would be in place for her father. But he deserved better than that. She'd already decided that even if she couldn't organise the funeral, she'd make damn sure of being there. In realistic terms that gave her a fortnight, or three weeks at best. She hoped that would be long enough away from Britain for the dust to settle, but she knew it probably wasn't. All the same, her father had been good to her, and she owed a lot to him. The problem was how little time she had to concoct a 'heist almighty' before flying home. It took months, if not longer, to devise such a scheme. She had fourteen days. It wasn't enough.

To make matters worse, the group's money was running out. Their emergency travel bags contained limited cash. Food, motel rooms and hiring guns from the armoury had almost cleaned them out. They needed money quickly, which meant Claudia's visit to the exclusive outlets of Sausalito was nothing more than window shopping. She had good taste but didn't have the finances to match. Sophie obediently followed her around the shops, silently keeping her company, but still the moment of inspiration Claudia needed so desperately did not arrive. That was until she visited the Boutique Exclusif in a quiet alleyway beside the yacht-filled harbour.

On arrival, the front door didn't open. Claudia had to push a buzzer, after which the snooty proprietor appeared and inspected the two young women on her doorstep. She didn't open the door, opting to press the intercom instead.

"Appointments only," she snapped. "We're not open to tourists."

With that, she turned on her heels and marched back into the darker recesses of the store. Claudia had heard about shops so exclusive that only the 'best' people were admitted, and resented being regarded as inadequate to join their ranks. She felt belittled and humiliated. The only consolation was that the alleyway was so quiet, nobody except Sophie witnessed the scene.

"Well that was friendly," Claudia complained to herself. Sophie shrugged, removed the Magnum from its holster and started loading bullets. Claudia rested her palm on the barrel, tipping it downwards.

"No," she advised, shaking her head. Sophie reluctantly put the gun away; she seemed almost disappointed. Claudia looked back at the store.

"Boutique Exclusif; no kidding, nobody can get near it," she sighed. Claudia then noticed how quiet the alley was, and the apparent lack of security cameras. The clothes in the window were all designer labels, with presumably much more inside.

"Sophie," she remarked. "I think we've found our first job."

*   *   *

Several miles from Sausalito, Ian was also indulging some retail therapy. He'd returned to the Mezzogiorno Warehouse, the grand building where, the previous day, he'd been transfixed by the Mediterranean-looking young woman who'd glided into its grand revolving door, vanishing into the building's mysterious interior. Today he was going through the door himself.

Within seconds, Ian was in love. He was yet to find the woman but was besotted with the venue. Calling it a warehouse didn't do it justice. In reality, it was a grand department store packed with every Italian delicacy, fragrance and fashion. He wanted to live in this place. He wanted to buy everything in it, right down to the ornate décor and beautiful frescoes on the walls. Mezzogiorno, as Ian already knew, meant 'land of the midday sun', referring to Italy's southern half. However, he was bathed in a radiance of a different kind – the suits he craved, the food he coveted and somewhere in all this splendour was the most beautiful woman he'd ever seen.

He was going to enjoy the next couple of hours.

Ian suspected the woman worked at the venue. He wasn't sure where, but that provided the perfect excuse to browse all four storeys of the grand building. He stopped for coffee in the atrium, olives in the fourth floor restaurant, and browsed the fashions. He was wearing the better of his two suits, which was two more than his male accomplices had brought to America. It meant he fitted in seamlessly, but he hadn't worn the suit to blend in – it was meant for the woman he'd seen the day before. Yet, as the afternoon slipped past, she was nowhere to be seen.

Ian headed to the exit reluctantly, deducing she wasn't working that day, or worse still, was a customer and their paths would never cross again. Just as he was ruing his luck, it changed. On the last counter before the revolving door, he finally found her. She was standing elegantly behind the main perfume stand. There was no way Ian could have missed her on the way in – she must have been on a break. Now Ian had his own huge break, and had to capitalise.

The thing is, men don't usually buy perfume for themselves, even in San Francisco. He needed a cover story. Another fine espresso in the atrium gave him the mettle he needed and time to hatch a plan. Twenty minutes later, during a lull at the perfume counter, he made his move.

"Can I do something for you?" She asked.

Ian could think of at least a hundred things she could do for him, but had to stay focused. Her accent was southern European, probably Italian, but he wasn't immediately sure.

"I'll be honest, I need some help," he blushed. "It's my mother's birthday next week."

It wasn't. It was three months earlier, and Ian had barely remembered.

"And you were thinking of buying her a fragrance?" The woman inquired.

"Yes, but something new, which suits her."

The woman placed her palms on the counter and fixed her rich, dark eyes, straight at Ian.

"Describe her," she smiled.

"Dark, almost Italian, refined, elegant, and it's not for me to comment, but most men would say beautiful."

In truth, Ian's mother had freckles and grey hair. However, he wasn't describing her, but the woman tantalisingly separated from him by just a thin glass counter of fine Italian fragrances.

"An impressive lady," she smiled. "Do you take after her?"

Ian couldn't believe his luck. He knew he was handsome, and had dated a couple of girls at university but avoided anything serious. He was holding out for a woman who wasn't just pretty, but magnificent. Finally, he'd found one, and better still, she was drawn to him.

"My name's Ian. I'm a trainee doctor," he said.

"Martina," she replied.

"Are you Italian?" He asked, desperately hoping the answer would be yes.

"In a way," she conceded. It transpired she was Slovenian by birth and her family crossed the border in her teenage years, settling in Trieste. She was also a student, and on a gap year in America, working at the Mezzogiorno Warehouse to fund her studies.

The conversation was running more effortlessly than the Tiber through Rome. Everything was going perfectly. For a moment, Ian considered asking her out on the spot, but fought back the urge. It was never wise to ambush someone with such a proposal; he needed to let the idea brew in her mind like a good macchiato. If he gave Martina a few days' grace, she'd hopefully start to regret he hadn't asked her out, and gladly accept if he returned, feeling that she'd made the decision herself. Ian's plan included a perfect excuse for coming back, but there was a major flaw he'd overlooked, which was about to become painfully obvious.

Whether it was the commission, or not wishing to offend Ian's absent mother, Martina recommended one of the most expensive perfumes on the counter. Ian had to buy it, as his excuse for returning was to report back a week later that his mother was delighted with Martina's choice. At first he took the price on the chin, writing it off as necessary expense. It was only when he fumbled through his banknotes that he saw the catastrophic hole in his perfect plan.

He didn't have enough cash.

Admitting he couldn't afford the perfume would ruin everything. He had to exude the aura of a man of means, even if he was a medical student. In desperation, he produced the only thing that could save his skin – his credit card. Martina took the payment and wrapped the perfume.

"Your mother's lucky to have such a kind son. I hope she likes it," she added.

"I know she will. See you again," he smiled.

The smile was returned. Ian knew the next few days would pass agonisingly slowly, for both of them. However, his jubilation was tainted as he knew he'd made a fatal mistake. Instead of using cash, he'd resorted to his credit card. If they were being followed, it would almost certainly be traced. In effect, he'd painted a huge cross over San Francisco for anyone tracking the Falmer Spiders.

*   *   *

Returning from Sausalito, Claudia and Sophie visited a hardware store to buy the items for their first 'freelance' job. It included half a dozen high-visibility vests, which had also been essential for the Cuilfail Tunnel project, or at least, an early stage that led to the Falmer Spiders' greatest triumph. Claudia wouldn't allow herself to reminisce about that job, as it reminded her too much of her father. She thought about him constantly, but kept fighting the urge to break down as she didn't want to look weak in front of the others, especially as she didn't have their unanimous support.

At the motel, a meeting was scheduled at six o'clock. Marcus had spent the day visiting the San Francisco 49ers stadium, returning with a replica no.16 shirt as worn by team legend, Joe Montana. As the electronics expert, Eddie had conducted a spectacularly dull-sounding pilgrimage to Silicon Valley. Doug had invested the afternoon in getting drunk. He'd over-indulged on locally brewed Anchor Steam beer, and was now steaming himself. Ian was the last to return and decided not to mention Martina and the perfume. He'd also bought something else on the way back which he didn't want anyone to know about, especially the police.

On this occasion he'd used cash, but was now virtually broke, along with the rest of the gang. Ironically, it was that very reason which forced the Frisco Spiders to tackle their first job long before they were fully prepared.

"So what's the target?" Marcus inquired.

"It'll be easier to explain on the way," Claudia replied. She led the gang to the Edsel. All six members climbed aboard and the ancient engine fired up reluctantly. As the classic sedan rolled through the iconic San Francisco streets, heading north towards the Golden Gate Bridge, Claudia outlined her plan.

"Designer goods," she explained. "Easy to move, and there's a small boutique tucked away in Sausalito which looks like an easy target."

"Excellent," Doug smiled inanely, "a cosy bit of armed robbery."

"Don't be an idiot," Claudia sighed. "We'll wait until it's closed."

It was extremely rare for the Black Widows to resort to armed robbery. If it went wrong, jail terms were lengthy. However, sentences for burglary weren't so harsh, and takings were greater as more valuables could be gathered compared to the limited and usually chaotic window offered by a raid involving guns. As a result, armed robbery was usually off the menu. All the same, burgling the boutique wasn't without risk. Claudia knew they weren't fully prepared, but their cash was running out. She was also painfully aware that jobs tackled in desperation to avoid the bread line were often the ones that landed you in jail.

As the Edsel passed over the Golden Gate Bridge, Claudia told Eddie his expertise would be needed to outsmart the boutique's security system. He was thrilled; the idea Claudia needed him for something – anything – was hugely flattering.

"What do you want from me?" Ian asked warily. Claudia replied he'd be the lookout, which was his usual role unless somebody required medical attention. He nodded and stared out of the window. The sun was setting majestically above the Pacific

Ocean but the beauty was lost on him. Only one beauty was on his mind, and she'd caused him to do something really stupid that afternoon. Now he'd have to hope there wasn't a severe price to pay.

It was dusk when the Edsel arrived at Sausalito. The boutique was now closed, along with the shops beside it, but there were still lots of people milling around the scenic harbour. It was quieter in the alleyway, away from the bars and restaurants, but the gang couldn't risk being seen breaking into the store, or even sizing up the job. They needed an excuse for loitering around after the shops had closed and thanks to the visit to the hardware store, they had one.

"This is horrible," Ian complained, pulling the high-visibility vest over his favourite suit. The rest of the gang also wore them, and either brandished clipboards or surveying equipment. Claudia knew they'd arouse suspicion in an alleyway of closed shops unless they had a plausible reason for being there. Their excuse was a university geography project, mapping the street for contours and gradient. To make them appear even more harmless, Claudia issued geeky glasses to her colleagues, except Eddie, who could provide his own.

As another precaution, Marcus went to steal a second vehicle in case the Edsel couldn't be used for the getaway. Secretly he hoped it might break down, as he'd finally be rid of it, but sourcing another car wasn't easy as there was nothing nearby and his search led him increasingly further afield.

Back at the boutique, Eddie was examining the external security. He was keen to impress his colleagues, especially Claudia, but a horrible sinking feeling was gripping his soul. He didn't recognise the system. He trudged back to the rest of the gang and admitted he was beaten.

"Good, can we go now?" Ian asked. Claudia looked into his eyes and knew something was wrong. She took him aside while the others packed up the surveying gear.

"What have you taken?" She muttered. Ian fell silent and looked ashamed.

"A mix of Benzedrine and ecstasy," he admitted. "It helps when I'm forced onto a job against my will, and I figured we'd be up late."

"I won't ask where you got it," said Claudia, remaining calm, "but where did you hide the rest?"

"None of your business."

"It is," she replied, sternly. "What happens if it's found and traced back to us? Is it stashed at the motel?"

Ian nodded, looking ashamed.

"Right, first thing when we return, I want that stuff hidden far away or thrown off a bridge, and while you're at it, think about hurling yourself off."

Claudia marched back to the rest of the gang. Doug was beaming from ear to ear.

"Great first job, boss," he mocked. "What's next? Raiding the tuck shop?"

Just when it seemed things couldn't get worse, Claudia heard an engine rumbling so deeply that the ground began to shake. Moments later, a Hummer range vehicle sailed into view. Its lights were blazing, its wheels studded with fake jewels, and it was a limousine conversion stretching to some forty feet.

In shock pink.

It halted beside the alleyway. The driver's window lowered to reveal Marcus grinning smugly as the strains of *It's Raining Men* by The Weather Girls wafted from the cabin.

"What the hell is that?" Claudia demanded.

"Stretch Hummer," shrugged Marcus, nonchalantly adjusting the door mirror.

"I told you to find a spare car. This sticks out a mile," Claudia groaned.

"But when we stole the Edsel, you said the best disguises were the most outrageous," Marcus reminded.

"I know what I said," she replied, barely keeping her temper. "Just get rid of it before anyone notices. It's probably been hired for a hen party."

"Really?" Doug asked, who needed no further invitation to board the vehicle, and let himself into the passenger compartment. The rest of the gang waited outside, including Ian, who couldn't stop pacing around.

"I hope you're proud of yourself," he muttered to Claudia.

"At least I'm not a junkie. You've only been here two days and look at you," she whispered. Ian decided to make his reply audible to the whole group.

"And in two days you've sourced handguns, automatics, money laundering services and two stolen cars," he hissed.

"God bless America," Marcus smiled, running his hands over the Hummer's steering wheel. At that moment, the passenger compartment door burst open.

"Hey, there's some great stuff in here," cackled Doug, emerging with a gargantuan bottle of fake champagne. He was also carrying a box of phallic-shaped chocolates, a greetings card and a life-size inflatable man.

"You'd better read the card. I'm too smashed," he told Eddie, handing it across.

"Happy bachelorette party Kiana-Star – fifth time lucky," he recited.

"I wonder what happened the other four times," Marcus reflected.

"Well I doubt if anyone stole her ride," Eddie speculated.

"Yes, and I reckon the driver was only having a number one, so he'll have spotted it's gone by now," added Marcus.

Claudia shook her head. The situation wasn't good, or to use the technical term favoured by the Black Widows in such cases, everything had *gone to bollocks*. Most people in Claudia's position would have aborted the job. However, along with her manipulative charm and deadly accuracy, another crucial weapon was her ability to think on her feet. She'd often found that when multiple problems struck, they could be turned against each other. Eddie couldn't neutralise the security system and Marcus had stolen a ridiculous vehicle, but perhaps one problem could solve the other. Claudia looked at the boutique once more. She started to smile.

"The job's still on," she announced. She then instructed Marcus to drive the stretch Hummer around the corner and aim it towards the boutique.

"Oh no," Ian groaned. "You're going to ram it, aren't you?"

"Okay," Marcus shrugged, "but on one condition. I want to use the Edsel instead."

Eddie pointed out that it didn't have an airbag.

"I'll take the risk," he replied.

"Too slow as well," added Doug.

"I could give it a push," Marcus suggested. Claudia overruled him, and once the Edsel had been parked next to the store to await the stolen goods, the Hummer was manoeuvred around the block. Crucially, Marcus lined it up to reverse into the store. While he'd never executed a ram-raid, he'd been trained, and knew the schoolboy error was driving forwards. Reverse ramming cut the odds of the vehicle becoming wedged in the wreckage. Marcus also appreciated having thirty feet of upholstered limousine cabin between himself and the 'bang'.

Reverse gear was engaged. While the Hummer didn't accelerate quickly, it soon built a menacing head of steam. Marcus braced for impact as the others watched on from the deserted alleyway. Moments later, the vehicle smashed into the reinforced windows with a deafening crash. Bricks toppled down noisily into the newly created lake of shattered glass on the cobblestones. No sooner had that ended but the burglar alarm wailed into life. Eddie was first into the building once the Hummer edged forwards. He found the security system console. Taking a chance, he removed the fascia, snipped some wires, and smiled as the alarm was silenced. Only then could he hear the pronounced hissing noise.

"Is that gas?" Ian asked warily.

"No," Doug replied, gazing at the Hummer's wrecked tailgate. "We've punctured the inflatable man."

The air started escaping more rapidly. The hissing was replaced by a full-blown raspberry.

"How lifelike," Claudia observed.

Without wasting more time, the gang descended on the boutique like a plague of locusts. They grabbed armfuls of designer goods and loaded the Edsel's trunk to bursting point. It didn't take long with several pairs of hands, and within sixty seconds of the Hummer ploughing into the building, the getaway car was in motion. Any longer, and curious visitors to the nearby harbour might have drifted towards the commotion, but when the first few arrived, all they found was the wrecked limousine. The Frisco Spiders were already long gone, driving back towards the Golden Gate Bridge.

*   *   *

The haul from the ram-raid only fetched a fraction of the prices quoted by the boutique, but Claudia knew that would be the case. Eddie and Sophie were tasked with selling them the next day. Meanwhile, Claudia visited the secret armoury. Her customised shotgun was ready, but the underground range was too small to test it properly.

An hour later, Claudia felt the sunshine in her hair on the outdoor firing range. Marcus drove her to the gun club which had been recommended by the armoury. Claudia didn't mind having an audience for her test firing, in fact she welcomed it, as she loaded the first cartridges and slipped on her safety glasses.

Claudia specialised in skeet shooting, which involved aiming at clay pigeons fired from two 'houses' from a series of vantage points. The challenge was meant to simulate a duck shoot. She hit the first few clays but then paused. Most were only partially fractured, and only when they were destroyed in a loud crack of grey powder was she truly satisfied. Claudia readjusted the sights and a faint smile appeared on her face when she reckoned they were just right.

"Why did you quit?" Marcus asked. Until now, he'd been silent, lounging on a bench without a care in the world. Claudia frowned at the question.

"You know what happened," she replied. "I didn't make the Olympics."

"Why not try again?"

Claudia normally liked having Marcus around. He was easy company and the only member of the gang she was mildly attracted to, but she resented being interrogated. As a result, she turned the unforgiving spotlight back into his face.

"I might as well ask why you quit motor racing."

Marcus leaned back on the bench, gazed into the blue sky and shook his head ruefully.

"I had my Senna moment," he sighed, adding that the phrase was inspired by treble world champion, Ayrton Senna. Many top drivers, capable of winning titles themselves, were outpaced by the Brazilian.

"Once you face a better driver and lose, you realise you'll never be the best," added Marcus.

"Who was your Senna?" Claudia asked, loading more cartridges.

"I was eighteen; it was some lad from Norfolk called Nash. I'd won lots of junior races but that was the first time I was totally outclassed. He's on the verge of Formula One now. All drivers eventually find their Senna, except if you're that good yourself."

Claudia hesitated before she resumed shooting. She remembered the Olympic trials three years earlier. She'd finished second – narrowly – and drifted away from the sport into the clutches of the Black Widows. She no longer practised enough to return to competition. She wanted to be world class at something, but knew it wouldn't be skeet shooting. All the same, she decimated the next few clays. Marcus nodded as the shrapnel fell to earth after each blast. It seemed there was an agonisingly fine line between being a champion and an also-ran, and the latter often struggled to earn a living from their chosen sport. Claudia and Marcus had been forced to find other uses for their talents, and the criminal underworld had duly obliged.

*   *   *

Thousands of miles away, back in Britain, a powerful man reclined in a powerful chair behind a powerful desk in a powerful office. The air stank of cigar smoke and stale aftershave, and that barely changed when the door opened.

His visitor was a small man with thin-rimmed glasses and a kindly face. He could've passed for a rural vicar or the only accountant in the village. He was neither. In fact, he was reckoned to be the best in the business at finding missing persons, especially those who wanted to stay missing. Few people knew his true identity, but his nickname struck fear into those who never wanted to be found. He was simply known as The Seeker.

"The Falmer Spiders," said the man behind the desk. "Heard of them?"

"Another unit exposed by The Snitch?" The Seeker inquired innocently.

"Yes, two dead after a shoot out, while six escaped."

"Are you interested in them?"

"Not all," replied the man behind the desk. "A couple could be interesting. You can read the details on the plane."

"They're overseas then?"

The man behind the desk pushed a bundle of paperwork under his visitor's nose. The first page had a photograph of a suave man in a hand-tailored suit.

"Trainee doctor Ian Haslett," said the host, "who's either been sodding unlucky and had his wallet stolen, or sodding dumb and used his credit card while on the run."

The Seeker reckoned it was the former as the Black Widows rarely made mistakes. Wherever he was being sent, a wild goose chase seemed likely, but if the destination was exotic or fashionable, it had the makings of a free holiday.

"Where am I going?" He asked.

"Let's just say 'be sure to wear some flowers in your hair'."

The Seeker smiled.

*   *   *

There was much to digest in the dossier provided to The Seeker as his flight crossed the Atlantic. The information on the Falmer Spiders was good. He glossed over its previous leader and deputy who were confirmed dead. His main interest in them was that Gethin had recruited Doug while Bryan had brought Claudia into the fold, who'd recruited Eddie, Marcus and Sophie from the university campus. Ian had been coerced into the Black Widows separately through his drug problems, and it was the use of his credit card which had given The Seeker a crucial lead. All the same, he couldn't be sure if Ian was still in contact with the rest of the gang, or even, his wallet.

The Seeker studied the information about the surviving six members of the Falmer Spiders. They were all part of Section Seven, which handled field work, but it appeared their days in that department were numbered. Indeed, at the highest levels of the Black Widows there was talk of scrapping the section altogether as it netted a fraction of what the others generated. Section Seven had been kept alive for two reasons; first, it was useful to have a presence in the field, and second, while kidnapping and heists were hopelessly outdated, they still turned a small profit in the scheme of things. It certainly hadn't been given a stay of execution because the Black Widows were sentimental. The word was unknown in the organisation.

The exclusive inner circle of the Black Widows was known as Section One. Major decisions were taken here and the brightest talents were nurtured into the next generation of leaders. As The Seeker read the dossier he noted Claudia had already come to their attention. She was smart, resourceful, alluring and sly. Her prowess at shooting was referenced but it wasn't reckoned she had the makings of a cold, hard killer. Instead, the dossier noted she was ideally suited to seducing politicians and captains of industry to gather secrets. From there, the Black Widows could extort favours, both financial and otherwise. Claudia was destined for greater things than field work, or in the eyes of most right-minded people, much worse things.

Section Two handled the Black Widows' legal affairs. As a criminal organisation, it obviously needed good representation in the courts to defend its operatives, or at least, those deemed worth saving. However, it also needed legal eagles to advise on its legitimate business affairs.

Section Three handled training, pensions and medical care. Its name was synonymous with bleak humour amongst the Black Widows; operatives handed a suicidal mission would complain of being saddled with "a Section Three job" as they were likely to be wounded and pensioned off. Ian was destined for this part of the organisation and The Seeker noted he hadn't joined the Black Widows willingly and didn't know the rest of the Falmer Spiders before his enrolment. As a result, he might be less inclined to protect his colleagues and perhaps even sell them out. On the flip side, he was also the most likely to abandon the gang, and even if he was in San Francisco, there was no telling if the others were present.

The Seeker then turned to Marcus Hastings; the failed racing driver had been pressured into university by parents keen for him to find a proper career. To their knowledge, he had, as the Black Widows provided a legitimate 'cover' job for all operatives.

They were quietly added to the payroll of firms owing favours or protection money. As far as the tax office and his parents were concerned, Marcus worked for a dull but respectable accountancy business. In fact, he was a field operative for the Black Widows, but he'd also come to the attention of Section Four.

Section Four took care of the black market. Narcotics and prostitution formed its core business but it operated in any field where merchandise was illegal, scarce or both. Gemstones, fine art, wines and even stamps could be procured for the right price via the Black Widows. Luxury cars were also available, usually stolen in one country and given fresh identities in another. Marcus was destined for this side of the operation, which wasn't without its dangers, but cleaner than most of Section Four's activities. For instance, it hoarded lifesaving drugs, selling them to the highest bidder. The trade was morally disgusting but hugely profitable. After all, how much would people pay to stay alive? In most cases, all they had.

Section Five took care of the Black Widows' finances. It included money laundering, where The Maid had been employed, along with payroll and investments. Such were the enormous sums generated by the organisation, it needed a small army of financial wizards to preside over the cash, which not only needed to be invested safely, but smartly. Because the experts were paid by results, and handsomely so, Section Five had built a respected reputation for turning colossal stacks of cash into even larger ones. In fact, the only part of the organisation that turned a larger profit was Section Six.

On the face of it, Section Six was stupendously dull. It handled Information Technology, but that didn't mean installing computers in dusty offices. Its main activities were hacking and fraud. Its scams were infinitely more subtle than the amateurish emails begging for money on behalf of stranded relatives or offering untold riches in exchange for upfront cash. One example was hacking into reputable websites and slightly inflating prices with additional fees. The vendor still received the cash it expected, the customer paid what seemed a fair amount, but they'd used the Black Widows as middlemen without realising. The sums were nominal, but added up to billions as so many transactions were involved, making the deception almost impossible to track. After all, if two million pounds was stolen from a bank, detectives would investigate, but would you call police if two pounds was taken from your account? And even if you did, would they respond? In practice, nobody rang the authorities as the charges looked genuine and reasonable.

Section Six also made enormous sums from hacking into secure systems and selling the material, more often than not, back to its original owner. About the only organisation it didn't target was the British government, thanks to a highly secretive deal brokered between the organisations. Realising that cyber experts were the modern day equivalent of prized knights or aerial aces, the government wanted the very best minds working on security and intelligence. The trouble was, the Black Widows also wanted the same people. The deal – the only one of its kind between the two bodies – was that computer experts could work for both. They earned vast sums for the Black Widows, and themselves, via criminal activity. In exchange, they were granted immunity by working part-time to safeguard the nation from terrorists and cyber attacks (at nil cost to the taxpayer). Everyone got what they wanted, even if the whole deal stank to high heaven.

The Seeker noted Eddie Griffin was on the verge of joining Section Six. His electronics and internet skills were impressive, but needed development before he was ready to join the finest minds in the Black Widows...and the intelligence service. The irony was that he could have made a fortune in legitimate business if he'd stayed out of crime. It had been his futile pursuit of Claudia which set him on a darker path. The Seeker circled this information with a marker pen, realising it was a major weakness and could be exploited. Indeed, if he found Claudia, he reckoned Eddie would dutifully fall into his lap soon after, wagging his tail behind him.

As it stood, all the Falmer Spiders worked for Section Seven, but the only member of the gang likely to remain there was Doug Morgan...if he was lucky. The Seeker noted he'd been identified as a liability and there was talk of removing him. This was extremely grave for Doug, as when the Black Widows terminated your employment, they did not send you a P45.

Doug was totally ignorant about how precarious his situation was, indeed, he boasted it would only be a matter of time before he was promoted into the 'elite' of Section Eight. This part of the organisation had one job, and one job only. It was enforcement.

Section Eight was feared by anyone who knew of it, and the horror stories connected with its hand-picked enforcers sent a shiver down the hardest of spines. To ensure rigid discipline, the Black Widows had a zero tolerance policy for anyone who stepped out of line, such as The Snitch. The same extreme prejudice was meted out to sworn enemies. The lucky ones died quickly. Few were lucky.

It took a certain kind of person to work for Section Eight, and that wasn't Doug. It shunned those who glorified revenge. Section Eight coveted people to whom killing meant just one thing – which was absolutely nothing. Such individuals were in short supply, even in the Black Widows, but one member of the Falmer Spiders had caught their attention. Her name was Sophie Ashe.

Much of Sophie's background was incomplete in the dossier provided to The Seeker. What there was made him shuffle uneasily in his seat. Her record since joining the Black Widows was equally chilling. Her cold, efficient manner in the field was noted meticulously. In fact, the headhunters from Section Eight paid her one of the highest compliments bestowed on any potential recruit, and it stretched to just two words.

"A natural," The Seeker recited from the dossier.

The plane began its descent into San Francisco. From the sunshine at high altitude, the aircraft battered its way through the unforgiving cloud deck. A storm was brewing. Until reading the last entry in the dossier, The Seeker had been confident. He only had to find a bunch of students running scared with a token numbskull heavy. Claudia couldn't be underestimated but none of the others posed any threat. That was until he came across Sophie.

This wasn't going to be a holiday after all.

*   *   *

Things went wrong for The Seeker as soon as he landed, ironically because his flight was on time. Two hours later, by pure chance, he would have intercepted Claudia at the airport. Having tested her shotgun, she'd parted from her colleagues after collecting her share of the cash from the Sausalito job. She was alone because she was going to do something she didn't want the others to know about – she'd come to buy an air ticket.

Through The Maid, Claudia had learned her father's funeral would take place in ten days, which meant nine were left in California before she had to fly home. Acutely aware that buying a ticket online would disclose her location, she paid cash at the airport, which exhausted most of her money from the Sausalito raid. It underlined she needed to organise another job, and fast.

Another problem churning over in Claudia's mind was whether she'd be able to sneak back into Britain, and if she succeeded, was returning to San Francisco worth the risk? Abandoning her colleagues seemed a cowardly dereliction of duty, but then again, only Eddie and Sophie backed her to lead the group. Did she really owe anything to Ian, Marcus and Doug? Ian's loyalty was certainly questionable, and Doug openly disapproved of Claudia being at the helm.

Claudia needed space to think. Had she been near the airport coffee lounge, where she'd previously waited for her colleagues to arrive, she'd have bought an Americano. However, fate had other plans, as she found herself beside the terminal bar. She thought twice before crossing its frontier, but drifted over the border into the land of alcohol; she was an infrequent visitor, but when she made the trip, she damn well left her mark.

None of the bar stools were taken and the venue was almost empty. It was five o'clock – early enough to drink without suspicion – and the middle-aged stewardess served her without comment. She also didn't request ID. Claudia couldn't decide if that was a good thing; she was almost twenty-three and wondered if she'd reached the tipping point where looking older was no longer desirable. As the first sip of liquor warmed her throat, she decided looking about twenty-five was fine. That was the easiest question she had to answer as many harder ones were colliding around her brain like drunken bees in an unfamiliar hive.

Two of her problems were linked – a shortage of cash and coming up with another job. The gang had eleven weeks left on their tourist visas, but she only had nine days before her flight home. It wasn't enough time to devise a coup as complex and profitable as the Cuilfail Tunnel project. She smiled at the memory of that job, not just because of its success, but spending time with her father. She'd battled through the initial grief of losing him and now felt numb and, in many ways, emotionally exhausted. She then reminded herself that she was determined something good should come from her father's death, but wasn't sure what it would be; a haul large enough to retire was the obvious thing. Now she was back to the problem of finding the next job. Her thoughts were going round in circles.

Claudia's glass was at the halfway mark. She put aside the problem of the next job to confront a more pressing dilemma – whether to have another drink. Bourbon on the rocks was her drug of choice; wine was a tipple for soppy girls who worked in public relations. That wasn't Claudia, and when she hit the bottle, they both came off equally battered and bruised. What triggered it was usually a major mistake on her part, rather than sadness or despair. Had she analysed it closely, she'd have realised it was a form of self-harm. She chose to ignore that when she hit the bottle. It made her sick and miserable, but afterwards she felt purged of whatever had been in her system, physically and otherwise. Her approach was methodical. She never got drunk in public and chose a safe place – usually her room – and ingested bourbon until her body could stand no more. She also ensured somebody was there, which the other two times she'd done it, had been Sophie. Almost bungling a job caused the first bout and flunking one of her university exams triggered the other. Sophie hadn't been judgemental either time, as if she understood Claudia's mindset without need for explanation. Medieval monks flagellated themselves to purge their impurities. Claudia hammered herself with Bourbon. Was it really so different?

Claudia's glass was now virtually empty. It would be exhausted before she could devise another job. Instead, she dedicated what little time remained of the first drink to review the Sausalito raid. She had to evaluate the good and bad points of that job before tackling another. Her first mistake was selecting a target through revenge. Emotion shouldn't have played any part, and the job was also rushed. Expecting Eddie to neutralise the security system before he'd seen it, or at least studied reconnaissance photos, was asking too much. She'd also forgotten to instruct Marcus to find a spare car until the job was virtually underway, and using it to ram the boutique was an act of desperation when her original plan failed.

It was clear the Sausalito job was poorly conceived and executed in equal measure. Stubbornly pressing ahead with it when Ian and Doug were both under the influence was also a grave error. The more Claudia reviewed the previous evening's events, the more she realised it was a minor miracle they'd escaped with anything at all. She realised she couldn't keep relying on her talent for thinking on her feet – her luck would eventually run out. It was also obvious that while the Sausalito job was riddled with mistakes, the weakest link in the operation had been her leadership.

Claudia reached her decision. She would make herself drunk.

An hour later she returned to the motel. Sophie was reading quietly, as she often did. She absorbed so many books and conversations it wasn't surprising she'd excelled in her exams, even with a challenging background. Sophie saw and heard everything, but gave nothing away. She barely flinched when Claudia returned, and only when she heard the mournful thud of the bourbon bottle on the sideboard did she look up. A flash of disappointment crossed her face, but then she nodded at Claudia in resignation. There was nothing more to say.

*   *   *

Twenty-four hours later, Claudia left her bed. A quarter of the bourbon remained. She belatedly read the label and focused on the words "enjoy responsibly". She'd done neither, and with the bottle having served its purpose, dumped it cathartically in the waste.

Sophie was still sitting quietly on her mattress, and except for a different book and clothes, her appearance had changed so little Claudia could've been forgiven for thinking it was still the previous evening. Yet it wasn't, and she'd sacrificed a valuable day, leaving just eight before her flight home. While she'd made no secret of buying the bourbon, she hadn't shown the air ticket to Sophie, as she didn't want to advertise her departure. However, it was possible she'd mentioned it during her drunken ramblings the previous night. She remembered nothing of what she'd said, but assumed – correctly – that Sophie had contributed little besides an impartial ear. What had she told her? Once again, Sophie had divulged none of her secrets, and learned many of somebody else's. In many ways she was a valuable confidant, but would equally be an appalling enemy if the tables turned, and Claudia recognised she shouldn't take her university friend's loyalty for granted.

"I'll find us another job. A good one," Claudia promised.

Sophie snapped her book shut and took a moment to scrutinise her room-mate from head to toe. The alcohol had left her looking pale and tired. Her hair was a mess and she was dressed in the remains of the previous day's outfit.

"Have a shower, then fix your make-up," Sophie instructed. "You only function properly when you fancy yourself."

Sophie left the room without a word. It occurred to Claudia she would need some fresh air, having acted as her babysitter for such a long time. She cleansed herself in the shower, concealed her alcohol-beaten complexion beneath a Maginot Line of cosmetics, and unpacked her smartest outfit, a figure-flattering pinstripe suit. Her appearance was designed to make a statement – the Frisco Spiders were back in business.

Soon after, she gathered the team in her room. Sophie returned from wherever she'd been and Claudia started with a debrief of the Sausalito job.

"We'll need to sharpen up our act," she concluded, after running through her findings, "but most importantly, it was a success."

"And what's your next great plan?" Doug inquired, smiling sarcastically.

"We'll discuss that tomorrow. Meanwhile, we need to organise another sightseeing trip to bolster our cover," Claudia replied. In truth, she was playing for time, and even Doug was starting to see through her tactics.

"Sod this, I'm off to free some otters on the old thundermug," he scoffed, waddling purposefully towards the bathroom and slamming the door. The rest of the gang looked at each other in awkward silence, which against all odds, was broken by Sophie.

"Why did he have to use our toilet?"

"It's been through worse recently," Claudia muttered quietly to herself, not wanting anyone besides her room-mate to know about the bourbon episode. Ian then seized upon the fact

Doug was otherwise engaged to suggest the Welshman should be excluded from the next job.

"You can't rely on him," he added.

Claudia reckoned that was rich coming from someone who'd taken drugs at the scene of the previous raid. However, she responded with a different line of attack.

"We've already lost two people," she replied gravely. The others instantly recognised that one of them was her father. "We must stay together."

"I still reckon he's a stupid, foul-mouthed liability," said Ian.

"Is his language really that bad?" Marcus inquired innocently.

At that moment, the toilet door crashed open and Doug peered around it with a look of pure disgust.

"Bloody crapper's buggered," he announced, before slamming himself back into the bathroom. It was followed by the muffled banging of dangerously amateurish plumbing.

"I didn't know Doug could fix toilets," Eddie commented.

A telltale stream of water began oozing beneath the bathroom door.

"He can't," Sophie observed.

It wasn't long before the room smelt wretched. Claudia wasn't fully recovered from the bourbon and volunteered to visit reception to report the leak. On her return, she suddenly realised there was a problem. Before the plumber arrived, she had to ensure there was nothing in her room she didn't want them to see. As a result, she ordered the gang to sweep the room and remove anything suspicious.

"I had a spell on the bin lorries, so I'll empty the trash," announced Doug. At first, Claudia thought nothing of his comment, and only realised its significance when it was too late.

"Bloody hell," he chuckled, fishing out the bottle of bourbon. "Did you girls have a party without us?"

Claudia was wrong-footed but Sophie rushed to her aid.

"It's mine. I've had it a while, but didn't want it anymore," she explained.

"Waste of good hooch," Doug replied, wiping the suspicious residue on the bottle's exterior on his jeans before tucking the bourbon into his leather trench coat. Nothing else raised an eyebrow; no weapons were in the motel and the goods from the boutique had gone straight from the Edsel to the black market. However, there was one final thing to check, and when Marcus opened the toilet cistern he produced a bag of pills, powder, liquid and syringes.

"Shoot, there's enough to knock out a horse," he remarked, bringing the cache into the bedroom. This time Sophie didn't take the bullet. She had no need to, as Claudia was virtually certain who was to blame. Instead of exploding with rage, she measured her paces to Ian until they were barely inches apart.

"I told you to hide your drugs far away," she muttered quietly.

"I didn't have a chance. Ever since the raid you've hidden in your room."

"Exactly," she replied, perfectly calmly. "In my room. Not yours."

Ian realised there was no defence to his selfish actions. Deep down he was a good man, but his dependence on narcotics made him act like a totally different person. Claudia, who resisted the temptation to raise her voice, then played her trump card.

"Give me one good reason not to report you to Section Eight."

The very mention of its name made Ian shudder. Despite being on the run, technically they were still part of the Black Widows and Claudia was his acting superior. Surely she wouldn't turn him over to Section Eight? He looked into her eyes and realised he couldn't be sure. He'd challenged her authority at every turn and now his greatest betrayal had been exposed. He didn't have a leg to stand on, and needed to find a way out.

"I'll quit," he offered.

Claudia studied the bag of narcotics, which their getaway driver was still holding. She wasn't satisfied, but as the plumber could arrive at any moment, she realised time was short.

"Okay, Marcus will drive you somewhere and you can lose them," she replied.

"You don't trust me to do it alone?"

"No, I don't," she replied, "and now the others know about your habit, nor will they."

Ian glanced around the room. Everyone looked the other way. He retreated into the corridor and Marcus followed him, having carefully concealed the drugs in a travel bag. They drove to the city's outskirts. On the way, Ian reflected on his words to Claudia.

"I'll quit," he thought to himself, but he now realised he was referring to much more than just drugs. If he wanted to rid himself of narcotics, he had to escape the underworld, because the two were linked. It was time to move on, and he knew it, but leaving the Black Widows was easier said than done.

*   *   *

The next morning Claudia swapped her suit for casual clothes. She ate breakfast and it tasted good. Her system had recovered from the bourbon, her senses were heightened and her brain was sharper. It needed to be, as only seven days were left and she needed a plan to strike it rich, or at least, keep the gang afloat. On the subject of keeping afloat, their next visit to a tourist attraction required a boat trip. Their destination in San Francisco harbour was iconic, or more accurately, infamous. They were heading to Alcatraz Island.

The tourist-packed ferry departed from Pier 41. In the distance, the outline of the foreboding island, nicknamed The Rock, stood resolutely in the harbour. The gang stood in a line along the desk of the vessel. It had taken a while to get tickets, given the amount of visitors who were drawn to look around the most infamous jail in America, and perhaps, the world.

Alcatraz's place in prison folklore was founded on its harsh and brutal location. Supposedly it was almost impossible to escape, marooned on a tiny island. The water around it was allegedly shark infested and the currents so fierce they would carry even the strongest swimmer out into the ocean. However, the water looked nothing like that to Claudia as she leaned on the railings of the ferry. The sea sparkled under deep blue skies, both of which were being fed by the kind of powerful sunshine that brings out the best colours in everything the eye can see. The exception was the prison island one mile in the distance, which even in perfect weather looked dark and soulless. Despite the jail being closed for many decades, it still looked bitterly intimidating.

Claudia could feel her muscles tensing as they approached The Rock. Along with providing extra weight to their cover as tourists, she was keen that her colleagues should see inside the jail. Some of them, especially Doug, had been too complacent during the Sausalito raid. Claudia had to remind him, and anyone else who was becoming slack, of the penalties for getting caught, and in America they were especially hard. This was a country where drug dealing usually equalled twenty years in jail and many states still applied the death penalty. The police were armed and the mobs equipped with heavens knows what else in response. Just as there was potentially more money to be made, the underworld was harder and more unforgiving. Today was the day Claudia intended to make that point, and Alcatraz was the place to do so.

The gang headed towards the front of the ferry with a grandstand view of the approaching prison island. It took ten minutes to make the crossing, and for the first five minutes hardly a word had been spoken. Staring at the gloomy outline of the prison, Claudia broke the silence.

"There it is, Alcatraz, the price of failure."

"Thank heavens it's closed," Eddie replied.

61

"Jail's an occupational hazard," said Doug. "If it scares you, get out of the business."

"I think Alcatraz would scare anyone. By all accounts it's a living hell," Ian muttered.

"It's just a nick, how bad can it be?" Doug asked, casually, He was about to find out.

The ferry docked at Alcatraz Island and the gang made the short climb up to the prison. From the moment they arrived, the full horror of the building was apparent. The jail was bleak and rotting through neglect and the vicious winds of the nearby ocean. The bars were rusting, the walls were decaying, and every word spoken would bounce from one rotting wall to another in a ghostly echo. It was sunny outside, yet the prison was gloomy with faint sunlight and charcoal shadows. Despite the fact the prison had closed decades earlier it was still easily identifiable as a true house of pain where the term 'correctional facility' was a mere whitewash for a mental and physical torture chamber.

The gang were at the end of B Wing, staring at the cells along a corridor that seemed to stretch into the grim distance without an end in sight. Their pale complexions told a story. This was hell on Earth. All of them were welded to the spot as they studied their surroundings in silent horror. There wasn't a word. There wasn't a sound. Eventually, the silence was too much to bear.

"This is bad," Doug conceded.

The group started to pace along the cold, cracked flooring of B Wing. Every prison cell they passed was given a glance by one of the team, sometimes a brief look, or in other cases a prolonged stare. The harsh conditions were evident for all to see.

"Look at this place, it would break a man in twenty-four hours." declared Ian, staring into the endless line of iron bars.

"That's what it was built for," Claudia replied. "These walls have crushed more spirits than any cosy English jail. Over here, prison is something to avoid at all cost."

"Like it wasn't back home?" Doug snubbed.

"This isn't like home," reminded Claudia. "Here the prison system means hard reform. You'll struggle to find tougher criminals anywhere else in the world, so the jails have to be harder to break them down."

"The penalties in Britain seemed harsh enough," Eddie commented.

"They were," agreed Claudia. "But here it's tougher. America may be a land of opportunity but while the rewards are higher, so are the penalties for failure."

Getting arrested in Britain was calamitous, but the consequences were usually bearable. It was also much easier if you had the protection of the Black Widows. Those who stayed loyal to the organisation behind bars were always taken care of well, in contrast to those who told the police too much, who were simply taken care of. For a Black Widows operative stuck in a British jail, life wasn't horrific or frightening, it was merely dull and frustrating. Yet without that level of protection in an American jail, every day would be a struggle for survival.

Claudia stopped in the corridor and gazed into one of the cells. The rest of the gang joined her and stared at the dark flooring, which was rough and cold. The bed was bare and rusting, the shelving chipped and rotting; it looked more like torture equipment than furniture. The cell was small and squalid, not much larger than a kitchen table. Surely nobody could stomach two months of this, let alone two years or two decades. The only comfort was that no jail was likely to be as brutal as Alcatraz, but the gang was in no mood to put that theory to the test.

When the gang emerged from the prison building, hardly a word was spoken. All of them wanted to leave the island but they would have to wait for the next ferry. They headed to the picnic area, which looked back towards San Francisco. That something as horrific as Alcatraz could be so close to an iconic holiday destination beggared belief. When the weather was calm, you could hear the bustling and cheerful sounds of the city drifting across the bay. What torture it must have been to hear and see the normal world in the distance, and been so far removed from its clutches.

The gang draped themselves in an untidy formation across two picnic benches. It didn't matter as nobody else was there; it was only eleven o'clock and those intending to have lunch in the picnic area wouldn't arrive for at least another hour. Claudia knew the visit to Alcatraz had weakened the team's morale, but in the long run, it was necessary. Marcus was often too laid back and Doug certainly needed a wake-up call. She pitied Eddie, who didn't need to see inside America's most infamous jail to grasp what was at stake. Sophie certainly understood, but was bulletproof enough to stomach the trip without sugar-coating. Ian also knew the risks, and Claudia recognised his nerves were hanging by a thread. The previous day she'd told him they needed to stay together, but she already suspected Ian was destined to quit. The only question was when he'd leave, and if he'd take anyone with him.

Doug took one final glance at the jail before they left the picnic area and walked to the ferry.

"I'm damned if I'm ending up in a joint like that," he announced, rising awkwardly to his feet.

If Claudia had achieved nothing else that morning, she'd reminded Doug that life outside the law wasn't a joke, but deadly serious.

The gang boarded the ferry without a word. Claudia could tell they were grateful to leave Alcatraz, and looking forward to returning to the warmth and freedom of San Francisco. Claudia found herself at the front of the vessel and was admiring the view when a dangerous thought crossed her mind. She was running desperately short of cash and her ticket to Alcatraz was steeper than she'd hoped, indeed, all her colleagues had grumbled at the cost, especially as none of them really wanted to go. She estimated the number of people on the vessel, and crucially how many paid cash for their tickets. She multiplied the result by the number of daily sailings. A large figure dared to suggest itself.

Claudia had noticed on boarding the vessel that a new company had recently taken over its operation, which was a virtually meaningless fact to any typical tourist. However, Claudia wondered if it presented an opportunity. Had the incoming firm's security been properly tested yet? As the ferry docked beside Pier 41, Claudia's fascination continued to grow. Such a raid was unlikely to net a king's ransom, but potentially enough to tide the gang over until she returned to San Francisco…assuming she was coming back.

On returning to the ferry office, Claudia was in no rush to leave. She captured a few images on her phone, which she then passed to Eddie.

"Can you take my picture?" She inquired. Eddie didn't need to be asked twice. He could've taken photos of Claudia all day. He only regretted she was wearing so much. After checking the first couple, Claudia said she wasn't satisfied, and asked for a couple more from a different angle. Eddie reckoned she looked perfect in the first images, but didn't mind as it was a good excuse to take more. It was just a shame they would be on her phone, not his own.

"Those are fine," she nodded, checking the second batch of pictures.

To complete their sightseeing, the gang headed to Fisherman's Wharf to board one of San Francisco's famous cable cars. Such was their popularity, there was an extensive queue to board them, regardless of your intended destination. Doug had never been noted for his patience and muscled his way through the tourists like a human snowplough with his colleagues in tow. As a result, they boarded a service much sooner than if they'd waited politely. Claudia reminded herself that for all Doug's failings, he could be useful at times.

The cable car was busier than the last helicopters out of Saigon and it seemed a miracle that the ageing machine could haul itself up San Francisco's brutal gradients. Perhaps it was no surprise that it didn't move rapidly uphill. The steady progress allowed the gang to admire the view, and in the case of Ian, gaze over the shoulder of a hopelessly outnumbered commuter reading a copy of the *San Francisco Chronicle*. Always curious about the news, Ian scanned the two pages he could see, and something caught his eye.

"Police offer Black Widows amnesty," was the headline.

The commuter turned the page before Ian could read the story. Frustrated, he turned to his colleagues and said they needed a copy of the *Chronicle* without delay. Without asking why, Doug set about finding one, and had no intention of troubling a shopkeeper in the process. The first copy he came across was the one being read by the commuter. He inquired, in no uncertain terms, if he might have the copy. The commuter wasn't in a mood to be persuaded.

However, Doug could be very persuasive at times.

He returned to his colleagues with ninety-eight per cent of a slightly ripped newspaper and some coarse feedback from the commuter. Claudia shook her head. Doug had to stop committing needless crimes, even if it was just stealing newspapers. The grim lesson of Alcatraz had either worn off, or was yet to sink in.

"What's so important about this paper?" Eddie asked. Ian snatched the copy and rifled through the pages until he found the crucial story. Above the traffic noise and the jolts and bumps of the historic cable car, Ian read the article.

"Police offer Black Widows Amnesty. Amid rising casualties amongst police and gangsters, authorities in London have offered an amnesty to members of the Black Widows. The criminal organisation, the largest in Britain, was recently undermined when an informer passed details to police exposing many of their members."

"Bloody Snitch," Doug complained. "Section Eight was too good for him."

"Police efforts to arrest those identified have met stiff resistance," Ian continued. "Eighteen police officers have been killed in the past six months, with similar casualties estimated on the opposing side."

Claudia shuddered. One of the eighteen deaths was at her hand. Another of the uncounted was her father. Ian kept reading.

"To avoid further bloodshed, British authorities are offering a blanket amnesty to all members of the Black Widows with a pardon for past crimes."

The gang fell silent. Only the clanking of the ageing cable car was audible. The rest of the article explained that the amnesty – which would last three months – required operatives to join a registration scheme, sever ties with the Black Widows and consent to microchip monitoring.

"Talk about Big Brother," muttered Doug.

"But don't you see, it's a way out," said Ian, smiling for the first time since he'd arrived. He then read the last paragraph, which outlined the only exceptions to the amnesty.

"Senior members of the Black Widows," he recited, "and those guilty of murder."

Sophie exhibited a rare moment of emotion as her mouth opened, but she suppressed the gasp with her left hand. It was noticeable that her eyes were fixed on Claudia, who turned pale when she realised that avenging her father placed her in the category of those who wouldn't be forgiven.

"I'm sorry," said Ian, looking at the two female members of the group.

Claudia wondered if he truly was.

*   *   *

The weather had turned again. Rain was battering the windows, demanding entry to the motel room. The glass held firm, but the second storm in three days confined the gang to barracks. Claudia summoned them to her room, but Marcus still hadn't returned from the convenience store. Meanwhile, the remaining five members killed time playing poker. It was just as well for Doug that it was only small stakes. Ian was also struggling while Eddie was level. Claudia was slightly up, but the low-value notes were chiefly drifting towards Sophie as if caught by the gravitational pull of the other green backs nestling beside her mineral water. Eventually, and not soon enough for Doug, Marcus returned with supplies.

"Car wouldn't start," he explained.

Eddie replied that he thought Marcus had found a spare key behind the driver's sun visor, meaning he didn't have to keep hot-wiring the Edsel.

"The ignition's faulty," the getaway driver replied.

Claudia noted the problem. She didn't want the car's reliability to undermine the next job, and on that note, she started to reveal her plan.

"I hope you enjoyed your trip to Alcatraz," she said. Nobody agreed. "Our visit wasn't a coincidence. Our next target is the prison ferry office."

Ian shook his head. Sophie was impassive, but the other three were impressed.

"Knock over the Alcatraz ferry," Marcus smiled. "Kinky."

Claudia outlined her estimates of how much cash passed through the office, and the three enthusiastic members of the gang were hanging on her every word. However, Eddie then found the courage to raise a potential problem.

"What about security systems?"

"You tell me," Claudia replied, sliding her phone across the table where the poker match had been in full swing. From the debris of cards and low-value bills, Eddie cradled Claudia's phone and caressed it into life. He saw the pictures he'd taken earlier that day.

"Recognise those?" Claudia asked, striding around the table to hover above his shoulder. Eddie scanned the pictures. In the corner of each one he could see burglar alarms, motion sensors, and in the final image Claudia had requested, a bulky square object tucked neatly into the corner of the office. It was the safe.

"I recognise it," Eddie smiled. "I busted a similar one open just before the Cuilfail Tunnel job."

Claudia couldn't believe her luck, but also recognised that sometimes you made your own luck. It also gave her the ideal opportunity to remind her colleagues of their finest hour.

"Ah, the Cuilfail Tunnel job," she smiled.

And so the story began.

*   *   *

It started long ago, and came from a chance remark in a Dublin pub. An underling at an Amsterdam diamond house was on holiday and saw a girl he liked. She wasn't interested when he approached her, so he raised the stakes, implying he was a major gemstone merchant. Still she wasn't drawn, and yet, a group of four men on the neighbouring table were captivated. Their gang was affiliated to the Irish Republican Army (IRA), which was keen to augment its war chest to bring about a united Ireland. When the holidaymaker left the pub, the object of his desire didn't accompany him, but the gang were only a few paces behind. When the time was right, they bundled him into a waiting Ford Cortina.

Ten minutes later, the holidaymaker was thrown from the moving car onto the pavements of Dublin. He was lucky to be alive, but traded his soul for telling the gang everything they needed to know about robbing the Amsterdam diamond house. Wasting no time, the gang was in Holland long before the holidaymaker was due to arrive home.

The heist was rushed and unsubtle, but successful. Enough diamonds to finance a small war vaporised from Amsterdam into the underworld. The man entrusted with smuggling the stones back to Ireland was a specialist, and not part of the gang. His codename was Rabies, because every customs officer north of Calais was desperate to keep him out. Yet, as so often, he passed through the border checks without challenge, carrying his priceless loot. The IRA had confidence in Rabies as they'd used him many times before, but crucially, never with such a lucrative payload.

Rabies disappeared. Despite the IRA's contacts and resourcefulness, it took months to find him. When they did, despite all their 'persuasion', he wouldn't divulge where the diamonds were hidden. They pressed him further, but to no avail, as he died under interrogation. And with that, the proceeds from one of Europe's greatest diamond heists had been lost forever.

Or had they?

It was purely by chance that the chase resumed, and it happened in the strangest of circumstances. The second of the two Dartford Crossing tunnels, passing beneath the River Thames east of London, was completed in 1980. Rabies, who still needed a day job besides his underpaid smuggling work, worked in highways construction. Decades after the second Dartford Tunnel was built, it received an overhaul and contractors were amazed when they unearthed several million pounds of emeralds buried beneath a seam in the concrete. Honest to a fault, the engineers declared the loot, and it was traced to a heist in Antwerp on 15 September 1978. The newspapers covered the story with glee, but missed the crucial element in the case – Rabies had been the smuggler and siphoned some of the loot.

The significance wasn't lost on The Black Widows. If Rabies was in the habit of burying gemstones amongst construction projects, it raised the possibility that he'd stashed the Amsterdam diamonds wherever he'd been working shortly after the heist. The job was executed on 30 March 1981, so all the Black Widows had to establish was where Rabies has been spreading asphalt that spring. It required a few pints to be bought in the right pubs, but eventually they found the answer. He'd been hired to excavate a tunnel beneath the chalk cliffs on the eastern side of the River Ouse in Lewes to provide a relief road for the historic county town of East Sussex.

The 430-metre underpass was known as the Cuilfail Tunnel.

It was also a handful of miles from the Sussex University campus. This is where the Falmer Spiders came in.

Their assignment was to search the tunnel and find the loot. It sounded easy, but thousands of vehicles used it daily. Anyone checking the road surface would risk being mown down, and police would be alerted as pedestrians weren't allowed. Even with specialist equipment, the only way to search the quarter-mile long tunnel would be to close it for several nights running.

So that's exactly what the Falmer Spiders decided to do.

Obviously, the highways authority – East Sussex County Council – wouldn't allow any old chancer with a shovel to close one of its major arteries. Therefore, the first thing was to plant one of the team in the highways department. A temporary admin post was being advertised and Claudia applied. She was finishing her degree and it was perfectly plausible she'd want a short-term job until something better came along. As expected, her interview panel was comprised of middle-aged men. They didn't stand a chance. Claudia judged her appearance to perfection, looking smart and a picture of youthful beauty, but crucially she hadn't overdone the glamour. She could've gone further, but had learned a bitter lesson from the only time a job had failed because of her actions.

The assignment was a raid at a bonded warehouse at Shoreham Docks near Brighton. Claudia didn't need her shotgun; her role was to distract the guard on the main gate while the others broke into the rear entrance. She'd unleashed the full fury of her cosmetics, and guessing the guard wouldn't be sexually sophisticated, left nothing to the imagination with her outfit. Indeed, her father looked visibly uncomfortable when he'd seen her, but conceded it was necessary. However, Claudia realised she'd gone too far when she met the guard. She claimed to be lost and asked for directions but he looked straight through her. The guard had a face only his mother could love, and it was

71

unbelievable Claudia could be attracted to him, so the diversion failed. The guard provided the directions and sent Claudia away. She returned to her colleagues in defeat. The mission was aborted. Worse still, the job was handed to another group who weren't so delicate. They raided the warehouse, fatally shooting the guard. When Claudia found out she felt terrible. Had she succeeded in her part of the job, he wouldn't have been killed. She bought a bottle of bourbon. The rest was history.

It didn't take long for Claudia to find her way around the council offices. Her job was dull, so she had plenty of time to snoop around, flirt with the necessary members of the male-dominated office, and crucially, find out who authorised road closures. Sadly it was one of the few female managers, and most applications arrived online, but a handful of paper copies resided in a safe in her office. Claudia noted the specification and Eddie found a similar model and rehearsed cracking it until he could do it blindfolded. However, breaking into the office would be risky and could arouse suspicion, even if done skilfully. As a result, the Falmer Spiders decided upon a bolder tactic – they'd target the safe during office hours.

Claudia's next job was to find a fire alarm that wasn't covered by security cameras. She located one in the basement and, on the allotted day, pushed the button. A mass evacuation of the building followed, and against the flow of irritated-looking employees trudging towards their muster points, three individuals went the other way. Each wore a high-visibility vest, and upon the back, the words "Fire Marshal". As with most large-scale employers, nobody knew everybody who worked there, and in the upheaval following a fire drill, no security checks were made on who was entering the building. The three bogus marshals were Eddie, Sophie and Ian. Meanwhile, Claudia was outside with her co-workers, looking innocent and equally confused. Inside, the trio followed her directions to the safe. As it happened, Eddie didn't need to crack it as was left unlocked during the chaotic evacuation. Eddie wasn't totally surprised, and while he was disappointed he couldn't demonstrate his skills, the job had become easier. The trio sourced the necessary forms and left the building long before the baffled employees were allowed back inside.

Three days later, once the paperwork had been forged, Claudia smuggled it back into the building. Cracking the safe wasn't required, as completed forms were kept in a seldom-locked filing cabinet. Her job was complete, but to avoid suspicion, she would see out her three-month placement. As a bonus, she'd get to keep the wages.

The next stage was closing the tunnel. The Falmer Spiders used the name of a maintenance firm overdue in its protection payments as cover, and rang the council. When the department manager was alerted to their request to close the Cuilfail Tunnel on seven successive nights she had a fit. Worse still, checking the paperwork, everything was perfectly in order. Thanks to Claudia's research, the forged signature granting approval came from another manager who'd recently retired and emigrated. The council had no grounds to refuse.

As dusk fell on the first Monday in August, traffic cones blockaded the Cuilfail Tunnel. Inside, The Falmer Spiders set to work. Gethin, who except Doug was the only member with construction experience, led the operation. Eddie used monitoring equipment to search for cavities beneath the road. When he found one, the others broke it open, then patched the damage after it had been eliminated from inquiries. At first morale was good, but as the nights passed, frustration began to ferment. Ian was the first to suggest they were wasting their time, and before long Doug agreed, who viewed patching the tarmac as too much like proper work.

By the sixth night, Bryan was struggling to keep his troops motivated. He'd told Claudia to stay away to maintain her cover at the council, but she couldn't stand by when her father needed help. At first he asked her to leave, but relented, and Claudia took the last high-visibility vest to join the search.

Claudia made a point of building up Eddie's confidence as he continually tried, and failed, to locate the diamonds. Then at four o'clock in the morning, as Claudia was drinking tea with Sophie, sitting on the tracks of the digger hired by Gethin, the breakthrough came. Eddie found an ice cream tub beneath the tarmac. He sprinted to the digger and the team gathered for the moment of truth. The lid was opened.

At once, the grey concrete walls sparkled as the contents of the box reflected every light in the tunnel. The missing diamonds had been found.

Doug was the only member of the gang stupid enough to suggest pocketing the loot. The others knew Section Eight wouldn't take kindly to such behaviour, and they'd still be rewarded, albeit with small payments over a long period. However, with the remnants of the Falmer Spiders on the run, it was unclear if the payments would continue. It also had to be recognised the Cuilfail Tunnel job took months of planning and was decades in the making. Claudia only had a week to devise something of equal scale, which seemed impossible. However, California was a land of opportunity, and a chance would present itself. When it came, she'd have to decide whether it was a risk worth taking.

*   *   *

Back at the motel, Claudia finished outlining the ferry office proposal. Her colleagues were cautiously enthusiastic, except for Ian, who made no secret of his opposition.

"If you hadn't noticed, there's an amnesty," he said.

Claudia resumed her seat at the poker table, directly opposite the trainee doctor.

"It lasts for three months," she reminded her colleagues, "so we'll do a couple of jobs here, then register back home."

"You can't if you've killed someone," said Sophie, barely audible. Claudia nodded in resignation.

"The rest of you can register," she added, "and without regret if you've made a fortune in America."

Eddie then asked if Section Eight might start eliminating those who joined the scheme.

"Unlikely," Ian replied, though he was still trying to convince himself. "They're so overstretched they can't eliminate hundreds of operatives if they all quit at once."

"I guess they've better things to do," Marcus agreed.

"Or worse things," Sophie corrected him.

For a moment, silence descended on the poker table. Eddie realised Claudia needed support, and provided it without hesitation.

"I like the idea. I'm familiar with that safe," he said helpfully.

"Robbing the Alcatraz ferry," Marcus smiled. "It's so ironic it's got to be done."

Neither Sophie nor Doug vetoed the idea but Ian was shaking his head.

"You fools. You'll get yourselves killed," he warned gravely. He then picked up his cards and was reminded instantly that his hand wasn't strong enough. He tossed the cards across the table, which landed on Claudia's winnings.

"Deal me out," he said, removing the hand-tailored jacket from the back of his chair. He left the room. He was determined his future wouldn't lie with the Black Widows, but hopefully, with the woman behind the perfume counter at the Mezzogiorno Warehouse.

Little did the others know it, but they were destined to follow the same path.

*   *   *

The next morning Ian was gone. Claudia was disappointed but not surprised, and relieved nobody had followed him and deserted the gang. Five people would be just enough to tackle the Alcatraz job; four would not.

With just six days before flying home, Claudia hoped The Maid could to 'cleanse' some of the proceeds from their next job before she left California. The takings from the Sausalito raid were relatively small, so his services hadn't been required. On this occasion, she visited him alone, and was relieved to find his regular booth at Always Maxed Out had no other visitors.

"Ah, the femme fatale of the Frisco Spiders," he smiled warmly, as she placed her bag on the chrome-edged table. They ordered scones and cream tea.

"I might need some laundry doing soon," Claudia revealed. The Maid raised an eyebrow.

"Are you going to be a naughty girl?" He teased. Claudia smiled, but wouldn't have tolerated the comment from a straight man.

"And quickly," she added. The kindly-faced gent across the table looked sorrowful.

"Hard times?" He asked, sympathetically. "I'll buy the tea if it helps."

Out of pride, Claudia insisted on paying her share, explaining a tight schedule had caused her pressing need for cash, which was partly true. She looked inside her purse and had a shock. She'd expected to find just enough money to survive the next few days. Instead, it was filled with green backs. A note was clipped to the cash, which Claudia read under the table.

"Thought you'd need this after buying your plane ticket," it said. The note wasn't signed, but Claudia recognised Sophie's handwriting and deduced it was her winnings from poker. Once again, she'd rescued her from a tight corner, but it confirmed she'd told Sophie too much during the bourbon episode. What else had she revealed?

"Money's not a problem," Claudia told The Maid, revealing the contents of her purse. "Time's the issue."

"Indeed," he sighed. "Time's always more valuable than money because you can't make more of it. On that note, was there anything else?"

Claudia shook her head, collected her bag and made her exit. She decided against telling The Maid that the proceeds would be split five ways instead of six, as she didn't want to advertise Ian's departure, and it wasn't impossible he'd return. If so, she'd have to decide whether to take him back.

The Maid had also withheld a crucial piece of information. His only other visitor that morning had been a stranger, but a well-informed one, of similar age and demeanour to himself. His credentials seemed legitimate but he'd asked a suspicious amount relating to a particular Black Widows unit, to be exact, the Falmer Spiders. The Maid said he understood they were defunct, which was technically true, as they'd evolved into the Frisco Spiders. The visitor was so kindly and reasonable that The Maid had wanted to help, but knew in his line of business, it was wise not to trust a single soul more than necessary. He wasn't even sure if he could trust Claudia, as they'd only met twice, so he mentioned nothing to her either. Yet, there was a nagging doubt in his mind that he should have told her something, as the visitor had made an allegation that could hardly be more serious.

If the visitor was to be believed, one of the Falmer Spiders was an undercover traitor.

*   *   *

Ian's pulse was racing. It wasn't just because he'd left the Black Widows, but he was poised to do something monumental. It wasn't the first time he'd asked someone for a date, but this was different. The previous occasions he'd been a student or teenager, and it was simply a case of 'boy meets girl'. Now he was a man, and he would be asking out a woman. This was grown up, it was important, and he was nervous.

Ian headed to the Mezzogiorno Warehouse. Searching for a hotel could wait; his luggage was safe in the room he'd shared with Marcus. Whether he'd return to collect it in triumph or desolation hung in the balance. He couldn't stop thinking about Martina; she'd even entered his thoughts during the Sausalito raid. Ideally, he'd have left it a couple more days before returning to give feedback on his mother's present. However, he could wait no longer. He had to know his fate, especially as if Martina refused him, Ian would collect his bags and catch the first available flight. He wouldn't care where it was going, except that it would take him away, as there would be nothing left for him in San Francisco.

Terror and excitement competed for his attention as he climbed the ornate steps leading to the grand entrance. The former was winning, so he was secretly relieved she was taking a break from the perfume counter. He could walk off the nervous energy around the Mezzogiorno Warehouse and fortify himself with a macchiato before making his move. Touring the building, he was surrounded by sumptuous food and fashions. Settling at the espresso bar in the base of the four-storey atrium, he admired the palatial surroundings. As the caffeine took hold, blended with the Californian sunshine filtering through the atrium's glazed roof, Ian began to feel the necessary courage filling his veins. He started to believe he would succeed.

Ian finished the coffee. He strolled towards the perfume counter, looking as relaxed as possible. Martina had now returned. On purpose, Ian walked past until pretending to belatedly catch her in the corner of his eye. He drifted to the counter.

"Glad I saw you again," he began. "I didn't have a chance to thank you for that advice."

"Your mother's perfume?" She asked. Ian was delighted. Not only had Martina remembered him, but the substance of their conversation.

"Yes, maybe I should test your knowledge again for Christmas," he said. She reminded him that wouldn't be for several months.

"That's a shame," Ian replied. "Okay, let's try something else. If you were going for a date, what would you wear?"

Her warm expression suddenly became anxious. She studied Ian's features, as if trying to decide if he was alluring enough to brave the risky game he'd dared her to play. A faint smile crossed her elegant lips and she placed a bottle of Gucci Première on the counter.

"A lady of taste," Ian noted. He guessed it was even costlier than the fragrance intended for his mother, but this time he was ready. Besides food and drink and a small loss at poker, he'd spent none of the Sausalito proceeds and his wallet was bulging. He leaned a little further across the counter.

"Is that what you'd like?" He smiled.

Now it was Martina's turn to be nervous. It was obvious where this was leading, if she wanted it to, but she didn't have long to decide. Crucially, a few days had passed since their first meeting, and not that Ian knew it, Martina had also been reflecting on that encounter. Ambushing her immediately might have proved fatal, but he'd left just enough time. Martina made her choice.

"I hope you've enough left for dinner," she smiled.

"Don't worry," he replied. "I can always rob a bank."

Martina laughed – she thought he was joking.

Ian left the Mezzogiorno Warehouse feeling invincible. Golden sunshine followed him as he cruised down the ornate steps to the sidewalk. His next task was finding a hotel, and it had to be good. He didn't stop to savour the moment with a drink at the café opposite the grand department store where he'd first laid eyes on Martina. The table he'd chosen that day was occupied anyway, by a small and smartly dressed man with a kindly face who'd regularly watched the establishment since arriving in town. Even from across the street, he noted Ian's expression and the spring in his stride.

"Poor boy," he said to himself.

The Seeker left the café.

*   *   *

Around a mile from the Mezzogiorno Warehouse, three men were loitering at Pier 39 at San Francisco's waterfront. They were Eddie, Marcus and Doug, the first of which was wearing a top with a crocodile motif and the word "Lowcoste". Marcus had chosen a San Francisco 49ers jacket. However, Doug was dressed like a small-time drug pusher, undermining any hope of posing as harmless tourists.

The venue they'd chosen was plausible enough; Pier 39, which offered coastal dining and shopping, was one of California's most visited tourist spots. However, its appeal to the Frisco Spiders was its proximity to Pier 41, the location of the Alcatraz ferry office. Claudia had told them to reconnoitre the building, its surroundings, and plan the getaway. The bustle of tourists provided ample cover for the task. Claudia had learned from Sausalito that shirking on the homework, such as scoping the target, was unforgivable. She wouldn't make the same error twice, but the trio she'd chosen weren't taking matters seriously. In fact, they were halfway through a contest to see who did the best sea lion impression.

"Oaph, oaph, oaph," Doug barked, setting the bar higher than Eddie's lame effort.

Between Piers 39 and 41 floated a network of large wooden boards, garnished with around thirty sea lions. The dark brown beasts resembled overgrown slugs. They were lazing around, snoozing off their diet of fish and other putrid delights. Lounging in the Californian sunshine, aside breathing, the only thing they were doing was smelling...awful.

"Those bloody things stink," Doug complained. "I should chuck over some deodorant."

"They'd probably hurl it back at you," Eddie replied.

"No need; I smell great," boasted Doug, opening his leather trench coat and giving his colleagues a laboured twirl. "I'm a babe magnet."

Eddie and Marcus exchanged glances. They tried not to laugh. They didn't try hard enough.

"You'd be lucky pulling a sea lion," Eddie scoffed.

"At least I'm not obsessed with Claudia," he replied. Eddie was no longer laughing.

"Leave her out of this," he murmured.

"Oh, the geek's sensitive," taunted Doug. "Save yourself the grief and admit you've no chance."

Eddie knew Doug was right, but wasn't ready to admit the painful truth.

"She's given us a job, so let's do it," he replied.

"Staring at sea lions," added Marcus, who'd been scanning the area with binoculars. He added that parking the Edsel near Pier 41 would be difficult, given the lack of spaces. Bringing it to the waterfront long before the job was the only solution.

"What about the spare car?" Eddie inquired. Marcus replied that finding space for two vehicles would be even harder, so hot-wiring a nearby car ahead of the raid was the best option.

"We'll only need a five-seater now that Ian's gone," he added.

"Sodding wimp," Doug complained. "I bet he's already flown home."

The Welshman then stopped in his tracks. He heard music. It was the start of the guitar solo from *The Chain* by Fleetwood Mac, also known as the Grand Prix coverage theme. Doug stared at Eddie in bewilderment until Marcus produced his phone from his jeans, which was the culprit. Marcus examined the handset.

"Who's calling?" Eddie asked.

"Interesting," Marcus replied. "It's Ian."

*   *   *

When Marcus arrived he was convinced it was the wrong hotel. Even for Ian, it was flash. The Ritz-Carlton was a five-star venue in a grand building that opened three years after the devastating earthquake of 1906. Standing proud in the affluent Nob Hill district, it was the natural home of celebrities, tycoons and nobles. Marcus would've felt under-dressed in his 49ers shirt and jeans if he actually gave a stuff what people thought of his appearance. To Ian, such things mattered, and it was no surprise he was wearing his finest suit when Marcus found him in the regal hotel lounge.

"Won the lottery?" Marcus inquired, taking a seat. Ian replied that he could stay for five days before the Sausalito cash ran out.

"What's so bad about the motel?" Marcus asked.

Ian could've pointed to its lack of refinement, unglamorous location or the fact Doug had tested a toilet to destruction. However, he focused on the primary reason.

"I've left the Black Widows," he said. "I need a clean break."

Marcus gazed around at the prestigious setting.

"If this is going straight, count me in," he smiled.

"Seriously," said Ian, leaning forwards and lowering his voice. "Leave the underworld while you can. Two of our team are dead, and that could've been us. There's more to life than crime."

"And drugs?"

"And drugs," Ian confirmed, who reclined in his luxurious seat and gazed into the distance. "You know, it's only when you take your head out of the gutter you realise what a beautiful place the world can be."

Marcus wasn't the most observant of people, but even he noticed the smile on Ian's face and his changed manner.

"You've met a chick," he grinned.

"So what if I have?" Ian replied, his posture becoming defensive. Marcus now understood the other important reason why he'd left the motel. Ian had called him to bring over his luggage, to which Marcus had agreed, helped by Ian offering to pay for the fuel. Marcus tucked the green backs into his jeans when they were passed across the table.

"Thanks," said Marcus, "so I guess we're done."

Silence entered the conversation. The two men had no further business, and no pressing reason to stay in touch. Ian realised that along with leaving the Black Widows, he was walking out on his colleagues. Nostalgia started nagging at him like an annoying rash. He liked most of the team, even if he disapproved of what they did, and at times even Doug could provide amusing if unsubtle company.

"We're done," Ian agreed. "But keep in touch."

"Staying in town?"

Ian smiled and stirred his coffee.

"Let's just say 'Frisco's growing on me."

Marcus rose from the table, leaving Ian's luggage beside his seat. Soon after, the Edsel's keys were in the ignition. Had he checked his rear view mirror closely, he would have seen an unremarkable blue sedan hired the previous day from the airport. A kindly-faced gentleman was behind the wheel, who'd been a couple of tables away from Ian in the hotel lounge.

"So, the doctor isn't alone," The Seeker said to himself.

The sedan followed the Edsel across town, keeping a respectful distance. Marcus drove to the outskirts and the secret armoury. He was providing transport for Sophie, who'd been shattering targets on the underground firing range with the fearsome Magnum.

As the Edsel pulled up outside, Sophie let herself into the car without a word.

"Motel?" Marcus inquired, reflecting his passenger's lack of conversational skills. She nodded and the engine fired. The journey was unremarkable for the first mile until Sophie broke the silence.

"You've got a tail," she muttered.

Marcus looked baffled. Sophie added that a blue sedan had been waiting outside the building, left the venue at the same time, and had followed them ever since.

"Your trouble is you're too suspicious," Marcus chuckled. Sophie's dead eyes narrowed a fraction more. The journey continued, and as they returned to the bustle of San Francisco, the sedan was still visible. Marcus felt awkward as it appeared Sophie had been right.

"Just suppose we are being followed," he speculated casually. "Should I lose them?"

Sophie glanced towards Marcus. She didn't say a word.

"You're right," he conceded. "We should lose them."

Sophie tightened her seatbelt and waited for the injection of pace. However, it never came. Marcus pressed the throttle but nothing happened.

"This car's so fricking slow," he sighed.

"Take some random turns," Sophie advised, adding that the sedan wasn't close and might lose them as a result. Marcus turned the wheel, and eventually, the Edsel grudgingly agreed to change direction. However, they came across a stop light. Marcus was trained well enough not to drive rashly unless it was essential. Once the green light appeared, they set off, and the sedan was still tailing them. Sophie then suggested they should take several right turns.

"It's a grid system. We'll end up back where we started," Marcus reminded her.

"Which proves we're being followed."

Marcus nodded and turned right, then again, then for a third time and finally once more and back to where they'd started. He checked the rear mirror. The sedan was gone.

"Looks like you were being paranoid," he muttered. Sophie shook her head. Marcus then realised it was equally possible that his rapid succession of right turns might have shaken off their pursuer. It was probably the only way he could have done it, as the Edsel was unlikely to win a drag race.

"Shame we lost him," Marcus sighed. "We could've had a San Francisco car chase just like in *Bullitt*."

Sophie decided not to remind him that all the occupants of the vehicle being pursued in the film ended up dead.

"Careful what you wish for," she advised.

*　　　*　　　*

Ian applied his best after shave. Not much was left, which was ironic considering how much he'd recently spent on fragrance. He gazed at the bathroom mirror in his plush double room in the Ritz-Carlton. He'd tapered his sideburns perfectly, yet wondered for a moment if shaving his goatee beard the previous summer had been a mistake. Even if it was, it was too late to do anything about it; he'd just have to enter the restaurant clean-shaven.

Ian arrived seven minutes before eight o'clock. Martina was seven minutes late, judging it perfectly. They were dining in Parallel 37, the Ritz-Carlton restaurant. When Ian first caught sight of Martina, he was transfixed. She was beautiful, and yet, he regretted that her little black dress was cut too short. She looked sensational, but he didn't want her to reveal too much on a first date. Indeed, he couldn't take his eyes off her, which would compromise his plan for the evening. His intention was to make it clear that he had a double room in one of San Franciso's finest hotels, and for all her charm, Martina would get nowhere near it that night.

Ian knew that playing hard-to-get would take huge willpower. He began the evening on safe territory, exchanging stories with Martina about their formative years. Smiles and laughter graced the table as the drinks arrived. Ian chose a decadent bottle of Barolo, not because red wine suited his food, but because it suited the lady. She was ravishing, olive-skinned and her eyes were a vivid clash of pure white and richest dark brown. She deserved the finest wine, and Ian didn't care what it cost.

"Are you here alone?" She asked, as the first glass of Barolo neared the halfway mark. Ian was unsure how to reply. He didn't want to seem unpopular, but was hardly likely to admit his only friends in 'Frisco were estranged colleagues from the Black Widows.

"My friends are staying elsewhere," he replied. Ian didn't say where, but mentioned they'd met at university, which sounded better than working for a notorious criminal gang. He then avoided any further mention of his colleagues, which was just as well.

Sitting two tables away, delighted that he could dine at Parallel 37 on somebody else's money, was The Seeker. He could hear the conversation, but so far, had learned little he didn't already know. He had visual confirmation that half of the Falmer Spiders were in San Francisco, which made it probable the whole group was in town. Losing the Edsel's trail had been irritating but The Seeker wasn't upset. The moment he'd caught sight of Sophie, a chill had run down his spine. He'd scrutinised her file and knew it was unwise to get any closer than necessary. Besides, trailing Ian was much easier and enjoyable; the young doctor certainly embraced the good life, and The Seeker was able to shadow his indulgences on expenses. Arriving in California, he'd expected to end up in some dingy motel, not staying at the Ritz-Carlton. Life was good, and as less of it remained, The Seeker had started to wonder if it was time to leave his curious profession. As he pondered whether to order another glass of pink champagne, the idea of a dignified exit became ever more attractive.

Just like the Frisco Spiders, it appeared The Seeker was considering one last job before making his exit.

Back at Ian's table, the conversation with Martina was effortless. Ian had to stop his mind racing in terms of where their relationship might lead. Wherever it went, it promised a fresh life away from the Black Widows where he'd spent the last three years working under duress for the organisation that had so cynically exploited his drug habit. No more, he resolved; crime and narcotics would be buried away in a forgotten part of his life and he was going to move on, hopefully with Martina at his side.

Acting the gentleman, Ian escorted his date to her waiting taxi after their sumptuous dinner. He promised to phone her, and Martina's warm smile confirmed she would most definitely take the call. As he waved her farewell, he returned to his luxurious hotel room slightly disappointed he was alone, but more impressed he'd managed to remain true to his plan. He drew back the sheets and was soon dreaming of a whole new life.

Meanwhile, in the hotel lounge as the final cognac of the night was drained, The Seeker reviewed his notes. Ian was clearly taken with his new companion. Details about the rest of the gang were scant, but they were in town, he was virtually certain of that. The question is, what were they plotting?

*   *   *

"So that's the plan," said Claudia, concluding her briefing.

For a moment, silence fell on the circular table in the corner of the Oriental restaurant. The booth chosen by the group was secluded enough for their conversation not to carry. It was designed for six people and the empty space where Ian would have been seated had already been annexed by Doug to give his ample frame more room. Oddly enough, their absent colleague was less than a quarter of a mile away as the Ritz-Carlton was on the southern edge of Chinatown. Claudia suggested visiting a restaurant in the middle of the district for two reasons. First, it bolstered their cover as tourists, as Chinatown was one of San Francisco's top destinations, and second, she was a sucker for Oriental food.

Even though it was only lunchtime, the group ordered a feast of mixed starters. The Lazy Susan on the circular table creaked under the weight of spring rolls, seaweed, ribs, chicken satay and dim sum. The food served a dual purpose, as not only was it delicious, but Claudia had arranged some items to map out the ferry office and its surroundings. Just before midnight, they would break into the office (or chicken satay) and Eddie would neutralise the security system and open the safe.

Cash would be carried to the getaway vehicle with Marcus at the wheel. He'd bring the Edsel, while the spare car would have to be something hot-wired nearby as they were unlikely to find much parking near Pier 41. It was yet to be decided if the reserve vehicle (spring rolls) or the Edsel (seaweed) would be used for the getaway. Not that he voiced it, but Marcus had already decided whatever he stole couldn't be worse than the Edsel, which he'd leave at the wharf to amass a truly epic collection of parking tickets nobody would ever pay.

"We then return to the motel," said Claudia, pointing to an empty plate where the ribs had been. "Where is it?"

"Sorry," apologised Doug, mopping sauce from his mouth.

"Doug, stop eating the map," said Claudia. In truth, he'd targeted the ribs because it was one of the few things he could eat without chopsticks. Forks weren't available and the spectacle of Doug with chopsticks was like watching a gorilla trying to knit. In fact, he'd barely eaten more than Sophie, who seemed to exist on a diet of fresh air.

"The final thing is our cover," Claudia announced. As ever, the group needed a legitimate reason to hover around the target. Thankfully, as Fisherman's Wharf and Pier 41 were often bustling with revellers, it wouldn't be hard to slip into the crowds. From beneath the table, Claudia produced a shopping bag and handed the contents around the booth.

"What the hell is this?" Doug complained, as he was confronted with a pink feather boa.

"It suits you mate," said Marcus, wedging a glowing tiara onto his dreadlocks. Eddie joined the spirit by adopting a comedy moustache and joke glasses. Claudia explained that dressing in party gear and being cheerfully noisy, far from drawing attention to the group, would make them less conspicuous.

"Great, I can neck a few beers before the job," Doug smiled.

Eddie then asked which evening they'd target the ferry office. Claudia had picked Saturday night, as she suspected the day's takings would be good, and there would be lots of other revellers to cover their tracks. It also left three days before her flight home, and she was quietly confident she'd learned from the mistakes of Sausalito and planned the job to the finest detail.

"Tomorrow night then," Eddie nodded. "That gives us thirty-six hours to kill in 'Frisco."

This is where the plan started to go wrong.

As the group left the restaurant, stepping into the sunshine of Stockton Street, all five had different ideas on how to spend the next day and a half. Meanwhile, Ian had his own plans, and intended to lunch at the Mezzogiorno Warehouse atrium. The walk from his hotel took him through Chinatown, as the warehouse stood on its northern fringe. Stockton Street was the quickest route, but that put him on collision course with the Frisco Spiders.

When Ian saw the gang, his first reaction was to hide in a doorway. If they hadn't seen him, perhaps he could retreat and find another route. Whatever they were planning, he didn't want to be dragged into it, yet he was also reluctant to turn his back on his friends. Could he stay in touch without relapsing into the underworld? There was only one way to find out.

Ian left the doorway and strode purposefully along Stockton Street. He was noticed first by Sophie, but it was Doug who announced his approach to the others.

"Well, if it isn't Dr Haslett," he said, adding that he was looking pretty smug.

"Of course he is," added Marcus. "He's probably off to see his new girlfriend."

Ian's confident expression suffered its first dent, but he quickly regrouped.

"Caught me out," he smiled.

"So who is she?" Claudia pried. Ian didn't divulge every detail but revealed his girlfriend's name and where she worked.

"And our first date was last night," he added.

"When's the next one?" Eddie inquired.

"Never you mind," Ian smiled, and he sensed the moment had come to make his exit. Farewells were exchanged and he continued towards the Mezzogiorno Warehouse. Eddie, Marcus and Doug went their separate ways, but Claudia persuaded Sophie to join her for a bit of spying.

"You want to see this woman, don't you?" Sophie muttered.

Claudia shrugged, adding she was also curious to see the Italian designer department store where she worked. Given they had no commitments for thirty-six hours, Sophie agreed, and they started tailing their former colleague along Stockton Street. Ironically, they were so focused following him through the Chinatown bustle, they were unaware they were being tailed themselves.

When Claudia arrived at the Mezzogiorno Warehouse, just like Ian, she fell in love. However, in her case it wasn't with another person, but the designer outfits. She was already a two-wardrobe girl and predicted she'd require a whole room before long. She was so distracted by the clothes that, had it not been for Sophie, they would've lost track of Ian. He'd taken up residence in the atrium, flanked by the coffee bar and café, and was treating himself to bruschetta with olives. Claudia almost regretted having Chinese for lunch, as the food looked – as was so often the case with Italian cuisine – simple but brilliant. While Ian savoured his lunch, Claudia led Sophie around the various departments, admiring the imported luxuries. Sophie then noticed Ian settling his bill and the trail resumed. He was heading towards the exit, or so it seemed, but stopped at the perfume counter. From ten yards away, hiding amongst the cosmetics, Claudia and Sophie caught sight of Ian's mysterious new lady.

"She's certainly pretty," Claudia conceded.

"More than you," Sophie added. Claudia's eyes narrowed.

"Hang on," she countered, shaking her hair defiantly. "I could have any man I want."

"You never got Ian."

"I didn't want him," Claudia replied, which at least was true. He wasn't her type; she liked them rugged. She also felt Ian was inclined to narcissism, which ironically enough, also applied to her, but she tried to ignore the fact. What grated with Claudia wasn't that Ian was out of reach, but that he didn't respond to her charms, which meant he was outside her control. Marcus was easy to manage and she could normally bring Doug to heel, while Eddie was on a tight leash, having gladly tied the knot himself. She had no power over Ian, and he'd deserted her team. Setting eyes on his new girlfriend, she understood why.

"Okay, she's pretty," said Claudia, "but in a different way to me."

"Yes, she's classy," Sophie replied, not in jest, but a plain and brutal fact. This time, Claudia didn't argue, as she knew she was beaten. Her attractiveness was underpinned by cosmetics and showing the boys enough to keep them keen. Ian's new lady didn't have to display anything more than her flawless features and elegant fashions.

Claudia made a mental note that if she ever returned to the Mezzogiorno Warehouse she would look good – damn good – even if the make-up took all morning.

Ian's conversation ended, and before leaving the perfume counter, he glanced over his shoulder. He made eye contact with Claudia, and frowned. He made for the exit. Claudia trotted along with Sophie in her wake, wondering if she ought to catch up and apologise. However, there was no need, as Ian was waiting outside on the ornate steps.

"You couldn't leave me alone, could you?"

"Just checking you were okay," Claudia replied, sheepishly.

"Thank you, I'm fine," said Ian, frostily.

"I also wanted to see the designer clothes," Claudia added, trying to dig herself out of the hole. Ian studied her gravely.

"Just ensure you pay for them," he warned.

"As if we'd steal anything," she replied, innocently batting her eyelids.

"Seriously, if you know what's good for you, stay clear of this place," Ian advised.

"No point doing a job here anyway," said Sophie, cutting into the conversation. She added there were security cameras and motion sensors throughout the building, the store detective appeared to be armed and the front entrance and underground car park had armoured doors. Claudia felt embarrassed she hadn't noticed, but had been distracted by the designer goods and Ian's love life.

"I promise we won't pinch so much as an olive. We don't want to make trouble for you or Martina. She looks quite a catch," Claudia added, with a mischievous grin. Ian smiled for the first time in the conversation.

"Indeed she is," he agreed, "and we've just arranged our next date for Saturday."

"Second date, eh?" Claudia remarked, winking playfully.

"Don't get ideas. It's just dinner," he clarified. "Besides, Martina needs an early night. She's back here early on Sunday."

Claudia was surprised to hear that a department store would open at the crack of dawn on Sunday. Ian explained it was a special arrangement as an exclusive customer wanted to shop privately before the public arrived.

"Who is it? A pop star, an actor?" Claudia inquired, unable to resist the urge to be nosy.

"No idea," Ian shrugged. "But I'll know afterwards, as Martina's asked for some help opening the store."

"How sweet. She can give you a little apron," Claudia teased.

"I'll be having breakfast in the atrium," he corrected her, "and you can join me, if you promise not to steal anything."

Ian didn't suspect for a moment that Claudia or Sophie would accept the offer, given the early hour, but he was too much of a gentleman not to make the invitation. Besides, he didn't want to leave his colleagues on bad terms, reckoning he was unlikely to see them again for a while.

He couldn't have been more wrong.

Claudia and Sophie blended back into the bustle of Chinatown. They were still unaware they were being followed, and their movements around the Mezzogiorno Warehouse had been meticulously tracked. Sophie's subtle glances at the security systems had also not gone unnoticed.

The Seeker returned to the Ritz-Carlton, satisfied he'd learned enough to allow Claudia and Sophie off the hook. He rarely drank before sunset but felt uneasy and ordered a large scotch. He hadn't overheard the conversation on the Mezzogiorno Warehouse steps, but it looked highly likely that would be the gang's next target. Having read their files, he knew they couldn't be underestimated, but he also knew the significance of the warehouse.

"It'll be a massacre," he sighed to himself, and began to drink…heavily.

*   *   *

Friday night passed without incident. On Saturday, Claudia and Sophie tested their firearms while Marcus and Doug watched the San Francisco Giants playing baseball. Eddie made another dull-sounding trip to Silicon Valley. All were killing time ahead of the main event of the day - raiding the Alcatraz ferry office.

It was at ten o'clock that night, when the group met in Claudia's motel room, that she realised there was a big problem. It was about twenty stone, called Doug, and it was pissed.

"How much have you had?" She asked.

"A few beers at the baseball," he slurred. "Oh, and Sophie's unwanted bourbon."

He extracted the empty bottle from his leather trench coat and dumped it clumsily in the bin. Claudia glared at its label, ruing the day she'd bought the damn stuff. Its purchase had been triggered by reflecting on her mistakes at Sausalito; now a further job now hung in the balance, along with another pivotal decision. She had to choose whether to leave Doug behind, risk bringing him along, or to postpone the operation. She made her decision based on the Sausalito raid almost failing because it was rushed.

"Go to bed, Doug," she ordered.

"What?" He exploded.

"Isn't he going?" Eddie asked.

"None of us are," Claudia replied, adding they'd strike early the next morning instead. She was taking a risk, as they knew from monitoring the office that security vans didn't visit during the evenings, but it was possible they came at dawn and the safe would be empty. However, it struck Claudia as a lesser gamble than tackling a raid when Doug was drunk…again.

"I need every pair of hands for this job, and they must be steady hands," she said, throwing an accusing glance at Doug. "Now get some sleep. We've got an early start."

The male members of the gang started to disperse grumpily, but before leaving, Doug noticed Claudia was putting on her jacket.

"Hang on, what gives you the right to go partying?" He asked.

Claudia stopped in her tracks and took a deep breath to prevent her temper boiling over.

"Somebody has to find a shop that's still open to buy alternative disguises," she explained. Doug suddenly looked hurt.

"Don't I get to wear the pink feather boa?" He inquired, with disappointment.

"Get to bed," Claudia spelt out coldly.

Doug retreated to his room. Given his alcohol intake, he was soon snoring, but sleep didn't come easily to the others. Some were tense, some were worried, and all were full of adrenaline. They knew the next day would be hard, but none of them could possibly have known just how hard it would be. In fact, it would be the toughest day of their lives.

*   *   *

Dawn broke over San Francisco. Ian drew back the pristine covers of his queen-size bed at the Ritz-Carlton. The bedding had magical qualities which meant it looked untouched and smelt of alpine flowers even after a good night's sleep. Saying that, he'd only managed six hours as the second date with Martina had been wonderful and neither had wanted the evening to end. Once more, he'd returned to his room alone, but dared to dream it might be different on his final night at the hotel. That would be Tuesday, so he had more than two days, and the prospect of seeing Martina again that morning filled his veins with a wonderful wholesome joy. There was a world outside the Black Widows, which he was truly savouring.

However, this would be the day when his past caught up with him.

While Ian dressed in his palatial bedroom, Claudia was three miles away, dragging herself from a motel bed and feeling wretched. She'd had a lousy night's sleep. Sophie had clearly woken early and was sitting on her bed, re-reading the Magnum's instruction booklet.

"Most people wouldn't bother doing that," Claudia muttered.

"I'm not most people," Sophie replied, without lifting her gaze. Claudia threw on a dressing gown, grabbed a shopping bag, then left the room and knocked on the neighbouring door. Eddie answered it, having also slept very little after spending the early hours playing online chess with a Peruvian insomniac who'd routed him. Inside the room, Claudia heard pig-like snoring.

"No need to ask if Doug's awake," she yawned, filing past Eddie towards the occupied bed. She forced her heel into Doug's side until he stirred.

"Here's your disguise," she said, casting clothes from her bag onto Doug's torso. When his bleary eyes tried to focus, the first word he saw was "coach".

"What's this?" He croaked.

"We're posing as a running club. You're the trainer," she replied, casually tossing an old-fashioned stopwatch into his lap. Doug wasn't awake enough to understand and cupped his mighty hands over his stubbly bloated face.

"My head," he groaned. "It feels like it's been in a rugby scrum."

"Then take some pills. There's work to do," Claudia replied, and issued Eddie with his outfit, before doing the same with Marcus, who opened his door looking tired but better than the others. Claudia then returned to her room and unwrapped her outfit. She had to admit she looked fitter than she was and only troubled the gym when she needed to tone up rather than boost her strength or stamina. All the same, even if she was in running gear, she wanted to look good. It was no accident she'd bought neutral colours for her colleagues but her own outfit was cherry with cream flashes and boasted Lyrca and padding in all the right places. She refused to put up her hair; an Alice band was as far as she'd compromise, and she'd factored twenty minutes into her schedule to apply make-up. Sophie watched the operation without comment but Claudia knew she disapproved. The longer it took to reach the ferry office, the greater the risk that the safe would've been emptied, which meant every minute mattered.

As it happened, Claudia took just as long to arrive at the Edsel as Doug. He'd strung the stopwatch around his neck, but his refusal to relinquish his trench coat and the overt stench of stale booze undermined his cover. The rest looked okay as Marcus could pass for a sprinter, Eddie for middle-distance and Sophie was tailor-made for distance running. Claudia was sitting in the front of the car with Marcus. She turned around to check on the others in the back. She lifted her right hand above the bench seat. Sophie was the first to recognise the gesture and placed her hand over that of her friend, and the others soon followed.

"The Frisco Spiders," said Claudia.

"The Frisco Spiders," the other chorused. The hands were withdrawn and the engine fired. Marcus drove away from the motel. As he did so, Claudia suddenly realised it was possible they might never return.

*   *   *

There was a spring in Ian's stride, heading along Stockton Street from the southern end of Chinatown to its northern boundary and the Mezzogiorno Warehouse. Few people were around to enjoy the early morning air. The skies were blue and Ian could sense it would be a good day. He planned to help Martina with her extra shift, after which, they'd have the afternoon together. Wine tasting in the Napa Valley struck him as a fine way to spend it, and then a romantic dinner back in San Francisco. He didn't feel like starched linen and silver service this time; his mind was turning towards a cosy candlelit bistro where none of the quirky wooden tables matched. It had all the makings of a perfect day.

It was not meant to be.

Across town, the remaining Frisco Spiders collected weapons from the secret armoury. Claudia didn't expect her customised shotgun would be needed, but she brought it anyway. The Edsel then rolled through town, its occupants virtually silent as they drew ever closer to Pier 41 and the Alcatraz ferry office. As Marcus predicted, parking wasn't easy at Fisherman's Wharf but he found a space two hundred yards from Pier 41. Finding somewhere to leave a second car would've been even harder, but the plan was to hot-wire another vehicle nearer the ferry office.

"I'll wait in that car," said Marcus, as he finished parking, adding it would be closer to Pier 41 and he'd need to stay aboard to keep the engine running.

"What about the Edsel?" Claudia asked, stepping from the vehicle.

"No problem there," Eddie replied, adding that Marcus had a key to start the car.

"Sadly," muttered the getaway driver, who had every intention never to drive it again, and extracted the key from his black tracksuit. He examined it while the others started walking towards Pier 41. Crucially, Marcus was standing next to a bin. He glanced at the Edsel for what he hoped would be the final time, shook his head, and threw the key in the trash.

Despite the early hour, some people were milling around Fisherman's Wharf, but nothing like the crowds that would arrive once the main attractions opened. Most of the early visitors were dog walkers or those taking exercise, which meant Claudia's phony athletics club blended in perfectly, even if they were only walking at Doug's laboured pace. Despite the steady speed, Claudia felt her heart racing as they approached the ferry office. Nobody was standing nearby, and the building seemed empty. No police were visible but Claudia realised they could be unlucky and encounter a passing patrol. If she'd had more operatives, she could've sacrificed one to create a diversion. An old favourite was using a towel to whip all the cars in a quiet street to orchestrate an overture of burglar alarms. It was guaranteed somebody would call the police and to divert officers from the target area while the towel-toting operative slipped away. However, Claudia had nobody to spare. Tackling the job with six people would've been tough. Five was the bare minimum, which meant they had no room for error.

Before long, there was only four of them as Marcus had to find another vehicle and wait at the wheel. To his delight, a Jaguar

XJ was parked on the Embarcadero beside Pier 41. It was fast, large enough for five people, and most importantly, it was a fine car. They were notoriously hard to steal but Marcus had succeeded once before…up to a point. He managed to breach the car's security and set about firing the engine while his colleagues headed towards the ferry office. Once there, Doug would provide 'crowd control' for any onlookers who ventured too close to the target. He stood near the ferry office, pretending to time Sophie while she jogged along Pier 41. Claudia waited beside Eddie while he picked the door lock. Within seconds it was open and the pair were inside. Eddie went straight to the burglar alarm console, which was beeping angrily, demanding a code. What it received was a reprogramming that left the box of microchips under no illusion who was boss. Thanks to the images on Claudia's phone, Eddie had researched how to disable the system and security cameras. He thought the same about the safe, but the Frisco Spiders then struck their first problem.

"It's different," Eddie complained, kneeling in the corner of the office and staring at the safe in disbelief.

"They've changed it?"

"No, but it's the updated model," Eddie replied, adding that the pictures on Claudia's phone weren't detailed enough to capture the small "x" on the end of the model name.

"Can you crack it?" She asked.

Eddie took a deep breath, then puffed out his cheeks.

"Probably," he replied, slowly and without confidence. He added that even if he opened the door, the alarm could go off. Claudia had to make a split-second decision. They'd made it this far, but could they risk going further? They hadn't passed the point of no return and could stroll away from the office. If they opened the safe, they'd have to live with the consequences. She then remembered promising herself that something good had to come from her father's death. He'd been a brave man and she knew what he'd say if he was standing beside her.

"Bust the damn thing," she ordered. Eddie took a nervous breath, nodded, and set to work. It didn't take long and he opened the door. He also set off the alarm. He also managed to alert the police by doing so. Claudia cringed as the piercing siren tore through her system. She couldn't hear herself think. Eddie had crawled into a ball with his hands over his ears. He was trying to say something to Claudia, which she couldn't hear over the noise, but judging by his lips it appeared to be "sorry". He repeated the movement when Doug smashed the door open.

"Stupid geek," he barked, loudly enough so not even the alarm could silence him. Claudia immediately occupied the space between them in case a fight broke out. Now she had another split-second decision, which was whether to abandon the job to minimise the risk of capture, or take the loot. As she made her choice, Sophie slipped into the office without anyone noticing and headed towards the safe.

"Let's argue later," Claudia shouted above the alarm, "get the money."

By this point, Sophie had arrived at her shoulder. Her voice wasn't loud enough to carry above the noise, so she spoke directly into Claudia's ear. Only two words were spoken, but they made her feel sick to the stomach.

"What money?"

Claudia turned to look at the safe. It was empty.

"Awesome boss," Doug mocked, turning around and leaving the office. The rest of the gang followed. There were no more difficult decisions to make, at least for now. The priority was to get as far away from Pier 41 as possible. However, through a mixture of obesity and a hangover that wouldn't take the hint and leave, Doug was in no state to run. The others could've sprinted without suspicion, thanks to their cover, but sacrificed vital seconds pacing with him to the Jaguar XJ. The ferry office alarm continued to wail and the dog walkers glanced at the gang, weighing up if they were involved. Nobody challenged them, but they'd clearly been noticed.

The Jaguar's passenger doors slammed shut.

"Get us out of here," Claudia muttered. Marcus didn't need to ask how the raid went, and released the handbrake. The vehicle rolled away majestically from Pier 41 along the Embarcadero. Marcus was pleased he'd started the engine, but his previous attempt to liberate a Jaguar XJ went the same way until its security system detected something was wrong and cut the power. Two hundred metres from the scene of the crime, it happened again.

"Why are you stopping?" Eddie bleated.

"Damn," Marcus sighed. "I really thought I'd cracked it this time."

"I'm not running another bloody yard," Doug complained, not that he'd run anywhere so far. The Jaguar ground to a halt. The Frisco Spiders looked at each other, then at the vehicle parked across the street.

"There's the Edsel," announced Eddie. The XJ's passenger doors sprang open. The driver's door took much longer. Marcus trudged towards the geriatric car, which his colleagues were trying to open.

"Unlock it then," ordered Doug.

"Ah, might be a problem," Marcus admitted, who then confessed that the key, rather than being in his pocket, was residing in a bin.

"You muppet," Doug complained.

Sophie, who said nothing, grabbed Marcus by the collar and marched him towards the bin. He was surprised how strong she was, and wasn't prepared when she tripped him. It brought him to his knees beside the bin. His kneecaps were seized with pain, and worse still, he knew there was no option except to reach inside the trash.

"Go on," urged Eddie.

Many things were in the bin. Many things weren't the key.

"This is disgusting," Marcus complained, rummaging amongst the stinking waste. None of his colleagues were sympathetic, and their mood wasn't improved by a sound that soon eclipsed the distant noise of the ferry office alarm. It was a police siren.

"Hurry up," Eddie pleaded.

Marcus thrust his arm deeper into the trash. Still he found nothing. Finally, Doug's patience snapped and he shoved the getaway driver aside. In one seamless movement, he wrenched the bin from its sidewalk mounting, turned it over, and shook out its entire contents...onto Marcus.

The gang started searching desperately through the trash, except for Claudia, whose vanity couldn't permit her to sink that low. She gazed along the wharf and saw a police car in the distance.

"Anytime now would be good," she smiled, gazing at their getaway driver. However, it was Eddie who found the key, nestled in the festering remains of a mediocre cheeseburger. Marcus wiped the priceless slither of metal on his tracksuit and rammed it into the Edsel's ignition. Doug hauled the weapons back to the car from the Jaguar and the others climbed aboard as fast as they could, knowing the police were closing in fast.

Once the Edsel's engine fired, most people in Marcus's position would have floored the throttle. However, he knew that would attract attention, and a dignified cruise away from the scene offered the best chance of escape. After all, unless the police knew for certain they'd broken into the ferry office, and which car was theirs, it was unlikely the Edsel would be stopped. Marcus checked the rear mirror and spotted two police cars. One had stopped at Pier 41, presumably to investigate the scene. The other was behind them, heading along the waterfront, as if looking for anyone acting suspiciously.

"Can't this heap go faster?" Doug complained, as the sirens drew nearer. Marcus ignored him, knowing that if the Edsel bolted, the police would almost certainly give chase. He had to stay calm and limit his speed. For a moment, it seemed to work, as the police car slowed to a crawl, silenced its siren and it became more distant.

Claudia monitored the police car in the passenger door mirror. She realised the next few seconds were critical. By now it was inevitable that officers were speaking to the dog walkers at Pier 41. Some would have seen her phony athletics team leaving the ferry office, but did anyone notice them leaving in the Jaguar? Even if they did, it was unlikely the same people would've seen it grind to a halt two hundred yards away, and the enforced switch to the Edsel. Yet if officers spoke to the right two or three people they might just piece the information together. If so, Claudia suspected those details would be received by the second police car anytime now. Right on cue, its sirens exploded back into life and its engine roared.

Now the Frisco Spiders were in trouble. Marcus kept driving sedately in the hope they weren't the police car's target. The gap between the vehicles narrowed from fifty yards to forty, then thirty, twenty, and finally it was next to nothing. The police car's public address system burst into life above the wailing siren.

"Old black and white car. Pull over."

Now there was no doubt. It wasn't in the nature of Black Widows operatives to surrender, so they had three choices. The first was to stop and talk their way out of it, but given the firearms in the Edsel's trunk that was unlikely to work. The second was to use the weapons to fight. The final option was to take off. Given that if the last option failed, they could still try the second, the decision wasn't hard. Claudia gave Marcus the signal to floor the throttle. However, a rueful expression flashed across his face, because he knew what would happen, which was nothing. As he summoned all the horsepower the Edsel had to give, it only succeeded in making lots of noise. As the engine strained, and the speedometer failed to respond, Marcus realised he was about to embark on a chase around San Francisco in completely, absolutely, totally and utterly the wrong car.

*   *   *

Little more than a mile away, Ian was oblivious to the drama at Fisherman's Wharf. He was in the Mezzogiorno Warehouse atrium admiring the view, and above all, the silence. He'd never been inside an empty department store. The cleaners had left and there was no sign of the security guards who were tucked away somewhere. The only person he'd seen was Martina. She was waiting beside the armoured security door at the front entrance for their special guest. Ian didn't know who to expect but was intrigued to see who it was. In the meantime, he gazed around the opulent surroundings and could just about hear the distant hum of the air conditioning. It was likely to be a warm day, and one he expected to remember for a long time.

Ian felt adrenaline filling his veins. He recognised the sensation from previous jobs with the Black Widows. He knew this would be the calm before the storm. In that regard, he was absolutely right.

*   *   *

Back at Fisherman's Wharf, the Edsel left the Embarcadero, heading westbound into Jefferson Street. The police car was in pursuit but made no attempt to draw alongside; it seemed it was sizing up its prey. Marcus turned the wheel and drove south along Jones Street.

"Now what?" asked Doug. It was a tough question. The police car was gaining, and was likely to continue doing so because there was virtually no traffic around, given the early hour. Yet the Edsel was gradually building speed, and Marcus realised he might be able to escape if he could maintain the vehicle's momentum. They were nudging fifty miles per hour, and rising. Only when they turned right into Sacramento Street did the speedometer dip below forty.

"We need to lose the police and return to the motel," said Claudia. Marcus nodded; he knew the route, having practised it the previous day, albeit at a sedate and inconspicuous pace. It would be a hard journey through a maze of down-town streets. In case she could help, Claudia opened the street map which was hidden under her seat. Eddie shook his head. He didn't see any need for paper maps; the internet had made them obsolete. He switched on his phone and pinpointed their location instantly.

"Just finding a route," he added. "Turn left in three blocks, heading south on Route 101. That'll take us back towards the motel."

"Is that okay, boss?" Marcus inquired, seeking confirmation.

"Follow Eddie," she replied, folding up the map. Soon after, the Edsel screeched out of Sacramento Street into Van Ness Avenue with the police in pursuit. The squad car was remaining twenty yards behind, which suggested it expected support. Claudia recognised the strategy; rather than risking a solo confrontation with the Edsel, it would await reinforcements.

The Edsel's speedometer was approaching fifty miles per hour. The car was cumbersome, and the higher speed didn't improve matters. It drove like a concrete Zeppelin. Marcus hated it, especially the fact it offered no means to escape the police. It was too sluggish for a straight road, too bulky for the corners and stuck out like a sore thumb. Meanwhile, the squad car remained fixed in the rear mirror. It was like a towing a noisy caravan. Yet, it was still content to shadow the Edsel without making its move. It just stayed in their mirrors...waiting.

It didn't have to wait long.

"Look out; roadblock!" Doug yelled.

Another police car and a juggernaut had been slung across Van Ness Avenue at its junction with Broadway. The Edsel was heading south, rapidly bearing down on the scene. Marcus didn't have much thinking time, having already passed all the side streets before the roadblock. His only options were to ram his way through, or turn around. Marcus knew the important thing was to keep moving, and the second option seemed better on that score. The junction was wide, but it would still require great skill, and luck, to execute the manoeuvre. He'd practised handbrake turns before, but never in a bulky 1950s sedan.

"Hang on everyone," he advised. He took a deep breath, turned the wheel and pulled the handbrake. At once, there was a terrible screech of tyres as the Edsel started swapping ends. The police car behind also began snaking in a cloud of burning rubber. If its driver was caught out, it was forgiveable, as you don't often see a Ford Edsel perform a handbrake turn.

Slowly, but surely, the monolithic old car rotated on its axis with the grace of a lame walrus. Marcus knew the handbrake turn didn't have to be perfect; he just had to get the blasted heap pointing the other way. He reckoned he'd been too cautious with the turn, but in fact, the Edsel slithered around more than expected. Instead of 180 degrees, it was more like 230 when the rotating stopped, but it was close enough. He applied full throttle and, eventually, the ageing sedan got the idea and unhurriedly pottered off northbound along Van Ness Avenue.

"We'll need a new route," said Claudia, turning to Eddie. Meanwhile, the pursuing police car had turned around and had been joined by the one in the roadblock.

"Oh," sighed Eddie, staring at his phone. It would have been unforgivable to have run out of battery as it was standard practice in the Black Widows before a job to ensure they were fully charged. However, that wasn't the problem.

"No signal," he explained.

"Looks like we need the paper map after all," said Claudia. However, when she unfolded it, San Francisco just resembled a spider's web of gibberish. She hadn't been in town long enough to recognise the street layout. She desperately scanned the streets for any familiar names. Then she spotted one.

"Stockton," she muttered to herself. Why did that ring a bell? She noticed it went through Chinatown and remembered the

Oriental restaurant, and then following Ian...to the Mezzogiorno Warehouse. She then recalled his invitation to breakfast.

"Change of plan," she announced, "we're going to visit Ian."

Sophie asked if she intended to hide at the department store they'd visited.

"That's the idea," she confirmed, but getting there was another matter. She scoured the map, all the while, they were still heading north along Van Ness Avenue. Stockton Street lay to the east, so they had to turn right. Marcus did so, into the first road that was available. Now they were driving up Lombard Street with the police cars still in pursuit. They'd have to shake them off before hiding at the warehouse and a further problem was about to make itself known. Claudia noted that Marcus was muttering the word "Lombard" to himself, and asked why.

"There's something about Lombard Street," he replied, awkwardly lurching the Edsel around slower cars like a drunken slalom skier.

"Is it a tunnel, or a bridge?" Eddie asked, whose phone was still out of action. They were now three blocks east of Van Ness Avenue, and as they crested the hill, Marcus remembered the reason.

"No, it's this," he sighed. In front of them was a sheer drop, a road so steep it had been altered into a series of hairpin bends. The tarmac was pink, either side of the road were displays of flowers, and each bend had a maximum speed of five miles per hour.

"That's the twisty street they use in the films," said Doug.

"I'm not going down that," said the getaway driver, who halted the Edsel at the entrance to the sequence of hairpins. The following police cars hadn't expected Marcus to stop and swerved under braking either side of him, blocking his other routes of escape.

"Or maybe I am," Marcus conceded, and rolled forwards into the first turn. Ten of them lay between the Frisco Spiders and

107

open tarmac. The first police car followed them, and so did the second, but crucially it misjudged the first corner, arriving with too much speed. There was a sickening crunch as its front wing struck the barriers, followed by loud screeching as the damaged bodywork rubbed against the front left tyre. It would surely burst if the driver kept going, so they had to stop to carry out a running repair, which meant falling behind the other two cars. Even so, they weren't getting far away, as the hairpins were so tight that Marcus was unable to exceed five miles per hour. The ageing car lumbered down Lombard Street with the much swifter police car behind it, angrily flashing its lights and blaring its siren.

"This is embarrassing," Marcus conceded, as he slowly crept around another corner.

"Walking would be faster," added Doug, which was the first time he'd suggested doing so all day. Their pace was agonisingly slow but Marcus knew he couldn't be overtaken. However, he couldn't afford to spend all morning wheezing around the turns as the police might get another car to the foot of the hill and block the exit. Another problem was that a small crowd of early morning tourists had gathered at the penultimate hairpin to watch the spectacle. Claudia wound her window down as they approached the group.

"We're making a film," she announced to the crowd, who seemed content with her explanation. Doug was less happy with the continual whine of the police siren, which was intolerably amplifying his hangover. He started flicking a v-sign through the Edsel's rear window.

"Sod off, you're doing my head in," he complained. He wasn't the only one upset about the noise as several residents came to their balconies to see what was disturbing their Sunday morning lie-in. A few lobbed old boots and unwanted pillows at the Edsel in disgust. Marcus doggedly drove around the hairpins through the drizzle of discarded household goods.

"A five-mile-an-hour car chase," he sighed. "I'll never live this down."

Eventually, the Edsel left the final corner and Lombard Street opened up, allowing both cars to accelerate away from the tourists. However, they still had plenty to watch, as the second police car was now tackling the hairpins, having resumed the chase.

Further along the road, the Edsel was bearing down on the junction of Columbus Avenue, one of San Francisco's busiest roads. Claudia wanted to get across it, but fate had other ideas.

"Cable car!" Eddie yelled. To avoid it, Marcus had to swerve right and found himself on Columbus Avenue. Claudia checked the map to find another route to the warehouse. If they stayed on the road for half a mile and took a sharp turn into Pacific Avenue, they would still be okay. The police car kept following them as Marcus charged down the wide road, and with the second squad car trying to catch up, there was now a good reason to drive as fast as possible, as shaking off one pursuer was easier than two.

"Turn right into Pacific Avenue, and it looks tight," Claudia advised. She wasn't wrong. Just when Marcus thought he'd negotiated all the hairpins San Francisco had to offer, he faced another. Without Claudia's warning, he would have missed it completely, but the 1950s sedan slithered into Pacific Avenue and headed west. Now they were just two blocks from the warehouse. It fronted onto Stockton Street, which meant they'd approach it from the side. It didn't look much from Pacific Avenue, but the grand facade of the main entrance came into view as the Edsel lurched into Stockton Street with all the grace of a cow on roller skates.

"Here we are darling," announced Marcus, like a cheerful East End cabbie, but his casual tone couldn't distract from the question now firmly etched on everyone's lips, which was how to get inside the building.

"Keep going round the warehouse," said Claudia. Not only did she need time to think, but they still had to shake off the squad car, which was buzzing around in the rear view mirror like an angry wasp. If they built a small gap, they could dive into the underground car park unseen. However, its entrance was guarded by unforgiving armoured shutters, which somehow would have to be opened. Claudia reached for her phone and dialled Ian's number, praying he would answer. The phone began to ring, then rang some more.

It continued to ring.

*   *   *

Ian gazed at his handset. He couldn't decide whether to take the call. The department store was blissfully quiet, almost ghostly, and the ring-tone was shattering the silence. Claudia had made no attempt to contact him after leaving the gang, which made him wonder why she was calling now, and so early on a Sunday. Then he remembered his casual throwaway invitation to breakfast. He hadn't expected her to respond, but if she was on her way, it was only decent to accept the call. He pressed the green button on his phone.

Had he not done so, his life, and those of everyone else in Edsel and the warehouse, would have worked out very differently.

"You're up early," he said.

"New regime; I've started jogging," Claudia replied. Ian didn't believe her. He rarely believed her. He also heard a cacophony in the background, including what sounded like a siren.

"Just a passing ambulance," she explained, "and I was just passing the warehouse and thought we'd have that breakfast you mentioned."

Ian's heart sank. He asked if she was alone.

"No, the others are here, and we've got the car. Could you let us in?" She asked.

Ian rolled his eyes. Salami and espresso with Doug wasn't his idea of fun, and making conversation with Sophie was tough at the best of times. His former colleagues gate-crashing his previously peaceful Sunday morning was unwelcome, yet he had to concede he'd invited them, which meant being dignified, diplomatic and weathering the disruption.

"Okay, but opening the shutters is a two-man job," he said, recalling Martina had needed his help to open the front entrance for their expected VIP.

"Actually, could you open the car park instead?" Claudia asked.

"Same deal applies."

"Fine, I'll get somebody to give you a hand," she replied.

"Whatever," Ian sighed, "just knock on the shutters when you're outside and we'll lift them together."

"Thanks Ian. I don't know where I'd be without you."

The line went dead. Ian was suspicious about Claudia's final comment. It wasn't in her nature to show gratitude unless she was really pleased...or in dire trouble.

*   *   *

Claudia tucked away her phone. One problem was solved, but two remained. First, they needed to shake off the police car. Second, she had to get somebody safely onto the street to lift the car park shutter from the outside. She reviewed the list of candidates. Marcus was driving while Sophie was too slight, and Doug was about as equipped to roll out of the car as a particularly unmotivated sloth. Claudia could probably do it, if she really had to, but there was another option. She turned to Eddie, made eye contact, and knew she had his undivided attention before speaking so much as a syllable.

"Eddie, there's something you can do for me."

He didn't need asking twice. He was immediately intoxicated by her personal attention. Had it been a suicide mission, he still might have accepted. In comparison, rolling onto the sidewalk from a moving car to open a garage door was a cinch. By this point, Marcus had already circled the warehouse once and knew police reinforcements would arrive if they didn't act quickly. To make things awkward, Eddie was sitting behind him, which meant he'd need to clamber over Sophie and Doug to reach the rear passenger door. The former didn't flinch, but the latter exuded a tirade of foul expletives befitting a Rhondda valley miner who'd caught his foot with a pick axe. He followed his outburst by kicking the door open and jettisoning Eddie from the vehicle with the delicacy of an anarchist lobbing eggs at a politician. Somehow, like a desperate cat, Eddie landed on his feet, and sprinted with a painful lack of poise towards a lamppost that was his final hope of arresting his progress before an undignified head-on collision with the sidewalk. He wrapped himself around the lamppost with the embrace of an insecure lover and gently fell to earth like a seed in an autumn breeze. It took a moment before he caught his breath, but once the shock passed, he limped to the entrance to the underground car park.

Meanwhile, Marcus was still trying to shake the police car. He'd seen the entrance to the car park and knew what was required. As the Edsel passed the warehouse to start another lap, he spotted Eddie stumbling towards the armoured doors. He knew within thirty seconds they would pass the entrance again, and it would be crucial whether it was open or shut. Marcus trusted Ian to be efficient, and Eddie to carry out Claudia's wishes. He wrenched the steering wheel right, then slowed as they glided around the next turn. Two corners remained and Marcus built the speed from the geriatric engine through the first and floored the accelerator through the second. His trump card was applying the handbrake, and he wrenched it towards the heavens as the ageing sedan entered the last corner before the car park. It jolted like a drunken bull until the tortured tyres bit into the asphalt and catapulted it towards the building. If it struck the wall, all was lost. However, it was aimed with consummate skill at the shutters, which were being hauled open by Eddie and his former colleague on the other side. It required split-second timing, but as the Edsel jolted off the carriageway, its roof glanced the rising shutters and the car bounced down the ramp with the elegance of old socks plunging down a laundry chute. Marcus rammed both feet on the brakes and the vehicle snaked downhill with the grace of a freight train ramming a commuter station. The tyres were smoking, the brakes were steaming, yet somehow the vehicle ground to a halt a matter of inches before smashing into the basement wall. For once, Marcus exhibited some emotion as he puffed out his cheeks. It wasn't pretty but the car, and his colleagues, were safe.

*   *   *

At street level, the second police car finally came to the aid of the one which had been doggedly pursuing the Edsel. By this point, the first vehicle was stopped opposite the Mezzogiorno Warehouse. The officer who'd been driving it was on the sidewalk looking baffled. How could a hulking 1950s sedan vaporise into thin air? It was there one minute and gone the next. The second officer stepped from their car and joined their colleague. Their brief conversation amounted to the suspect vehicle vanishing without trace. They then heard a dull drone and looked to the skies to see a police helicopter overhead, which had also arrived a fraction too late. The officers knew security cameras around the city were being monitored, so the Edsel ought to be spotted before long, unless it had gone to ground. If that was the case, it was somewhere in the vicinity of the warehouse. As a result, the officers knew it was time to leave their cars and dust off the tried and tested practice of door-to-door inquiries. The Edsel, and its occupants, must be somewhere. They couldn't just disappear.

*   *   *

"We need to disappear for a while," said Claudia, stepping from the Edsel into the basement car park. It was spacious, well lit,

113

and deserted apart from their vehicle. The rest of the occupants vacated it while Eddie and Ian trudged down the ramp towards them, having closed the armoured shutters in the Edsel's wake.

"You were in a hurry," Ian observed, making eye contact with Marcus. His comment wasn't light-hearted.

"You know me. I like showing off," he replied. Ian shook his head.

"You're a getaway driver for the Black Widows," he reminded him. "You only take risks if it's essential."

"Ah, but we're freelance now, so we do things with style," Claudia smiled.

"Like nearly running me over, and your long-suffering geek?" Ian replied, gesturing his thumb towards Eddie, who was visibly shaking.

"Who cares? Nobody's hurt," muttered Doug, who opened the Edsel's trunk to check its contents. Ian also spotted them, which confirmed his suspicions.

"You don't bring automatic weapons to breakfast," he said gravely. "You're on a job, aren't you?"

Before Claudia could summon a smart reply, Doug waded back into the conversation.

"Yeah, but not anymore. The whole thing went to bollocks," he complained, staring right at Claudia.

"And whose fault was that?" Eddie countered, rushing to her defence.

"You set off the alarm," shouted Doug, his temper rising.

"So what? That safe would've been full if you hadn't got drunk the night before," Eddie responded.

"I was ready," he protested. "It was your fancy tart who bottled the job."

Insulting Claudia was the one thing guaranteed to make Eddie lunge at Doug, even though it was a complete physical mismatch. It was also the kind of comment that Claudia's pride would find hard to stomach. Sophie instantly recognised the danger. A single shot rang out and echoed around the deserted car park. Everyone stopped in their tracks and the only movement was the wisp of smoke puffing from the barrel of the Magnum. She said nothing after discharging the firearm into the ground. Her expression said enough. The silence was eventually broken by Ian.

"I think you should go now."

*   *   *

The Seeker made his coffee last to delay ordering a second. He was the first customer of the day in the café opposite the Mezzogiorno Warehouse and expected to be there a while. Not much happened after Ian's arrival until the dramatic reappearance of the Ford Edsel. He couldn't believe what he was seeing as the vehicle circled the building four times with the police in pursuit. His heart then skipped a beat as the car looked certain to ram into the warehouse, but it vanished as if by a miracle into the underground car park. The police didn't follow, either because they'd missed the manoeuvre, or more likely, they knew better than to venture inside. Instead, they were making inquiries nearby, and The Seeker knew they'd arrive at the café soon. He wondered if he should tell them about the Edsel. If police stormed the building, a massacre was inevitable. What was Claudia thinking to lead her team into such a place? It was either remarkably brave or fatally stupid.

The coffee cup was almost empty. Across the street, an armoured black limousine with dark windows halted beside the warehouse. The Seeker didn't recognise the suited ogre who disembarked from it, but recognised his sort, and was unsurprised his next duty was to open the rear compartment door. From it stepped a woman half his size, wearing sunglasses that weren't justified by the early hour. The chauffeur, who'd stayed in the limousine, drove off while his passengers headed towards the main entrance, hidden behind steel shutters.

The plot was thickening. The Seeker didn't recognise the woman but surmised she boasted wealth, connections and probably arrogance. A thought then crossed his mind in terms of what Claudia was planning. If his hunch was right, it was brilliantly audacious, but extremely dangerous. The only comforting thing, The Seeker surmised, was that he wasn't inside the building himself.

The Seeker ordered a second coffee. It was going to be a long day.

*　　　*　　　*

"Oh no," Martina sighed. Even peering through the shutters, she recognised the woman coming her way. She wasn't familiar to Ian, who'd left his colleagues in the car park to help with opening the entrance. He wondered if she was a celebrity whose fame hadn't crossed the Atlantic. She certainly looked important and came equipped with a monolithic bodyguard.

"It's Romana," added Martina. Ian looked at her blankly.

"Is she an actress?" He asked.

"More like a drama queen," she replied. "Romana is The Don's only daughter."

Ian's mind went into overdrive. The crown princess of the local Mafia was heading his way, and he realised he was in totally the wrong place at totally the wrong time.

"Does her family own this place?" He asked.

Martina nodded sorrowfully.

"I must apologise," she added. "If I'd known it was her, I wouldn't have invited you."

The colour drained from Ian's face. It seemed he'd never escape the criminal underworld. Now he was mixed up with the Mafia, having just left the Black Widows, and his colleagues.

Who were hiding in the basement.

"Oh, God," he muttered to himself.

"Just help me with the shutters, then you can go," Martina smiled, trying to sooth his nerves, without realising the gravity of the situation. Ian hadn't told her about his colleagues, hoping they'd leave quietly before anyone found them. He certainly didn't want to add to Martina's problems now that the identity of their mystery shopper was known, and with that in mind, Ian realised he couldn't leave. Not only was he uncomfortable leaving Martina alone with the Mafia, but he also dreaded to think what would happen if they stumbled on his colleagues.

Ian was now very nervous. He also detected Martina was increasingly anxious as Romana approached the building.

"Why did it have to be her?" Martina sighed. "She's a total bitch."

This was the first time Ian had heard anything coarse pass her lips, but her next statement justified the description.

"She gets people fired for kicks."

At that moment, Ian would've happily settled for nothing worse than Martina getting sacked. He knew how serious the situation was, and agonised whether to tell her anything. In the end, he said nothing, as Romana was bearing down on them, and there simply wasn't time.

Ian and Martina took a deep breath and opened the shutters. The door was unlocked, but not swiftly enough to prevent Romana waiting a fraction of a second. She was best described as a sneer on legs. She wasn't attractive and her frosty demeanour didn't help matters. She crossed the threshold without a word, delegating the talking to her bodyguard.

"You took long enough," he muttered to Martina, before glancing at Ian. "Who's the guy?"

"My boyfriend," she replied. Ian smiled; it was the first time she'd called him that. "I needed help with the shutters."

The bodyguard glared at the uninvited guest. Ian's smile evaporated. He knew he was on thin ice. For a moment, he wondered if Romana's minder would shoot him dead on the spot. The atmosphere was crackling with tension and the suspense was unbearable. When the bodyguard finally made his move, Ian was quietly relieved.

"Beat it," he ordered.

Ian and Martina exchanged glances. She smiled sweetly and shrugged apologetically, recognising she'd placed him in an impossible position and his only option was to leave. Ian didn't want to desert her, but realised digging his heels in might put them in even greater danger.

Ian trudged down the ornate steps from the entrance to the sidewalk. Behind, he heard the armoured shutters rattling down as the bodyguard sealed the building. Martina was trapped inside. To make matters worse, his colleagues were probably still in the basement.

Ian considered his options. He could run away, but wasn't prepared to abandon Martina. He also felt a tinge of loyalty towards his colleagues, even if their arrival had been timed appallingly. Then again, along with causing a major headache, the Frisco Spiders could also be the answer to his most immediate problem, which was re-entering the building. If they lifted the car park shutters, he could hide with them until Romana left, then depart safely with Martina. He was determined not to leave the building without her, and if he stopped the Mafia and Black Widows coming to blows, he'd prevent a bloodbath, saving a host of lives.

"A coward," Ian muttered to himself, recalling what Sophie had labelled him when choosing a leader for the Frisco Spiders. The truth wasn't so simple. He wasn't a coward, but only risked his neck when the cause was right. On this occasion, it was. He marched towards the car park.

*   *   *

"Somebody's coming," warned Eddie, peering through the shutters inside the underground car park. He'd been told to keep watch in case police tried entering the building. He'd seen officers making inquiries across the street and their next stop would be the café opposite. Marcus strolled up the ramp to glance at the outside world.

"Relax," he said. "It's just Ian."

Moments later their former colleague knocked on the shutters, which were raised, then closed swiftly in his wake before the police saw anything.

"Still here then," Ian muttered, pacing down the ramp towards the car park.

"You haven't given us breakfast yet," Marcus reminded him flippantly.

"I've lost my appetite," he replied, "and you were supposed to lose yourselves somewhere else."

"We can't do that until the cops disappear," Eddie reminded him.

"And whose fault is it they're here?" Ian asked, as they joined the rest of the gang beside the Edsel. Claudia was studying the map, planning their route back to the motel, but first they had to leave the warehouse.

"Does this place have a back door?" She asked.

Ian was, by now, familiar with the building's layout, even if the back offices were a mystery. Along with the main entrance and car park ramp, he said there were two fire exits. Eddie asked if they could slip through those unnoticed.

"You'd have to walk through the store, which means Romana and her bodyguard would see you," Ian replied. Claudia looked at him quizzically.

"Who's Romana?" She asked.

"Never you mind," he replied.

"Hang on," she said, wagging her finger. "She's that exclusive customer you told us about."

"Is she a singer? Is she sexy?" Doug inquired lecherously.

"Neither," Ian replied, "but her arrival means it's even more vital to get you out."

"What's so special about her?" Marcus shrugged.

"None of you get it, do you?" Ian sighed. "Don't you realise where you are?"

"The Mezzogiorno Warehouse bounded by Stockton Street, Pacific Avenue, Grant Street and Broadway," Sophie recited in a dull monotone without requiring Claudia's map.

"Indeed. It imports Mediterranean goods and the name refers to the southern half of Italy," Ian replied. "So who do think owns this place?"

At first the question was greeted with uneasy silence. Then, after a few moments, Eddie was the first to suggest what the others were already thinking.

"Oh, no," he muttered. "The Mafia."

Ian nodded gravely.

"And Romana, if you must know, is The Don's only daughter," he added.

"So why are you here?" Demanded Doug. "Have you changed sides?"

"No, but I want you gone before World War Three breaks out," Ian replied. Eddie returned to the shutters to see if the police had left. They were outside the café, pointing at the warehouse.

"There's still gendarmes on the street," he called down to his colleagues.

"And the Mafia upstairs," Marcus added.

"How many?" Claudia asked, turning to Ian. He replied that apart from Martina, he'd seen nobody except Romana and her bodyguard, though he understood there were a couple of security men hidden somewhere.

"Five of them, five of us," Marcus observed.

"It should be six of us," added Doug, glaring at Ian.

"Leave me out of this, and the same goes for Martina."

"Okay, without your bird, that leaves four," said Doug. "Would Romana give us any trouble?"

From their brief encounter, Ian reckoned Romana could cause all sorts of trouble, but not in a pitched battle.

"She'd rely on her bodyguard," he replied.

"Only three bad guys then," Doug smiled, reaching into the Edsel's trunk for the meanest-looking automatic he could find.

"The odds are improving," said Marcus.

"Yeah, if we need to defend ourselves," added Doug, loading the automatic...incorrectly.

"Or take a hostage," Sophie observed.

Claudia smiled. At first, she wondered if Romana could be their ticket out of the warehouse, but recognised crossing the Mafia was very risky. If they did so, it had to be worth it, and she then reflected on her pledge that something good had to come from her father's death. So far, the multi-million pound job they'd be seeking was nowhere in sight. Now, it had presented itself, and Claudia was first to recognise the opportunity.

"Not a hostage," she said. "But a kidnap."

*   *   *

At the café across the street, The Seeker watched the police officers walk away, their backs turned. He could have told them so much, but revealed so little.

As the second coffee arrived, he reviewed the sequence of events. The doctor who couldn't keep control of his credit card had opened the store with an employee he didn't recognise. The Seeker reckoned she might be the 'insider' and was clearly attractive if you liked that sort of thing. The rest of the Falmer Spiders then made a much less subtle entrance, chased by police. At first he reckoned they were trying to shake them off and hide in the warehouse. Up to this point, the events made sense.

Then the limousine turned up. It seemed likely there would only be a skeleton staff inside to greet the VIP, given the early hour. As a result, if the remaining Falmer Spiders intended to kidnap her as The Seeker suspected, they probably had the numerical advantage. All of that made sense, but what defied logic was how the police had become involved. More to the point, would it force the job to be cancelled? The gang's only hope was that officers wouldn't want to meddle with a building run by the local Mafia. Perhaps that was the reason Claudia had chosen it, and maybe their hosts would receive a cut of the proceeds. This was all speculation, and The Seeker recognised he must focus on the facts and not try to complete a jigsaw with half the pieces missing.

The police had now reached the other side of the street. The Seeker wondered where they were going. His pulse quickened as they scaled the ornate steps to the Mezzogiorno Warehouse's main entrance; clearly they were prepared to enter the lion's den after all. With the Falmer Spiders already inside, this had the potential to end extremely badly.

The Seeker began his second coffee...and started thinking about breakfast.

*   *   *

Three long, purposeful knocks resounded from the heavy shutters at the warehouse's main entrance. Martina froze in her tracks. Romana's bodyguard looked towards the front doors with suspicion.

"That better not be your idiot boyfriend," he warned.

Romana barely flinched and continued inspecting designer labels in the clothing department, removing garments from their hangers, snorting at their appearance and draping them wherever required the least effort. Martina kept tidying in her wake, but the noise from the shutters had thrown her off her stride. She'd assured her visitors that nobody else, except the two security guards, were present, and it was clear they didn't want to be disturbed.

Then it happened again. Three more knocks. This time they were more rapid, but equally purposeful. The bodyguard stared at Martina and frowned.

"Whoever it is, get them gone," he ordered.

Martina bowed, retreating backwards a few steps before turning to walk across the polished marble floor through the perfume and cosmetics departments to the main entrance. How she longed for her visitors to leave. Dealing with Romana was like treading on eggshells. Now there was the added complication of somebody at the entrance. She desperately hoped it wasn't Ian, not because she didn't care for him, but because she now did. She wanted him to be far away, and to join him as soon as possible. Martina was counting the minutes until the store was meant to open and Romana's visit would end, but then again, she could always order the venue to close for longer. She had those kind of connections. Martina was a clever and smart young lady but not from a wealthy family. Working at the Mezzogiorno Warehouse had, until now, been a pleasant way to fund her studies. Not anymore. She took a deep breath and peered through the shutters.

"Who is it?" The bodyguard yelled from twenty yards away. Martina cupped her hands over her mouth when she saw who it was. She could barely bring herself to speak, but realised she had to say something.

"It's the police," she replied, her usually smooth voice croaking on the final word. Romana hesitated in her dissection of the clothing department for half a second, then muttered something to her bodyguard. He nodded, and ambled awkwardly towards the entrance.

"Tell them we're closed," he ordered, and took up a position near Martina that would allow him to stay hidden behind the main doors while she dealt with the uninvited guests. Martina's pulse quickened. One wrong move and she would be in serious trouble. She hesitated before placing her hand on the security shutters, but her assistance to raise them wasn't required, as the hulking bodyguard lifted them single-handed and stepped back into the shadows.

Two police officers were outside. Neither looked intimidating. Not only were they a few inches below Martina on the ornate steps, but one was a rotund man of around forty while the other was a female officer who still looked fresh out of college and not remotely battle-hardened. She handled the introductions before moving onto the purpose of their visit.

"We're looking for a car," she said, before checking her notes and describing the Edsel. It meant nothing to Martina; she had no interest in old vehicles and, more importantly, was unaware that Ian's colleagues were in the basement.

"I haven't seen anything. I was just preparing to open the store," she blushed.

The rotund officer craned what little there was of his neck to peer into the venue's interior. He couldn't see past the perfume and cosmetics counters.

"Real good food in there," he nodded, before recounting an off-duty visit to the atrium café. For a horrible moment, Martina wondered if they'd ask to be admitted for coffee and breakfast.

"We'd love to have you back when we're open," said Martina. She registered a grudging nod of approval from the bodyguard hovering menacingly at her side. The conversation went dead.

"Sure you didn't hear anything?" Asked the female officer, trying to salvage something from the otherwise fruitless encounter.

Martina shrugged apologetically and shook her head. The rotund officer smiled at the way her hair effortlessly settled back into its immaculate shape. The female officer wasn't distracted and produced a card, which she handed to Martina.

"If you see anything, call us," she said, injecting a hint of frostiness into the conversation for the first time. She turned her back. The rotund officer smiled inanely, then followed in the footsteps of his younger colleague. They didn't have to go far before the armoured shutters rattled down behind them with a contemptuous crash. Having sealed the building, the bodyguard glared at Martina and said nothing.

"Was that okay"? She asked, fearing his reply. It took a long time before he responded.

"Let's hope we don't get any more callers," he muttered. "For your sake."

Martina retreated a few paces, then headed back to Romana, who suddenly seemed the lesser of two evils. Martina certainly could've done without the police arriving. Now she was worried why they had called in the first place. What was happening and who were they hunting? How she longed to be away from the building, and how she looked forward to being with Ian again. She'd hadn't wanted him to leave, but realised there was no option. She reflected that at least he was away from the building, and safe.

*   *   *

Ian couldn't believe what he'd just heard.

"Kidnap the only daughter of a Mafia boss?" He exploded. Fortunately, there was nobody else in the basement to hear his outburst, except his former colleagues, who were clustered around the Edsel, apart from Eddie, who was keeping watch by the shutters.

"Think about it," Claudia smiled. "When will we get a better chance?"

"Three of them, more of us," added Doug, heading towards Ian until they were virtually eyeball to eyeball. "So who's side are you on?"

"I told you, leave me out of this," he replied.

"Okay," said Claudia, raising her palms to calm the atmosphere, "we won't involve you, including when we count the money."

"If you count the money," he reminded her, "and even if there's only three of them, only two of you can shoot straight."

"He's got a point," Marcus conceded, fiddling with a scratch on the Edsel's paintwork which was upsetting him. "I know about cars, but not guns."

"Would a share of a multi-million pound ransom change your mind?" Claudia asked.

"Oh," said Marcus, who stopped in his tracks. "Well, if you put it like that."

"Anyone else against my plan?" She asked, knowing that Eddie wouldn't speak out of turn, and Sophie was unlikely to speak at all.

"A rumble with the Mafia," beamed Doug, relishing the prospect of what he considered 'proper action'. Claudia knew his enthusiasm could be useful, but would have to be curbed when it came to the crunch. She needed to know more about the building, and their target. Unfortunately, the only one of them with that knowledge was Ian, and he was shaking his head.

"You'll end up dead," he sighed, "and so might the rest of us, including Martina."

Claudia recognised Ian's girlfriend was in the forefront of his mind, and anything that placed her in jeopardy would be resisted. However, if she devised a way to protect her, the tables might turn. She walked across to her former colleague.

"I've seen Martina," she admitted. "You're a lucky man. She's a special lady."

Ian had expected to argue with Claudia again, but when she paused, he could only respond by nodding.

"And you've left her alone with the Mafia," she continued.

"I had no choice," he protested.

"Yes you do," Claudia corrected him. "You might not be in the Black Widows anymore, but your friends are, and friends stick together."

She noted some of her colleagues were nodding helpfully. Marcus even extended a casual thumbs-up to the trainee doctor.

"What is this? A ransom or a rescue?" Ian asked.

"Both," Claudia smiled. "We get the money. You get the girl."

Ian hesitated in replying. The point was hard to argue against, but he recognised there was still an option to walk away, or hold tight until the Mafia left.

"You won't get far," Eddie warned, gazing through the shutters. "Police are still hovering outside."

"But I haven't done anything," Ian protested.

"Exactly," Claudia soothed. "Martina's upstairs, all alone, and you've done..."

She didn't complete the sentence. She didn't need to, having seen the look on Ian's face.

"Okay," he conceded, having been worn down.

During the next few minutes, Claudia squeezed every drop of information she could from Ian, who'd resigned himself to the fact his colleagues weren't going to leave. Eddie kept watch at the shutters and noted officers were still making inquiries while a helicopter passed overhead regularly. The getaway wouldn't be easy, but if Claudia's plan worked, the police would be none the wiser about events inside the warehouse and would, hopefully, lose interest and leave.

Claudia recognised escaping the warehouse was just one part of a risky and dangerous plan. In truth, she wouldn't have considered it had she not been under pressure to find a job large enough on which to quit the underworld. The risks were enormous, but so were the rewards. In terms of the proceeds, Claudia was confident that The Maid could launder the cash. As with all large operations, Claudia knew the trick was to start at the end and work backwards. Most people would regard the heist as the climax of the process, but in fact, it's near the start and only preceded by the planning and training stage. The end is the successful deposit of clean cash into a chosen bank account with no loose ends. Those loose ends include not leaving behind evidence or anything to reveal the identities of those involved, or put simply, a clean getaway. Claudia reckoned that was possible, but being pursued to the warehouse by police was unfortunate. She hoped they only had a firm description of the car and not its occupants, in which case, they'd just have to dispose of the Edsel. It would be elementary if they could leave the building unseen, but if they were being watched, the car would prove a liability. Still, there wasn't time to create a perfect plan, but she had been handed a perfect opportunity.

Abducting Romana would be simple, Claudia reckoned, if they had the element of surprise. She was concerned about the two security guards who were allegedly somewhere in the building, who'd have to be neutralised if they chose to get involved. Even if they didn't, the Frisco Spiders might have to hunt them down to avoid any loose ends. As with all other jobs, Sophie would use tranquillisers in the first instance and only resort to the Magnum if required. She would need at least two tranquilliser darts, but crucially, only one that worked. Sophie didn't have any blank darts but was able to fashion one in a few minutes.

"Lucky you read the manuals," said Claudia, as her colleague set to work, using the Edsel's boot-lid as a convenient surface. Marcus was to remain with the car while Eddie monitored the exit. The others would execute the kidnap, which unfortunately for Ian, included him. As Claudia had pointed out, he was essential to the plan.

Ian desperately hoped it was a risk worth taking.

*   *   *

Romana studied the designer garments. They were draped over her bodyguard, who knew better than to protest about being turned into a mobile clothes stand. She was the one person he never questioned. A host of other garments had been strewn around the warehouse, which Martina had just finished tidying. Now the best four outfits – or the least worst in Romana's eyes – had been sifted from the mulch. She beckoned her bodyguard towards the changing rooms, stepped inside, and left him guarding the entrance. Martina was relieved. Unless Romana needed help she'd

128

have a few minutes to draw breath. She backed away from the bodyguard to the frontier of the menswear section. The warehouse used mannequins that were almost lifelike, with hair and facial features, and four of them were on a raised platform which Martina was standing beside.

"Psst."

Martina glanced around, wondering what had caused the noise. She could only see the bodyguard, who hadn't budged from his sentry duty outside the changing rooms a few yards away.

"Psst."

Martina turned round, still searching for the source of the noise. It wasn't coming from the floor or ceiling and all she could see before her was a quartet of dummies in fine suits. One was wearing a similar outfit to Ian. In fact, it even looked like him.

"Psst. Up here."

Martina's jaw dropped. The third mannequin wasn't a dummy at all, but her boyfriend. He'd adopted a pretentious pose to match his lifeless companions. Only his lips were moving, and barely so.

"What are you doing here?" Martina whispered.

"I sneaked through the basement," he replied. "Do you want Romana gone?"

Martina nodded slowly and purposefully.

"My friends are here," Ian revealed. "They can help."

"How?"

"Let's say they're not tourists. They can handle gangsters," Ian reassured her, while also trying to reassure himself.

"Are you a policeman?" Martina asked, with a hint of suspicion.

"Not exactly," Ian conceded. "Now listen carefully. My friends will soon appear and shoot the bodyguard with a tranquilliser."

"Are you insane?" Martina hissed, as loud as she dared. However, worse was to follow.

"There's no time to explain," he replied, still holding his unnatural pose. "Before he passes out, the last thing he'll see is that you've also been darted."

Ian had thought carefully about how to break this awkward news, and decided that "darted" sounded better than "shot". Martina said nothing. She stared at him with her mouth wide open in disbelief.

"It'll be a blank." he added. "For your safety, it must look like you're not involved."

"You're shooting me for my safety?" She hissed, again as loud as she dared.

"It shouldn't hurt," he replied, then fell silent. He knew the bodyguard would eventually spot them talking unless he ended the exchange. However, it wasn't Romana's minder that halted their conversation, but a clatter of mops and buckets. A trio clad in white overalls, protective glasses and face masks had emerged from the service lift. Their outfits were more suited to asbestos removal than cleaning, but they set to work mopping the floor. No sooner had they started but they incurred the attention, and wrath, of Martina's bodyguard.

"Hey, nobody's allowed in here," he barked.

The largest cleaner, who was almost his physical equal, ignored him. So did the small one. Only the third cleaner reacted, cupping a hand to their ear, suggesting the message hadn't been understood. The bodyguard left his sentry duty and loped across the marble floor towards the uninvited guests.

"You hear me?" He grunted. "Go clean elsewhere."

He was now just a few feet from the cleaners, and this time, only the small one reacted. They did so by whipping a pistol out from the cleaning trolley. The bodyguard had no time to react. He was shot in the neck before he could draw his gun. The last thing he registered before slumping to the ground was the same pistol being turned on Martina, fired again, and she clasped her neck in shock.

Then the lights went out.

As for Martina, her neck felt like it had been gorged by the mother of all mosquitoes. She sank to the ground involuntarily. Within moments Ian was by her side, and soon after, one of the cleaners arrived. It wasn't the large one, or the one with the pistol, and Martina detected a strong hint of mid-range perfume.

"She'll be fine," Ian assured the cleaner, who nodded and returned to their colleagues. Ian removed his jacket, placed it beneath Martina's head, and went to find a medical kit. He returned promptly, removed the dart and treated the puncture wound with antiseptic which made her wince. Martina gently rose to a seated position alongside Ian.

"You said it wouldn't hurt," she hissed quietly.

"I didn't think it would, but I've never been shot," he conceded.

"And Sophie's never fired a blank," added the largest cleaner cheerfully. Martina couldn't place his accent. It sounded British, but not English. She noted another cleaner was placing a finger to their lips, indicating the largest one should stop talking. Martina glanced at a nearby dress mirror, spotted her reflection, and expelled a sigh of frustration.

"I'll have to wear a scarf for days," she muttered. "Now, could you please explain what's happening."

As time was pressing, Ian chose the short version.

"The Mafia owns this place," he stated. "My colleagues work for another organisation and plan to kidnap Romana."

Martina's eyes bulged at the revelation. Then a mournful expression crossed her face.

"So that's why you asked me out," she murmured, staring at the polished marble floor.

"No, it wasn't like that," Ian protested. "I don't even work for these people anymore."

"Then why are you helping them?"

Ian sighed, and banged the back of his head ruefully into the mannequin platform.

"I'm asking myself that question," he replied.

131

"So you're not a doctor."

"I am, trust me," he said, rolling the blank dart between his fingers in examination.

"A doctor who fights the Mafia," said Martina, with suspicion.

"If you like," he smiled.

*   *   *

It was nine o'clock. At that moment, Romana's primary concern was that her chosen garments were smaller than the size they claimed to be. It was impossible she'd put on weight, so the store was to blame. She would complain later and recommend the assistant who'd served her should be fired. However, that was soon academic, as a far greater problem made itself known.

Without warning, the dressing room curtain was torn back. She was about to howl in protest until noticing something that made her stop in her tracks. Her intruder was armed. In fact, two more stood behind them, all identically dressed as if cleaning up after a nuclear spill. She couldn't make out their faces, but saw the weaponry. To compound the situation, she suddenly realised she wasn't wearing enough. Her mouth opened and she was about to scream, but then came the gag. It was bound so quickly and forcefully that not a sound left the changing room. The largest intruder, who'd fitted the gag, stood aside while the other two kept their weapons aimed at her. One had a shotgun and the muzzle drifted towards the discarded skirt on the floor which she'd just tried and dismissed. The gun was flicked upwards a couple of times and she understood she was meant to get dressed. Once she'd done so, the largest intruder bound her hands behind her back and marshalled her towards the exit.

The first thing Romana saw was her bodyguard. He was slumped on the floor. Other minders could always be found, so she wasn't worried about his welfare, but was increasingly concerned about her own. It had all happened so quickly. One minute she was

132

selecting outfits, the next, she was held prisoner by three intruders who only communicated by hand gestures and waving guns. She kept walking under protest; the powerful hands of the largest one were clamped around her shoulders, so she had little option. She wished they would talk. She wished she could scream. She wished her bodyguard could save her. She prayed her father would do so. She hoped there would be revenge.

*   *   *

Hidden amongst the clothing racks, Martina had watched Romana being manhandled towards the service lift. She vanished as the doors closed, along with the bogus cleaners.

"What will happen to her?" She asked.

"Nothing if Papa opens his chequebook," Ian replied.

"These are proud people," she warned. "It won't be that easy."

Ian feared she was right. Kidnapping the daughter of a Mafia boss would surely unleash a vendetta that would make a visit from Section Eight seem like tea with the vicar. His colleagues were playing with fire, and along with Martina, he could also end up being burnt.

The soft bell of the service lift chimed and the doors opened. Martina noticed two of the cleaners had returned. The large one was absent, while the others were removing their glasses and face masks. Martina heard them talking and noticed two things immediately; first they had similar accents to Ian, and second, to her surprise, they were female. The smaller one went to the front doors to guard the entrance. The other was heading towards her.

"I'm Claudia," she announced, cheerfully extending her hand. Martina shook it reluctantly.

"Who are you?" She asked.

"Who are we? " Claudia reflected with a playful smile. "We're the Frisco Spiders sweetie."

Martina didn't like being called "sweetie". She also didn't care for Claudia's perfume, which along with her make-up, had been used to excess. Claudia detected the frostiness.

"Don't be like that," she added. "It wasn't me that shot you."

Before replying, Martina went to the nearest mannequin in the women's department, unwound a white silk scarf from its neck, then wrapped it around her own. It complemented her outfit effortlessly, slightly to Claudia's annoyance, who was stuck in her running gear and felt under-dressed.

"Well, that's enough drama for one morning," said Martina, who started making for the exit. However, Claudia blocked her path.

"I'm afraid you can't leave," she said, adding that police were still outside.

"So? They aren't looking for me."

"But they'll ask questions, and sadly, you know too much."

"We're stuck here?" Ian asked. He glanced at the front doors and noted Sophie was guarding them with her arms folded.

"It's best if we leave together," Claudia replied, smiling sweetly at her former colleague. "And to show there's no hard feelings, we can split the ransom six ways."

Ian pondered her proposal for a moment.

"Seven," he muttered, casting his eye towards Martina.

"A share for your girlfriend?" Claudia asked, narrowing her eyes.

"She's helping, isn't she?" Ian replied. Claudia puffed out her cheeks.

"Okay," she conceded, reflecting it shouldn't be a major issue, as they could simply demand more cash to ensure the rest of the gang didn't lose out. They would have to pay a percentage for The Maid's money laundering anyway, so the ransom would need to be big. However, in the shape of Romana, they had a priceless bargaining chip.

Still dressed as a cleaner, Doug finished binding Romana's arms and legs. She was lashed to a pipe bolted to the basement wall, in a raised alcove beside the lift. It was only visible from a small part of the car park, which meant neither Eddie or Marcus had been seen by the hostage. Doug then took a white cloth sack from the cleaning trolley and stuffed it over Romana's head. He did so for two reasons, firstly to ensure the gang's identity remained secret, and secondly because he was sick of the sight of her.

Doug waddled past the storeroom where they'd found the cleaning gear and down the five steps leading from the alcove into the car park. He was armed with orders from Claudia. First, Marcus would take the lift upstairs, drag the unconscious bodyguard into the compartment, and bring him down to the basement. Doug would keep an eye on him, and Romana, allowing Marcus to move the Edsel into the far corner of the car park, safely out of sight. He would then relieve Eddie from keeping watch at the shutters, and the electronics expert would head upstairs where his services were needed.

It was a lot for Doug to remember, so Claudia had provided written instructions. The final item said: "Burn or eat this paper – your choice". Doug was still to have breakfast, but his hunger hadn't reached the point where digesting the list was more appetising. The paper burned on the ground while Eddie hurried past towards the lift.

*   *   *

With reluctance, Martina told Claudia everything she knew about the Mezzogiorno Warehouse. It was no surprise her knowledge was greater than Ian, especially regarding the back offices. She knew the top floor contained staff rooms and the likely location of the security suite. She didn't know where the two guards were, or even if they were on duty. Claudia was worried about the guards; they could appear at any moment. They had to be found. She also realised their movements had been recorded by security cameras from the moment they entered the building. If they were fortunate, nobody had been watching, but at the very least they had to find where the footage was stored, erase it, and disconnect the system.

"You sent for me," Eddie announced, having arrived from the lift.

"Just the man," said Claudia. "There's a security suite on the top floor."

"And how can I help?"

"Ruin it for me," she smiled.

"What about the guards?" Asked Ian, who was now sitting with Martina in the atrium café. Claudia picked up her shotgun, which she'd left near the changing rooms after Romana had been successfully abducted. She announced she'd guard the front door, releasing Sophie to accompany Eddie in case the security suite was occupied. Sophie led the way, and with Marcus minding the car park and Doug babysitting Romana, all five of the Frisco Spiders had jobs to do.

"What about us?" Ian asked, from the comparative safety of the café.

"Isn't it obvious?" Claudia replied. "You invited us for breakfast. Chop, chop."

*   *   *

The Seeker's breakfast was unsatisfactory. His favourite was a full English but that was rarely served abroad, and when it was, it usually disappointed. The bacon was never quite right, the sausages usually strange and black pudding wasn't there. He'd tried a Parma ham panini with sliced tomatoes. It was the closest thing south of the Alps to a proper bacon sandwich, but worlds away from the genuine article. The panini was excellent, but he'd dined so richly in San Francisco he was starting to miss the reassuringly naff comforts of home. Twenty years he'd spent finding people, usually in Godforsaken places. Those he uncovered were either dead or soon wished they were. What a life. Hunting the Falmer Spiders was about as good as it got, and it wasn't good enough. This would be the last assignment, and he started to suspect, his final day in the job.

The Seeker gazed across the street. His tired eyes settled on the grand entrance of the warehouse and its foreboding shutters. All seemed quiet but he knew it wouldn't last. Something big was about to happen, and would spell bad news for somebody. He wouldn't intervene; it would be his job to pick up the pieces.

The Seeker pushed the remains of his panini aside and waited for the action to start. He wouldn't have to wait long.

*   *   *

Eddie crept from the lift and felt the plush carpet of the top floor beneath his vintage pair of Adidas Gazelles, which he'd found online for a bargain. In future he wouldn't have to economise if they successfully ransomed Romana. However, there was a long way to go. His first job was finding the security suite. Sophie was already a few paces ahead, moving silently between the desks of the open plan office towards the rear of the building. In what was clearly a bustling environment during the week, there wasn't a soul around. The coffee cups kept their lonely vigil on each desk, waiting for their owners to return. The kettle in the kitchen was stone cold. The lights had been off, and sparked into life as Eddie and Sophie made their way through the workstations.

In that respect, they'd already surrendered the element of surprise. They had to hope they weren't being watched.

As the plush carpet gave way to bare flooring, Eddie knew they were close. The décor was more functional and they found themselves in a corridor enclosed by white walls and half a dozen plain doors. Any of them could lead to the security suite. None of them were marked, but each had a gap of roughly half an inch at its base, allowing the doors to open without dragging on the floor. Eddie ran his fingers along the gap of two doors, and then a third before stopping.

"Feel the heat," he whispered to Sophie. She placed her fingers in the gap and nodded.

"Computer suite," he added, "they're always warm."

Eddie started picking the lock, which didn't take long, as his Black Widows' skeleton key rarely left his pocket. It opened the vast majority of locks, but to his frustration, hadn't worked on Claudia's room at Sussex University. It was almost as if she'd anticipated the move and bolstered her security. Thankfully, the computer suite wasn't so well defended.

The door creaked open. The lights flickered and Eddie smiled as he came upon countless racks of circuit boards and telecoms gear.

"Now where's the security footage," he muttered to himself.

"Later," Sophie corrected him. "Cut the telecoms first."

"But Claudia said…"

"…she wants the guards neutralised," interrupted Sophie.

"But how does knocking out the phones and internet achieve that?"

"If your telecoms failed, where would you go?"

Eddie stared into Sophie's dead eyes for a moment. As ever, she was right. She hid behind the computer suite door with her tranquilliser pistol, with the Magnum poised if required. Eddie sorted through the circuit boards, found the most crucial ones, and began plunging the warehouse into the Stone Age. He then took cover in a store cupboard and waited for Sophie's signal. She kept watch behind the computer suite door. Her left index finger hovered on the trigger of her pistol, awaiting the moment to fire.

*   *   *

Martina muttered several choice Slovenian phrases while wrestling with the coffee machine. She'd been lumbered with it, as nobody else had the faintest clue how it worked. Ian had also been put to work, filling ciabatta rolls. Claudia had left the front entrance and assumed the comfiest chair in the café, her shotgun resting faithfully beside her in case her catering conscripts rebelled. Ordering breakfast wasn't a flippant command; an army marches on its stomach, and the Frisco Spiders had neither the time nor inclination to eat much before leaving the motel. With the situation mostly under control, or the least chaotic it had been since fleeing the ferry office, there was a window for sustenance.

Tucked behind the café was a small travel counter. Most of the holiday brochures were Italian, but as Claudia went to investigate she spotted the currency exchange rates display. Along with Euros, dollars could be exchanged for the Canadian equivalent along with Japanese Yen, Mexican Pesos and Chinese Yuan. If she was a common thief, she'd have pocketed some currency, but was wise enough to know that a professional criminal committed as few offences as possible. Much of the money was probably dirty anyway; a currency counter was a neat way to launder cash by packing it off in the wallets of unsuspecting tourists who'd exchanged clean funds. The same would inevitably apply to the money for Romana's release. Claudia weighed up how much to ask for; it was tempting to demand a fortune but she had to be realistic. As she looked at the exchange rates once more, an idea occurred. Her gaze settled on the figure for Chinese Yuan and she jabbed a few numbers into the calculator on her phone and saved the details.

Claudia returned to the café to find Ian and Martina loading the refreshments onto a pair of silver trays. There were eight rolls and coffees.

"Have you included Romana?" Claudia asked, with a hint of surprise.

"No, Doug's second stomach," Ian clarified.

"He normally eats Sophie's share," Claudia reminded him.

"Well I hope you don't expect me to make more for the customers," he grumbled.

Claudia's eyes narrowed, not because of Ian's attitude, but that he'd identified a serious problem she'd overlooked.

"Customers," she muttered to herself, before turning to Martina. "When's this place meant to open?"

"Whenever Romana wants it to," she replied, cleaning milk stains off the coffee machine.

"Yes," Claudia smiled. "She's a bit tied up just now, so I guess we're in charge."

"Surely you're not going to open for business?" Ian asked.

Claudia pondered the idea for a moment, as the bustling crowds might present a chance to leave undetected, but it didn't take long to see the fatal flaw. By opening the doors, she'd surrender control of who entered the building, and the police and Mafia could flood the warehouse and her gang would either leave in handcuffs or coffins.

Claudia realised she had to keep the warehouse locked down, which meant turning away customers, and more urgently, the rest of the employees who'd arrive sooner.

"Why would the warehouse be closed?" Claudia asked herself out loud.

"Strike action?" Ian suggested, trying to be helpful.

"Against the Mafia?" Martina asked with a wry smile, batting her eyelids to soften the put-down.

"The Mafia, that's it," Claudia smiled. She had a solution, and all it required was a pen and paper.

140

Sophie's left index finger was still poised on the trigger. She was waiting. Eddie was increasingly nervous in the store cupboard, but his one comfort was that he trusted Sophie as she never missed and never failed. Still the waiting continued until finally, in the bare corridor outside the computer suite, they heard footsteps. They weren't heavy or menacing, and were more of a nonchalant trot, but still sent a shiver down Eddie's spine.

Poised behind the door, Sophie didn't flinch as the footsteps drew nearer. She heard the screech on the bare floor as the heavy shoes changed direction and within a heartbeat, a third person entered the room. Sophie fired the pistol. She never saw their face, but a narrow portion of neck above the collar of the guard's uniform was exposed, and that was enough. Her dart hit the target, the guard stumbled for a moment, then fell to the ground.

Sophie glided silently around the body, confirmed it was unconscious, then headed to the store cupboard. She knocked on the door eight times, which was a well-known calling card of the Black Widows, but what most people didn't know is that subtle variations were involved. In the case of the Falmer Spiders - now the Frisco Spiders - there was a brief hesitation between the third and fourth and the sixth and seventh knock. It meant nothing to the untrained ear, but to Eddie, it meant Sophie had succeeded and it was safe to emerge.

From Eddie's experience, guards were usually retired police officers or people who'd wanted to be police officers. In this case, the poor wretch was old enough to be the former and unfit enough to be the latter. Eddie left him snoozing, restored the telecoms, and headed down the corridor with Sophie. They tried a few doors until finding the security suite. It was darkened with two desks, and crucially, both were vacant. The monitor at the first workstation was turned off while the second was halfway through a hand of online poker. Eddie deduced the guard had been gambling and hadn't been watching the security cameras. To compound the guard's failings, he appeared to be doing very badly. Indeed, being tranquillised was probably his first lucky break that day, as at least it stopped him incurring more losses.

Sophie began logging out of the machine while Eddie used the other to review the security footage, isolate the moment when the store had been opened that morning, and obliterated everything that followed. He also switched off the cameras so that nothing else was recorded. As far as the security systems would be concerned, the Frisco Spiders had never been anywhere near the Mezzogiorno Warehouse.

Sophie finished logging off the second computer.

"I'm hungry," she announced.

"There's a first time for everything," Eddie smiled.

*   *   *

When Eddie and Sophie returned to the atrium, coffee and ciabatta rolls were waiting. Sophie ate her rations without a word. Eddie had barely started his when Claudia pounced on him for another task.

"I need help with a phone call," she revealed.

He left his breakfast unfinished. Claudia noted that Ian and Martina hadn't eaten, prompting a potentially costly mistake. Instead of asking one of them to take breakfast to Doug and Marcus in the basement, she handed the job to Sophie. She dutifully queued outside the service lift while Claudia and Eddie rode it to the top floor. Each wall of the compartment was adorned with mirrors, which meant that everywhere Eddie looked, he saw countless Claudias. He could've spent all day in that lift. He was tempted to sabotage the control panel but recognised time was pressing, and she wouldn't appreciate the delay. As the bell chimed softly at the top floor, she left the compartment, but Eddie stayed behind for a brief second to savour the rich scent of her perfume.

His lungs full to the brim, he returned to the plush carpets he'd walked a matter of minutes beforehand.

"We need to find the manager's office," she revealed, heading through the maze of desks. It was located at the front of the building and the door was locked, but that was little match for Eddie's skeleton key. The office was grand with a regal table and chairs, bulging bookcases and an antique desk graced with a plush executive chair. There was a telephone and computer on the desk, which was precisely what Claudia had been seeking.

"And now we call the Mafia," she revealed.

"From their own phone?"

"It's impossible to trace," she smiled, assuming the executive chair and swivelling smoothly from side to side as if she owned the place. "We just need a number."

Eddie fiddled with the phone but there wasn't anything obvious stored on its memory, which is what he'd expected, so he turned to the computer instead. It was booting up when Claudia's curiosity got the better of her and she opened the top drawer of the desk. It contained a battered book with a list of names and numbers.

"What's that?" Eddie asked, poised to hack his way into the computer.

"I think it's an address book," she grinned, smugly handing it across. Eddie scanned the pages.

"You're right," he nodded, but then a pained expression crossed his face. "But it's a jumble of names and numbers. I don't understand any of the notes."

Claudia scowled and snatched the book. Her expression didn't improve when she reached a similar conclusion.

"The notes look Italian," Eddie suggested.

"Yes," she sighed, before a glint entered her eye. "So all we need is somebody who speaks Italian."

*   *   *

143

Ian finished his breakfast. Martina had nearly done so, but it tasted like ash in her mouth. She wanted to leave, and her gaze settled on the front entrance. Not for the first time it was unguarded, but crucially, none of the gang were anywhere to be seen. The others were upstairs or in the basement, as Sophie had gone to deliver the refreshments.

"Do you think we could leave?" She whispered.

Ian glanced around and reached the same conclusion as his girlfriend.

"Maybe," he smiled. "It's worth a try."

As if creeping out of a library, the couple tiptoed away from the atrium and through the clothing department. One of Martina's designer shoes scraped on the floor as they entered the cosmetics section, muffling what Ian thought was a muted bell. They kept going, past the perfume counter where they'd first met. How long ago that now seemed. They reached the front entrance and there was still nobody around. Ian wrenched the shutters with Martina's help and they rattled up towards the roof. Now they just had to unlock the doors and Martina had the key. She opened them and Ian smelt the fresh air of freedom. They stepped through the entrance onto the ornate steps, bathed in morning sunshine, and dared to smile.

"That's far enough."

Ian didn't have to turn around. He recognised the voice.

"Sophie, we're going if that's okay," he stumbled, clearly nervous.

Having returned from the basement, Sophie had caught up and was standing behind them. She said nothing.

"We've done our job," Martina added, before daring to take another step forward. No sooner had she done so, but Sophie drew a gun from the light jacket covering her running gear. Tellingly, it wasn't the tranquilliser pistol. Martina could have responded in many ways, but the emotion that boiled to the surface was one that Ian had never seen before. It was frustration.

"What?" She scolded. "You'd shoot your own friends?"

Sophie hadn't been aiming the Magnum, but now she turned it on Ian's girlfriend.

"Actually, she just might," Ian warned.

*   *   *

"Where's Ian when you actually need him?" Claudia bemoaned. The address book was riddled with Italian footnotes. Without knowing what they meant, the names and numbers were useless.

"Should I fetch him?" Eddie asked, standing loyally beside the grand desk in the manager's office at which Claudia was enthroned.

"Yes, but first I need your help with the ransom demand," she replied.

Eddie's phone contained a tool to distort voices, which Claudia would use to record their message. It would then be played into the landline in the manager's office. If the Mafia traced the call, as expected, it would confirm the demand was genuine without revealing any useful information, such as the caller's accent.

"How much will you ask for? Ten million, twenty?" Eddie inquired, his excitement rising as he dared to mention the larger sum. Claudia didn't reply; she merely tapped her phone which cheerfully displayed a figure of $14,194,925. Eddie looked baffled.

"Why that much?" He asked.

"Exactly. Why?" Claudia beamed. "It'll drive them crazy trying to work it out."

A wry smile crossed Eddie's lips. He had visions of Mafia men desperately racking their brains regarding whether they'd ripped somebody off by precisely that much, or whether the numbers contained a hidden message. In fact, there was a subtle significance, which Claudia had engineered into the demand to throw the Mafia off the scent.

She started recording the message. It was brief, containing the crucial points and nothing more. Romana had been kidnapped by a heavily armed gang and her life depended on a ransom being paid. Claudia included delivery instructions for the cash, recited the figure twice, then hesitated for a moment. She wondered if she was being too clever, and added a brief sentence that, as it turned out, dramatically affected the kidnap's outcome. In fact, it would be a matter of life and death.

"Or we'll accept the equivalent in Chinese Yuan," she added.

Eddie looked quizzically at Claudia, but assumed she had her reasons. Such was The Maid's talent for money laundering, Chinese currency was unlikely to faze him. The key thing was that untraceable Pound Sterling came out the other end. One final matter remained, which was the deadline for the cash.

"By ten o'clock. Message ends," said Claudia. The recording ceased. Eddie gazed at the antique carriage clock on the grand desk. It was already twenty past nine.

"A forty minute deadline?" He gasped.

"Thirty by the time it's sent," Claudia added.

"Is that long enough?"

"Just," she nodded.

Snap ransoms were a favoured Black Widows technique, but were sometimes used by other gangs, so it wouldn't identify Claudia and her associates. Not only did snap ransoms reduce the waiting time to receive the cash, but data compiled by Section Five proved they were most likely to work. The deadline was so harsh there was barely time to think, much less mobilise an opposing force to mount a rescue. There were no exhausting days of negotiations. Instead, it was all over before anyone could blink, with the kidnappers escaping in the ensuing chaos.

"Anything else before I fetch Ian?" Eddie asked.

Claudia nodded and gave him a sheet of paper to fix on the exterior side of the front entrance shutters. There were only eight words, but they made Eddie shudder.

"Store closed due to death in the family," he recited.

"Why else would the Mafia shut for the day?"

Eddie nodded, read the words one final time, and realised there was a serious risk they would come true.

*   *   *

"Are you going to kill us?"

Martina asked the question, but not with the fear you might associate with such an inquiry, but a clear overtone of contempt. She was three steps down from the grand entrance with Ian beside her. The Californian sunshine was at their backs. Hidden inside the darkness of the building, the barrel of the Magnum was pointed firmly at her chest. Sophie remained silent.

"I've never seen her murder anyone," Ian advised his girlfriend, "but she has a reputation."

Martina rolled her eyes before staring directly at Sophie.

"You're no better than the Mafia. Are you proud of yourself?"

Just for a moment, the briefest flinch rippled across Sophie's face, but the Magnum didn't waver. Ian sighed and trudged back up the steps. Martina shook her head before joining the reluctant retreat.

"Let me guess," Ian groaned, "we're all in this together."

"I'm trying to save your life. Not end it," Sophie replied, finally breaking her silence.

The next contribution came from the soft chime of the service lift. Eddie stepped from it, brandishing a hastily inscribed sheet of paper. Before he reached the entrance, Sophie holstered the Magnum in her jacket.

"Need fresh air?" Eddie inquired, noting the doors were open. Nobody replied. He stepped through the no man's land between Sophie and the others before taping the notice to the shutters as instructed. With grudging help from Ian, the shutters were rolled down and the building was sealed again.

"Claudia needs your help," Eddie informed Ian. The trainee doctor sighed at the news.

"Why me?" He pleaded.

Eddie replied that his Italian language skills were required. When Martina heard this, a difficult decision presented itself. Her boyfriend spoke good Italian but she was fluent. She had to decide whether to keep a low profile to maximise her chances of survival, or stand beside Ian in his hour of need. She took a deep breath and made her decision.

"We'll go together," she resolved, placing her hand in Ian's soft and reassuring palm.

"Oh," Eddie blushed, "I guess the more the merrier."

He led them to the service lift and the doors rolled shut. Sophie remained at the front entrance, hoping she wouldn't have to reach for the Magnum again.

*   *   *

"Can you make sense of this?" Claudia asked, casting the address book over the desk with disdain. Ian and Martina, having been led to the manager's office, craned their necks to study the pages.

"It's full of gibberish," Ian confirmed.

"They use Italian for anything secret," said Martina, seizing upon the book and studying the pages, "and this is about Sambuca imports."

Claudia scowled at the revelation. Ian shrugged helplessly. Eddie nuzzled beside a filing cabinet hoping he wouldn't be seen. Martina sighed and began flicking through the pages.

"You want to phone The Don?" She sighed, holding the first page of the book open. "Go ahead."

Even Claudia, with her limited knowledge of Italian, understood "Il Don". She frowned, dialled the number beside it, and awaited the reply. The call was answered. The voice on the other end sounded dishevelled, but that wasn't her concern as they didn't need to talk, they just had to listen.

Once the recorded message was played, Claudia hung up. She knew what would happen next. Within seconds, the mobile phone which had been in Romana's designer handbag started to ring. Only it wasn't in her possession anymore. It had been brought upstairs and was vibrating cheerfully on the antique desk next to Claudia. She noted the fact it was ringing and smiled. She cancelled the call, noted the number, and sent a message.

"Yes we are serious. We have her phone," she texted back.

In the unlikely event the initial phone call hadn't triggered an earthquake at San Francisco's Mafia headquarters, the subsequent message certainly did.

There was no turning back now.

*   *   *

The Don's weekend retreat was a coastal villa south of San Francisco. He'd been hosting a party. Many guests had stayed over and the house was littered with empty wine bottles and discarded bow ties from dinner jackets which had once been pristine but in many cases were now being used as makeshift pyjamas. The house stank of alcohol, smoke and people who'd ingested too much of both.

The Don was too old for late night parties, but told himself otherwise. He perched on his grand bed, which was occupied by one of his three mistresses. He couldn't remember if they'd attempted anything the previous night. She'd woken briefly when he'd taken the call, but went back to sleep assuming it was

149

business and it was best not to intervene. The Don struggled off the bed, but felt adrenaline filling his veins as he marched towards the door. He was a large man, and had lived well enough to become larger still in recent years, which slowed his progress. However, he was determined to get even with whoever had intruded into his Sunday morning so impertinently. He rarely saw Romana; she was the daughter of his long-estranged wife and The Don reckoned she was becoming as disagreeable as her mother. However, she was still family. While he disapproved of her, Romana being kidnapped made his blood boil. It was not because of love, for that had faded, but something Martina had already recognised was even more fundamental to a man in The Don's position...pride.

The door to the neighbouring guest room crashed open. The Don staggered through it, the veins bulging on the side of his bronzed neck. He was looking for the man he trusted more than any other, his deputy, Angelo. He was younger, slimmer, smarter and had a magical ability to solve even the toughest problems. Crucially, he didn't party excessively, and was already dressed and sipping espresso, having slept alone.

"It's Romana," The Don roared, verging between panic and rage. Angelo was troubled. Her name hadn't been mentioned in months. For Romana to cause a stir, something awful must have happened. She was either dead, arrested, seriously injured or something equally grave.

"They've kidnapped her," The Don added, brushing past his deputy and storming into the room.

"Who?"

"The Triads. It must be."

"Why would they do that?" Angelo asked, who immediately recognised the consequences of such a move.

"I don't know, but they want a ransom," he snorted, adding that a precise sum had been demanded, but was also payable in Chinese Yuan. Angelo drifted to the window and gazed at the gentle waves of the Pacific Ocean.

"What's the deadline?" He asked.

150

"Ten o'clock."

Angelo choked on his espresso. For the first time, he looked concerned.

"Professional guys," he diagnosed. "Amateurs don't use snap ransoms."

The Don, who could feel his adrenaline melting away to be replaced by desperation, then asked the question which had been at the forefront of his mind when he crashed into Angelo's room.

"What do we do?"

Another sip of espresso was taken.

"Pay up," he conceded, adding they could follow the kidnappers, discover if they'd been hired or were working alone, then reclaim the money and administer a suitable revenge.

"Yeah, and I'm pulling the trigger myself," The Don added, before realising a crucial clause in the delivery instructions, which was that he wasn't allowed anywhere near the warehouse. Instead, somebody else would hand over the cash, and only one car would be admitted to the underground car park. The Don then divulged the rest of the delivery details. Angelo nodded and realised he had to make three phone calls.

The first call was to mobilise a quartet of trusted men, or failing that, the least incompetent ones he could find in down-town 'Frisco on a Sunday morning. Angelo was too far away to reach the warehouse by ten o'clock but would head there urgently. While he couldn't preside over the pay-off, he hoped to identify and track the kidnappers when they left the building.

The second call was to the Mafia's favourite bank. Such was the nature of its business, the mob often needed large sums of cash at short notice. Most banks wouldn't scramble a manager to serve a customer on a Sunday, but it wasn't an ordinary bank and the Mafia was its best customer. Fourteen million dollars was needed urgently, in fact, a little more than that. Angelo typed the mysterious figure into his phone and converted the currency. It was exactly one hundred million Chinese Yuan.

151

The third call was to his opposite number in the Triads to find out what the hell was going on.

*   *   *

The Seeker had no idea what the hell was going on. From the café across the street, he'd watched the warehouse shutters being raised and the trainee doctor stepping into the light. He was joined by the attractive woman, who was the suspected insider. They'd been talking to someone inside the building, and judging by the body language, it was an argument. The Seeker wasn't surprised as he knew something the rest of the gang probably didn't - one of them was a double agent.

After a while, the couple returned indoors and a slight figure with chunky glasses appeared. He fitted the description of Eddie Griffin and was outside just long enough to tape some paper to the shutters before they were rolled down to seal the building once more.

The Seeker had to know what the notice said. He was reluctant to approach the warehouse, so he span a yarn to the café waiter that he wanted to know when it opened but a leg injury made it difficult to cross the street. The waiter gladly pocketed ten bucks for the errand, which struck him as easy money. The Seeker recognised it was danger money. However, he read the notice and returned unscathed.

"What did it say?"

"Store closed due to death in the family."

The Seeker nodded slowly and mournfully. He now knew what the notice said, but not if the death had just occurred, or whether it was about to happen.

*   *   *

"Are you trying to get everyone killed?"

It was Angelo asking the question. He was on the phone to his opposite number in the Triads. Fong was young, unusually so for such a role, but also very smart. He wasn't on Angelo's Christmas card list, but there was mutual respect. They could do business, and harboured similar views of their leaders in that they both considered themselves better, and were just waiting for the moment to manoeuvre them aside.

Angelo was calling from the passenger seat of the Maserati Quattroporte, having borrowed The Don's car and driver. They weren't speeding; reaching the warehouse by ten o'clock was impossible and being stopped by police would delay them further. However, there was urgency in the phone calls Angelo had been making, none more so than his conversation with Fong.

"The Don's seriously mad. I reckon he'd shoot anyone without round eyes just now," Angelo warned.

"We'd never kidnap Romana."

"Because you'd know what we'd do."

"And she's much too annoying," Fong added knowingly. Angelo chose not to comment, but replied that if the Triads didn't have Romana then somebody was trying to frame them.

"Which is serious," Fong agreed. "I will advise The Master at once."

The line went dead. Angelo recognised his opposite number had to inform his boss, which left him uneasy. The Master and The Don had distrusted each other for many years. Only careful diplomacy between their deputies had prevented an outright war, and if the Triads had kidnapped Romana, it would surely ignite a wildfire of violence.

Angelo placed two more calls as the Maserati entered the San Francisco suburbs. He tried the warehouse security office and then Romana's bodyguard. Neither phone was answered. He checked his Rolex; fifteen minutes remained before the pay-off. The quartet tasked with delivering the ransom should be at the bank. With more time, he'd have chosen a different team. Three of the gang were unreliable. Bianco was the only one he trusted and Angelo hoped his competence would be enough to carry the others. Their orders were simple enough; collect the cash, exchange it for Romana and follow the kidnappers. However, there were still many things that could go wrong, even if the Triads weren't involved.

*   *   *

As soon as Fong ended his conversation with Angelo, he sought The Master. They both resided in the same palatial apartments in Nob Hill, overlooking Chinatown, but there the similarity ended. Fong was westernised and well educated. The Master was neither. He was at least awake when Fong knocked his door. In fact, The Master hadn't slept. He had two addictions, which were smoking and gambling, and he'd spent the night indulging both. His mah-jong table was fabled, amongst those in the know, as boasting the highest stakes games in America. Millions were won and lost, and that night, he'd fared poorly. He certainly wasn't in the right frame of mind for bad news.

"Angelo said what?" He exploded, once Fong outlined the situation.

"A personal call to The Don could be the answer," his deputy suggested. However, that was easier said than done. While the deputies could do business, their superiors distrusted each other. The Master would gratefully seize upon any chance to disgrace and humiliate his old foe. He also resented the Mafia having a Chinatown foothold in the shape of the Mezzogiorno Warehouse. Yet it now presented an opportunity, as the Triads were much closer and could mobilise a gang to reach it before the ransom arrived. His thinking was also influenced by his costly night of mah-jong. He'd lost millions, but now there was a chance to cover the losses at his rival's expense.

"So the Mafia intends to give us a ransom," he smiled "It would be rude not to accept."

"You're taking the cash?" Fong inquired, with a hint of concern.

"The Mafia expects to see Triads," The Master noted, "so they will see Triads."

*　　　*　　　*

Everything was set. Doug watched Romana and her unconscious bodyguard, who Marcus had dragged to the basement. He'd also hauled the guard who'd been darted in the computer suite to the same spot. When Marcus returned underground, Claudia, who'd been covering for him at the car park entrance, returned upstairs. Sophie was guarding the front entrance in case Ian and Martina tried absconding again, but they seemed glumly resigned to their fate in the atrium café. Eddie had finished wiping the security footage on the top floor and deactivated the cameras. He then liberated a laptop from the offices and arrived in the café.

Ian watched Eddie with mild curiosity as the electronics expert hacked his way into the building's network and produced, of all things, a snazzy presentation. He wasn't doing so for fun, as the computer would act as the middle man between the Frisco Spiders and the Mafia. When the mob arrived with the ransom, they'd find the laptop in the car park with delivery instructions. If all went to plan, the only person the Mafia would see was Romana when she was released. Claudia had marked a red 'X' in the centre of the car park where the money should be left. She'd also taken the precaution of ensuring the Edsel was tucked around the corner where it couldn't be seen. Doug would retreat from view when the Mafia arrived and the shutters would be opened by Marcus, with help from Eddie, just before the cash arrived.

If the exchange went to plan nobody would get hurt and the Mafia wouldn't know who'd arranged the kidnap. What Claudia didn't realise is that the Triads were also on their way, and as their base was closer, they were going to arrive first.

Eddie placed the laptop in the centre of the seemingly deserted car park. He then raised the shutters with Marcus and they headed to the café. Claudia didn't like leaving the entrance open but Marcus, who'd kept watch, had informed her that police had apparently left. She didn't share this information with the others. In theory, it was a brief window to flee the building, but she'd risked too much to leave empty handed. She didn't want an argument about going through with the kidnap, she just wanted to get it done.

Sophie was peering through the shutters at the front entrance. Claudia wasn't sure what to do with her; where would she be most useful? Guarding the entrance was important, but if things turned sour in the basement, Sophie and her Magnum would be invaluable. Claudia was trying to decide when fate intervened.

"We have guests," Sophie announced.

Claudia raced to the shutters and spied a black Mercedes E-Class rolling along Stockton Street before turning into the car park. Four people were aboard, and suddenly, all too late, she realised she'd made a big mistake. She had the trump card in the shape of Romana, giving her the power to dictate the conditions of the pay-off. She'd allowed a single car into the basement, but now realised it should have just been one person carrying the cash. Four people were in the Mercedes, but only two of the Frisco Spiders were competent with firearms. If a battle ensued, they were probably outnumbered, and having surrendered control of the car park to allow the ransom to arrive, the rest of the building could follow. As ever, in times of crisis, she turned to her most trustworthy colleague.

"Sophie," she said, "you'd better come along in case this gets nasty."

The dead eyes didn't flinch. The two women went downstairs and met Doug in the alcove overlooking the car park. Romana was still bound and gagged, but her captors couldn't risk a conversation in case their accents gave away their identities. Claudia was careful to place a finger to her lips as they arrived. The trio then laid in wait as the Mercedes rolled menacingly into the seemingly deserted car park. The engine stopped. All four doors opened. As the occupants stepped from the vehicle, Claudia was seized by shock. Something had gone horribly wrong. The car didn't belong to the Mafia, but the Triads.

Claudia recovered just quickly enough to give a playful wink to Doug and a smile. He didn't know the terms of the handover, hence she reckoned it was possible to humour him that everything was fine. He looked baffled but stayed quiet. Sophie was also silent, but tellingly, was checking each chamber of the Magnum to ensure the bullets were primed for action. When the pistol snapped shut, the noise was drowned out by another powerful car. It was an Alfa Romeo Guilia which thundered into the basement as if the driver had been racing all the way. Claudia checked her watch. It was precisely ten o'clock. All four doors of the crimson Alfa Romeo flew open. Three of the occupants were adorned with stubble and sunglasses, one of which carried a large metal suitcase. The fourth was taller, with long fair hair and sideburns. His suit was crisp and he had the appearance of being the only person in the car who'd been awake more than ten minutes.

"Bianco," smiled one of the Triad delegation, pointing a finger at the man in question. "You owe us money."

"So I heard," he replied. His voice was lighter than his muscular stature suggested. "Hope you know what you're doing."

"That's not your business," said the second Triad, thrusting his palm forward to receive the ransom. The four men from each gang faced each other. A few uneasy metres of neutral concrete stood between them. All of them were armed, either visibly or secretly. If the money had been surrendered, it was possible none of the firearms would have been fired. That was not to be the case.

"Hand over Romana first," said the man with the ransom.

A difficult silence settled over the bare concrete. The Triads could see a hooded and bound figure in the nearby alcove, but were unsure if they could run the risk of releasing her. Fong had told them another gang had organised the kidnap, but there was no sign of them. Claudia and her colleagues were hiding around the corner, and the laptop they'd left on the ground had so far been ignored. The Triads hadn't touched the computer as their orders had been clear and simple – they were to collect the ransom and leave. Now it seemed, after his all-night Mah-jong session, that the Master had failed to anticipate a major flaw in his plan. The Mafia wouldn't pay until Romana was released, and the Triads weren't sure if they could do so.

"Money first," the leading Triad insisted.

"Romana," was the Mafia response.

"Money."

"Romana."

"Money!"

"Romana!"

Nobody ever knew who fired the first shot. The crucial thing is that someone did, and while the bullet missed, those that followed did not. The Mafia man clutching the metal suitcase was first to fall. However, it didn't prove the Triads started the battle, merely that they scored the first hit. The fourth Triad, who'd delivered the fatal shot, was next to die. He was riddled with bullets from the automatic of the third Mafia man, dispensing instant revenge for his colleague's death. The exchange that claimed both lives took little more than a heartbeat.

A few yards away in the alcove, Claudia had to think fast. Her immediate concern was Doug. For all his bravado, he'd never experienced a fire fight before. It was impossible to tell how he'd react. At one end of the scale he might fall to pieces, at the other, he might join in recklessly with all guns blazing. Neither was good. Claudia ushered him through the nearby door, ordering him to shoot anyone who opened it without giving the Frisco Spiders' secret knock. She added that he was their last line of defence,

158

which was meant to flatter him, and seemed to work. In truth, Claudia knew if the survival of the others rested on Doug, they were probably finished. As a result, she had to hold the line in the alcove with Sophie, and checked her shotgun while her colleague lay in wait with the Magnum. They couldn't see the battle unfolding round the corner, but crucially, the rival gangs were also unaware of their presence.

In the centre of the car park, the metal case dropped by the deceased Mafia man was spinning on the concrete floor. It was tantalisingly out of reach of both gangs, but having been ordered to collect the ransom, there was more pressure on the Triads to seize the cash. The third member of their team lunged for the case. The remaining Mafia men, by contrast, were retreating towards the Alfa Romeo. Two were firing indiscriminately, as if seized by panic, but Bianco remained focused. While his colleagues' bullets flew in every direction, including towards the alcove, he produced his gold-plated pistol from his immaculate suit, took aim, and eliminated the Triad who'd dared to seize the abandoned ransom. His body lay five metres from the Mercedes, behind which the two remaining Triads had taken cover. They were firing automatics without precision, but in the general vicinity of the Alfa Romeo and the trio of Mafia men, one of which made the fatal mistake to trip over his own feet. As he fell to the ground, both Triads turned their weapons on his helpless frame and pumped dozens of bullets into the body, which within moments became a corpse.

Two were dead and two remained on each side. The survivors were hiding behind their respective vehicles; the only other cover in the otherwise barren car park was the alcove. Neither gang had ventured that way, possibly deterred by the five steps that led into the uninviting shadows. Claudia was still there with Sophie. They couldn't see the fire fight but the noise was deafening, or at least it had been, for suddenly it stopped. Yet the ceasefire hadn't arisen thanks to a truce. Instead, both sides were considering their next move. In many ways the situation was simple; the Triads had to capture the cash while the Mafia had to stop them, or at least until Romana was safely in their care. However, her welfare had been the last thing on anybody's mind as bullets had flown around the basement. The Triads weren't concerned about her, while the Mafia men were too busy saving themselves to worry about anyone else.

A few seconds later - which seemed an eternity after such an intense exchange of fire – the deadlock was broken. The Triads hatched a plan where the leader of their gang unleashed a hail of bullets at the Alfa Romeo, pinning down their opponents. Under the covering fire, the second Triad tried to recover the case, sprinting into the bloodstained no man's land between the vehicles once the barrage began. The Mafia men cowered behind the remains of their car as every last piece of glass which had so far survived was shattered by the blitz of Triad bullets. Meanwhile, the recovery of the case was underway, but agonising seconds were lost as the Triad undertaking the task struggled to release it from his fallen colleague's posthumous yet resolute grip. Finally it was free, but the Triad barrage ceased as his colleague was forced to reload. Both Mafia men sensed it was time to reply. Bianco did so instantly and clinically. Again, all it took was a single shot from his pistol, and the Triad carrying the ransom fell to the ground. This time the case wasn't held firmly but spilled onto the concrete and slid invitingly towards the Mercedes. The remaining Triad starting crawling towards it, shielded by his vehicle. The case was within his grasp but the hail of Mafia bullets deterred him from reaching out. He knew he was outnumbered, but his slight change of position presented an opportunity. From where he was lying, he could see the feet of the second Mafia man. Without hesitation, he opened fire and the bullets hit their target. As he'd predicted, the Mafia man tumbled to the floor and the back of his balding head appeared in his sights. A second round of bullets settled the matter.

Now just two men remained. The Triad climbed into the Mercedes. Bianco wondered what he was doing, until the passenger door of the German saloon sprang open. Within a flash, a hand reached out from the comparative safety of the vehicle's interior to seize the suitcase and snatch it back inside the car. The ransom had been lost, at least from the Mafia's point of view, but not necessarily the battle. The Alfa Romeo, which was significantly more damaged, was closer to the ramp leading to the street outside. The Mercedes would have to pass it before making its escape, assuming it could still be driven. Its bodywork was riddled with bullet holes, and yet, the engine started. Even though one of the tyres was flat, the Triad wasted no time in screeching away. There was no time for Bianco to think. He produced his pistol one final time, took aim at the driver's head, and squeezed the trigger. Despite the Mercedes' glass being toughened, it couldn't withstand the bullet, which passed through the front window with precision and accuracy. The Triad behind the wheel slumped forwards but the car didn't stop. Instead, it drove towards the foot of the ramp, clipped the concrete, and smashed head-first into the opposite wall. A deafening crash echoed around the car park, but then, at long last there was silence. All Bianco could hear was his own rapid breathing. Then there was something else; a dull crack emanated from the alcove. He felt a sudden pain in his neck, which was soon eclipsed by the agony he felt in his left shoulder, where he'd been shot during the Triad barrage without even noticing because of the desperate battle. Despite that, it was the tranquilliser dart in his neck that finally brought him down.

"He won," said Sophie, almost cheerfully, while gesturing towards Bianco's unconscious frame in the middle of the bloodstained battlefield. She was standing at the top of the five steps, above the grim carpet of corpses and destruction that now covered the previously bare concrete. Claudia viewed the apocalyptic scene with as much resolve as she could muster. It took everything not to lose control, scream and be violently sick. Instead, she took a few deep breaths, consciously doing so through her mouth to prevent the stench of the bloodbath entering her system. Never before had she experienced and witnessed so much devastation. There was death and destruction everywhere. She didn't know where to turn, and in the end, her eyes settled on the only comforting thing in sight, which was Sophie. Her colleague was surveying the carnage without comment, then turned towards Claudia. Her expression gave no suggestion of being appalled or perversely gratified by the bloodshed. The only thing she wanted was orders.

"Let's close the shutters," Claudia murmured softly. She realised she'd temporarily lost control of the basement and the consequences had been devastating. It was imperative to reseal the building. Thankfully when they reached the car park entrance, no reinforcements for either gang were outside. They hauled down the shutters, locked them, and returned to the horrific scene that awaited in the basement. It comprised two wrecked cars along with eight bodies, of which seven were dead. In fact, as they soon discovered, the death toll was actually eight. Several rogue bullets had strayed into the alcove, and while Claudia and Sophie had been protected, Romana was less fortunate. The cloth sack placed over her head, which had once been white, was now completely red. Meanwhile, her bodyguard and the security man were unscathed, thanks to being unconscious on the floor, beneath the wayward bullets.

"Head shot," Sophie diagnosed, glancing at Romana, whose body was slumped to one side. "Unlikely to have felt anything."

Claudia didn't reply. She just turned away, but unfortunately, that meant facing the even greater devastation in the car park. There was death everywhere she looked.

"All this killing," she muttered to herself. Sophie appeared silently at her side, and nodded.

"We'll never know who started it," Claudia added, before turning to her colleague with a suspicious glance, "unless it was you."

"No," she replied. "I'm just an animal. It takes a human to understand genocide."

Claudia gazed around the basement, trying to come to terms with the aftermath of the worst violence she'd ever experienced. Technically, it was a battle she'd caused, but she forced that unhelpful thought to the back of her mind as soon as it surfaced. After all, she didn't have the luxury of sufficient time to review her actions. She was in extreme danger, along with her colleagues, and before long her weary eyes settled on the source of all the violence. It was a metal case, and inside, was more than fourteen million dollars.

*   *   *

The Seeker smiled as the third coffee arrived, not because he particularly wanted it, but the gunfire had confirmed his suspicions. The Mezzogiorno Warehouse was normally quiet on a Sunday morning, but not today. Even though it was muffled, the noise of the fire fight was unmistakable. It was inevitable that police would be called, indeed, the café proprietor had already done so.

Aside the satisfaction of predicting it, The Seeker wasn't remotely excited by the gun battle. He'd seen the Falmer Spiders arrive, followed by the Triads and finally the Mafia. Unless they were working together, which seemed unlikely, it was about the most toxic combination in the criminal underworld. As a result, the violence that ensued was hardly surprising. However, what did surprise The Seeker was spotting Claudia and Sophie lowering the car park shutters after the battle had ended. Somehow they had survived whatever hellish struggle had unfolded inside the warehouse. They went up another notch in his estimation, and there was no sign of the Mafia or Triads. Was it possible the Falmer Spiders had eliminated the operatives from both rival gangs? If so, The Seeker was doubly pleased he'd avoided wading into their operation and keeping a respectful distance across the street.

What would happen next, The Seeker concluded, was less clear. The Falmer Spiders might try to leave, and if so, he would tail them. Indeed, that was probably the most likely scenario unless they were still waiting for the ransom. However, if that was the case, they couldn't afford to wait long. Police would be returning to the warehouse, and this time in greater strength. It was also likely that the Mafia and Triads would send reinforcements if their initial teams had been liquidated. The Seeker deduced that a large number of police, and an even greater number of gangsters, would now inevitably collide at the Mezzogiorno Warehouse.

He was right.

*   *   *

Claudia's fingers rested on the catches of the metal case. She'd brought it to the atrium café, joined by Sophie and Doug. All of the Frisco Spiders along with Martina were clustered around the table on which the scratched but otherwise undamaged case rested. Eddie had already checked it for booby traps and concluded it was safe.

One of the catches was unlocked. Several of those gathered around the table took a sharp intake of breath. Pulses were rising. Claudia glanced around, then flicked the second catch. The lid didn't spring open automatically and she paused for a moment before lifting it by hand. The hinges creaked and the contents of the case were slowly exposed. Once they were visible, there was complete silence around the table. Mouths were wide open, but no sound came from them, until Doug found what he reckoned were the appropriate words.

"Bugger me with a leek."

He reached into the case and took something out. It was money. A lot of money. Some of his colleagues gasped and began to smile. Ian and Sophie watched the spectacle impassively. Claudia nodded to herself and was too busy feeling smug to notice Martina was doing precisely the opposite, shaking her head ruefully. Her boyfriend was next to join the conversation.

"Can we go now?"

"Yes, after we've cleaned up," Claudia replied.

"Bit of a mess in the basement," Sophie added, her deadpan comment being the understatement of the year. Only she and Claudia had seen the aftermath of the shoot out. They'd taken Doug upstairs without letting him view the bloodbath; Claudia was unsure if he'd derive some macabre kick from it or run screaming for the hills. It was simpler not to find out. However, the Edsel was downstairs and they'd have to drive through the battlefield to leave the warehouse. Claudia knew she couldn't fully shield her colleagues from the grim reality of what lay in the basement. However, she'd endeavour to provide the sugar-coated version, and began her debrief after sending Sophie to the front door to check if police were outside.

"The Triads arrived unexpectedly," she explained, after setting the scene.

"Who invited the noodle gang?" Doug asked.

"No idea, but when the Mafia arrived, things turned ugly," said Claudia.

"That's putting it mildly," Ian scowled. "We all heard the gunfire."

"I thought you'd been killed," Eddie added, gazing at Claudia, his lower lip trembling slightly.

"I'm fine," she beamed, "and the bad guys are all dead, having shot each other."

Martina suddenly went pale and slumped into the chair behind her. She found her eyes pointing at the ransom and looked away in disgust.

"And the last man standing turned the gun on himself?" Ian inquired, with an overdose of sarcasm.

"He'd already been shot," Claudia replied, adding that Sophie then darted him.

"Shot where?" Ian demanded.

"Shoulder I think; it was bleeding a lot," she replied.

Ian rolled his eyes, stared at the floor, then returned his gaze to Claudia. His expression was bitter and resigned.

"I'll need a first aid kit, sterilising gear and a tool box if you can find one," he muttered.

"What?" Doug scoffed. "You're going to fix him up?"

"I'm a doctor," he snapped. "We take an oath to heal the sick and wounded, no matter whose side they're on."

Martina gazed at her boyfriend with a subtle hint of pride. Ian added he'd require somebody to assist him, ideally Sophie.

"She's got the strongest stomach," he added.

"Can't see why; she never uses it," Doug muttered.

Right on cue, Sophie returned from the front door. Her colleagues heard the distant sound of sirens.

"Any police?" Marcus inquired.

Sophie nodded, adding three cars were outside along with a support vehicle.

"So much for a clean getaway," Ian observed.

Claudia frowned at the comment, but a quick glance at the metal case reminded her why they'd risked so much. She told Doug to guard the front entrance while Eddie found the equipment Ian had requested. Once it had been sourced, the trainee doctor would go to the basement with Sophie while Claudia "made the scene safe", which was her coded description of covering the bodies and making the car park's appearance less horrific.

"What about me?" Marcus inquired.

"Count the cash," Claudia replied. "Martina can help you."

"I'm not touching that blood money," she frowned.

"Wear some gloves then sweetie," Claudia scoffed.

Marcus allowed himself a brief smile and began flicking through the cash. Martina stared at the ransom with grim fascination, and once a couple of minutes had passed, reached into the case.

"This will take you ages," she muttered. "I might as well help."

"Thanks," Marcus smiled. "Welcome to the Frisco Spiders."

*   *   *

Angelo was troubled. It wasn't the urgent journey to the warehouse that fazed him, or even the fact Romana had been kidnapped. It was the silence. Something had gone horribly wrong.

Angelo's instructions had been clear; to hand the ransom to the kidnappers and then follow them, keeping him updated. He trusted Bianco, if not the other three, but had heard from none of them since they'd left the bank. It was unlikely Bianco had fled with the ransom; he had the right blend of loyalty mixed with enough sense to understand what the Mafia did to traitors. The others were less reliable and might have overpowered him. If they'd been led into temptation, the Mafia certainly wouldn't deliver them from evil. Indeed, exactly the opposite would apply. However, there were other possibilities. Bianco and his colleagues might have been captured. They could even be dead, and if they'd disappeared with the money, they soon would be.

The Maserati parked up in Broadway beside the warehouse's less glamorous northern side, with the grand façade of the main entrance around the corner. Shuffling awkwardly in the passenger seat, Angelo was unsure what to tell the driver. The main options were to take off, continue to wait, or storm the building. The latter seemed foolish, especially if Bianco's gang was already captured or worse. There was also nothing obvious to chase, but sitting around felt too much like doing nothing. Angelo knew something was wrong and he had to act, realising that time was ticking and delaying his response could prove fatal.

Based on the evidence, or lack of it, Angelo deduced the plan had failed. He realised this would reflect badly upon him, and compromise his ambitions to take over the San Francisco operation. In fact, not only would he have to work hard to keep his position, but also to keep his head attached to his shoulders. However, Angelo was smart and knew how to play the game. If the operation ended up as a success he'd take the credit, but if not, he needed to smear his superior's fingerprints liberally over the calamity to ensure he was the fall guy.

Angelo dialled his boss. He was still tired, hungover, grumpy and annoyed.

"Bianco's team hasn't emerged," Angelo informed him.

"Where is he? Where's Romana?"

"Hard to say unless we storm the place," he replied, which was true enough. Angelo's next move was to ensure that if his next suggestion failed, it would be The Don who was held responsible. He put the call on speaker phone to ensure the driver heard the exchange.

"Do you want to send more guys to take the warehouse by force?"

The phone connection to the beach house crackled for a few seconds, but otherwise there was silence. Even from several miles away, Angelo could hear The Don thinking; it was a painful exercise which had never come naturally to the over-promoted ogre. Once again, it was pride that forced his hand.

"I'll send all the men you need, and bring me whatever's left of the kidnappers."

"And Romana?"

"Oh," said The Don, pausing for a moment. "Yeah, bring her too."

"Okay."

"Alive," The Don added belatedly, in case clarification was needed.

The call ended. Angelo had what he wanted – the chance to lead a successful operation, or the insurance policy of passing the buck for a botched one. He couldn't lose, which was vital if he wanted to assume control the local Mafia, just as Fong had ambitions to take over the San Francisco Triads.

And on the subject of Fong, his driver and their Mercedes S-Class had just pulled up on the southern side of the warehouse in Pacific Avenue, and he was poised to make a phone call to The Master.

*　　　*　　　*

If there's one thing the Black Widows had taught Ian it was how to treat a bullet wound. However, he'd never handled a live subject; he'd practised on dead pigs. It probably helped that he didn't know his patient. He didn't even know Bianco's name, merely that he worked for the Mafia and was the sole survivor of a pitched battle that left eight people dead including Romana. Claudia covered the bodies, then guarded the car park entrance with her customised shotgun. He wasn't sure if she was there to stop police entering the building, or prevent him leaving.

Ian set to work on the wound. He'd been trained to use tools and even the contents of cutlery drawers if medical equipment couldn't be found. Sophie, having already anaesthetised the patient by darting him, proved an able assistant. She wasn't squeamish and was better than most trainee nurses Ian had encountered. He, on the other hand, felt nervous. Despite his training he was in unknown territory. It underlined how fortunate the Falmer Spiders had been up to this point that Ian had never treated one of his colleagues. Their luck couldn't hold forever, and with more police vehicles arriving outside the warehouse all the time, Ian suspected it had already run out.

Once Ian had finished treating Bianco, he cleared away his things. Sophie helped until Claudia placed her on sentry duty at the car park entrance. They had to climb over the bonnet of the crashed Mercedes to swap places, which had embedded itself in the basement wall.

"Done your good deed for the day?" Claudia inquired cheerfully.

169

"He would've bled to death," Ian replied sternly. Claudia nodded; she had to concede there had already been too much bloodshed. He then asked if they could leave.

"Only if you ask the cops nicely," Claudia replied, adding that the wrecked Mercedes was also blocking their exit.

"Well done. You've got us surrounded with no chance of escape," Ian muttered, removing the delicatessen apron he'd been wearing over his suit.

Claudia wouldn't admit it, but he was right. She'd managed to get the ransom money, and had the means to launder it, but her assumption they'd be able to stroll off once the Mafia had left and the police were sufficiently bored had been wrong. In fact, more vehicles were appearing outside with every minute. To make matters worse, Sophie reported that not all of them were police.

"I wondered how long it would take the Mafia and Triads to send reinforcements," said Ian, nonchalantly adjusting his cuff links. Claudia felt her heart slipping down her spine and into the overpriced cherry-coloured suede trainers she'd bought the night before. How long ago that now seemed. From the comparative safety of the motel that morning, she was now surrounded by police and gangsters, outnumbered and outmanoeuvred. However, the game wasn't up just yet. Escaping the building was clearly their goal, but stopping the others entering it was the immediate priority. If she could keep them out, and buy some time, a solution might emerge.

"Whoever tries entering this building first will soon wish they hadn't," Claudia announced, cranking her shotgun with purpose.

"Wonderful," Ian sighed. "I might as well put that apron back on."

*　　*　　*

170

Fong briefed his reinforcements in the back of an unmarked van which had pulled up behind his Mercedes. They were heavily armed and already aware of the rumours regarding the warehouse. Something had gone badly wrong with the handover, and neither the ransom or their colleagues had emerged. Fong realised he wouldn't need to motivate his men for the looming second round of the battle. In fact, his biggest problem was ensuring their hunger for vengeance didn't get the better of them.

"Right, the first thing is to ensure your guns are hidden and you move this van three blocks away," Fong announced. His orders were met with confused muttering. He was forced to explain that because police had already surrounded the building, it was likely nearby vehicles would be searched.

"And if police open the doors and find eight men armed to the teeth, what will happen?" He added.

"They'll run screaming; that's what they usually do," came the joke from the back of the vehicle. Fong wasn't laughing.

"I'll keep watch and call when you're needed," he muttered, resisting the growing urge to discharge his firearm into something, or someone.

Fong stepped from the van which drove off as instructed. On the other side of the warehouse, a vehicle packed with Mafia gunmen pulled up behind Angelo's Maserati where a similar conversation was about to occur. Meanwhile, the police vehicles outside the main entrance had swelled to half a dozen and Stockton Street had been closed. Rather than evacuating the adjacent buildings, officers chose to keep everyone inside, which in the case of The Seeker translated into a fourth coffee as neither he, nor the café owner, were leaving anytime soon. However, the police were planning a more imminent move, as a seventh vehicle had just arrived. It was the SWAT team.

*   *   *

171

"It's getting busy out there," said Doug, gazing through the main entrance shutters, his finger poised on the trigger of his automatic. It might have been dangerous, had Sophie taught him how to remove the safety catch. She was still in the car park, but Claudia had returned while Ian drank a mineral water in the atrium café without saying a word to anyone.

"We have to stop police entering the warehouse," said Claudia.

"I'm your man," Doug smiled, proudly brandishing his impotent gun. Claudia shook her head.

"I think the man for this job is a woman," she announced.

Moments later, Doug was carrying a hefty metal table from the café; he was lifting about eighty per cent of its weight, while Eddie strained to guide its other end towards the front doors. Laid on its side, it made a bulletproof shield, but Claudia didn't intend to use it to repel an assault on the warehouse. Instead, she planned to deter such an attack before it began. From behind the table she'd have clear vision of all seven police vehicles once the shutters were raised, and through its gaps, she noted officers were preparing for action. They were swarming around their vehicles but there was no sign yet of firearms besides pistols. The heavy artillery was still in the SWAT van, and there Claudia knew, it had to stay.

The customised shotgun was loaded. Claudia knelt behind the table. Eddie was beside the shutters and reported police were looking increasingly ready to storm the building. Claudia realised if her plan was going to work, she could delay no longer. She gave the signal and Eddie raised the shutters with Doug. Strong Californian daylight swept into the previously darkened lobby, but from the street, it would still be too dim to see what was happening inside. The police had no time to react. Claudia sprang up from behind the table, took a heartbeat to steady herself, then fired at the SWAT van. Its siren was blown to pieces by the first shot. Then she aimed at the patrol car beside it, and again, its siren was destroyed in a cloud of smoke and glass.

As Claudia reloaded, officers scattered for the nearest cover they could find. A couple toyed with the idea of returning fire with their pistols but couldn't identify the source of the shotgun rounds. As a result, they also went into hiding, which meant Claudia only saw the vehicles and no officers. This made her job easier as she didn't intend to shoot anyone. In fact, peculiar though it sounded, she was firing her shotgun to ensure nobody got hurt. Two more rounds were unleashed and two more sirens were destroyed. Her accuracy from skeet shooting meant she was perfectly suited to hitting medium-range targets at rapid speed. She then blasted the three remaining police sirens into pieces before taking cover. Eddie and Doug lowered the shutters.

Outside, all was quiet, at least for a while. The officers, who were still under cover, began hasty discussions to decide their response. Gunfire had come from the warehouse but it was hard to know from where. However, seven shots were counted, and the sirens of all seven vehicles had been destroyed. It was message – whoever pulled the trigger really knew what they were doing. More to the point, if they'd targeted the officers, there would now be seven bodies in the street. Maybe next time they wouldn't be so lucky. It would certainly give the local police chief lots to think about, and he was nearing the warehouse at a rapid rate of knots.

Once the shotgun blasts stopped echoing around Stockton Street and the officers emerged from their bolt holes, the police chief arrived. His car was grander than the rest; it even had a working siren. He was a good but overworked man stumbling towards retirement after a career that was almost glittering but never quite blossomed. Sunday was his day off, or should have been. Instead, he'd been scrambled at short notice, which explained his appearance.

"Uh, chief?" Ventured the scene commander, checking it was indeed his boss.

"What's the matter?" He asked, stepping from the car. "Never seen a clown outfit before?"

"Not on you, chief."

"It's my granddaughter's fifth birthday and Mega Tubby The Clown didn't show up, the useless drunken slob."

The scene commander could see where this was going.

"The outfit's not perfect," the chief continued, "but the best we could fashion from household items."

"Yeah, the mop makes a good wig. Not sure about the pink MC Hammer-style pants though."

"I know; my wife hasn't worn them since George Bush was president."

"Right."

"Senior," the chief clarified. "Now what's happening?"

The scene commander gave his briefing in the back of a support van. As the chief listened, he realised he wouldn't be returning to the party any time soon.

*   *   *

Just a few feet from the police lines, The Seeker had a grandstand view of the action. He wondered why the nearby buildings hadn't been evacuated. He deduced it was because leading dozens of civilians outside, within firing range of the warehouse, just wasn't safe. Indeed, that was the only option unless the properties had rear access.

"Does this place have a back door?" The Seeker asked the café owner, who was the only other person present.

"If it did, would I still be here?" He muttered.

The Seeker heard the coffee machine hissing and burbling as it made his fourth cup of the morning. This time he'd ordered decaf as he felt an overdose of adrenaline coursing through his veins. He increasingly felt like a coiled spring as the action unfolded through an alarmingly fragile pane of glass. It was tempting to retreat further inside the café but he had to keep watch in case the Falmer Spiders fled the warehouse. However, as time dragged past, it seemed the only way they'd leave the warehouse was in a hearse. However, they'd surprised him before, and he was fascinated to see what happened next.

In that regard, he was secretly pleased the café didn't have a back door.

*   *   *

"Surely this place has a back door," said Claudia.

All the Frisco Spiders were clustered around the central table in the atrium café, except for Sophie who was guarding the car park entrance.

"I've already told you there isn't," Ian sighed, reminding her there were four exits, namely the front door, car park, and two fire escapes, all of which led straight into the police's clutches.

"What about a secret exit only staff know about?" Eddie suggested. Martina rolled her eyes.

"If there was, would we still be here?" She replied.

Claudia noted the subtlety of her response. She hadn't said "I" but "we" and noticed her hand was entwined with Ian's on the café table. Martina had made it clear they would only leave the warehouse together; Claudia was yet to decide if this was useful or a problem. For now, the main issue was finding an escape.

"What's behind the warehouse?" Eddie asked. It was a fair question, as it didn't occupy the entire block. Martina informed them an office building stood behind it, but there was no communicating door.

"No bother; just drill through the wall," Eddie smiled, hoping it was the stroke of genius that would save the day. It fell to Doug, of all people, to put him right.

"Never worked as a builder have you," he sighed, which was a withering diagnosis rather than a question.

"I made a bird box at school," Eddie replied, clutching at straws. Doug wasn't impressed.

"First, we haven't got a drill, and second, these walls are solid stone topped with marble," he said, elbowing a nearby column to underline his point.

Eddie looked sheepishly at Claudia. She tried to look sympathetic, as while she had no romantic interest in him, due to his unwavering loyalty, she felt bad if he was made to look stupid. As it happened, a thought crossed her mind that might spare his blushes.

"What if there's a weak spot?" She asked.

"You mean a thinner section of wall?" Doug asked.

"Or a botched repair job," Eddie suggested.

"Wouldn't know anything about those," muttered Doug, intently studying his shoes. Claudia smiled; they had a new plan. She would split her personnel into teams and probe every darkened recess of the warehouse to find another way out. As a bonus, Martina and Marcus would be available, having counted the money.

"To the dollar, it's all there," said Marcus, reclining in his chair with a satisfied grin. Claudia noted a collection of small-value green backs rested on top of the numerous bundles of one hundred dollar bills. She was impressed the Mafia had counted the cash so quickly, but then the whole point of a snap ransom was leaving just enough time to meet the demands, and no time for anything else.

"Time," she muttered to herself, quietly enough so that nobody else heard. It now seemed their greatest enemy. They'd be safe in the warehouse for a while, thanks to her warning shots destroying the police sirens, but the officers would regroup and surely try again, and if they didn't, the Mafia or Triads might attempt an assault. Exploring every inch of the warehouse couldn't be done quickly so she'd have to buy more time. Somehow, she had to ensure the police and rival gangs hesitated in storming the warehouse. Thankfully the Black Widows had trained her well and she knew what to do.

"Eddie, find me a phone," she smiled. "It's time to call the press."

*   *   *

The police chief's heart sank. As if matters weren't bad enough, the last thing he needed was a media circus. The vans of the major outlets and shoddy sedans of the freelancers descended on the warehouse like a plague of locusts. They'd arrived within the past few minutes, which the chief had to concede was always likely to happen. You can't cordon off a busy street in Chinatown without somebody noticing, and in the age of social media, it only took one person with a camera phone and time on their hands to start a press frenzy. In some ways, it was surprising it had taken the haggard hacks and geeky bloggers so long to arrive, but that still didn't make things easier.

From a police perspective, the arrival of the press – regardless of who tipped them off – made a complicated situation worse. In a tense stand-off you couldn't afford to make a mistake, doubly so if the cameras were rolling. Police would be under intense scrutiny with live pictures beamed into the homes of those who knew nothing about law enforcement but would still argue with their televisions that they knew best and the officers on screen were idiots. The chief was not an idiot (even if he was dressed like a clown) and knew he had to tread carefully. After all, he didn't just have the media to worry about, but also the Mafia and Triads.

The police knew what Angelo and Fong looked like. They were ninety-nine per cent sure what they did and one hundred per cent sure they couldn't prove it before a court. Both had been spotted in their vehicles on opposite sides of the warehouse. Neither was making any effort to conceal themselves and the chief opted against extending the cordon to push them further away. He

177

was certain if they searched Angelo's Maserati or Fong's Mercedes they'd find nothing more than aftershave, crucifixes and a box of stale noodles. Neither was there to mount an assault or challenge the police, the chief knew that. Both were there to send a message that the Mafia was watching its building and the Triads were guarding Chinatown. If the police made a mistake, harsh stories in the press would be the least of their concerns.

As the chief gazed at the warehouse he realised he was staring at a gunpowder barrel. One wrong move and it would explode, and he feared the fuse was already lit. Through a mixture of Mafia, Triad and media scrutiny, the reputational damage to the police, and himself, could be incalculable. The arrival of the press was the final ingredient in a recipe for disaster. The chief understood this all too clearly as he gazed at the media circus encircling the flimsy cordon, but it fell to his deputy to succinctly summarise the political and reputational ramifications resulting from press intervention.

"Well that's fucked things up," he said, drawing alongside his boss.

"Inevitable I guess," he sighed.

"Do you want to talk to them?"

"What's there to say? We know the Mafia and Triads are involved, and someone inside the building is a crack shot at damaging city property."

"Guess we can't tell the press any of that," his deputy conceded. "Could we pretend it's an exercise?"

The chief reflected on the idea for a moment, which certainly held some appeal, but if, and more likely when it was exposed as a lie, he'd look pretty daft, or as daft as a police chief already dressed in a home-made clown outfit could appear. His heart then nearly stopped when a sudden "honk" rang out around the police compound. He glanced at his waistband and saw his deputy's hand on the comedy horn strapped to his belt.

"Sorry chief, couldn't resist," he blushed.

"Easy on the surprise noises, will you?"

"Okay, but how about some planned ones? You know, playing loud music until the people in the siege can stand no more and surrender."

Again, the chief gave it some thought, but dismissed it when he recalled a similar tactic backfiring in response to a student sit-in at Berkeley.

"We tried playing the Spice Girls on a loop but the speakers kept getting shot at," the chief recalled.

"I didn't know the students were armed."

"They weren't doing the shooting," the chief added, throwing a telling glance to the SWAT van. His deputy nodded sympathetically, then asked a brilliant question that deserved a brilliant answer, but sadly there wasn't one.

"What do we do, chief?"

His superior fell silent.

*   *   *

"Now that's a car," Marcus smiled. He was happy, in fact happier than when he'd finished counting the ransom, for if there's one thing he valued more than cash it was a vehicle money couldn't buy.

"What is it?" Eddie inquired, who was usually out of his comfort zone dealing with anything lacking microchips.

The car was exhibited on a platform on the fourth floor of the Mezzogiorno Warehouse. As with most department stores, products for women dominated the prime floorspace while those geared to men were exiled to the upper levels. However, Eddie and Marcus weren't shopping but seeking a way out. Claudia had split the Frisco Spiders into three teams. She'd paired herself with Doug, chiefly because she didn't trust him not to steal anything. While they explored the basement, Ian and Martina checked the lower retail floors with Sophie for company. Claudia reckoned

179

Eddie and Marcus didn't need a chaperone as they were the least likely to cause trouble. She would live to regret her assessment.

"It's a Lamborghini 350GT," Marcus announced, running his hand seductively along its burgundy bodywork.

"Right," Eddie nodded, trying to pretend that meant something.

"It's the first proper Lambo," he added. "It came before the Miura."

"Miura?"

"Come on," Marcus sighed. "The car that got wrecked at the start of *The Italian Job*."

"I thought they were Minis."

"No, that was the end, and the Miura was trashed by the Mafia."

"Oh," nodded Eddie, gesturing at the 350GT, "so what are the local Mafia doing with this one?"

A display board stood on the platform. On closer examination it revealed that one lucky shopper could win a chauffeur-driven day in the classic 1960s super car.

"You should buy something and enter," Eddie suggested.

"The trouble is we're not meant to be here," Marcus reminded him, as he removed a screwdriver from a convenient pocket.

"Too bad."

"Not really. The best thing about old cars…" said Marcus, as he forced the driver's door with the screwdriver, "…is they're dead easy to nick."

Seconds later he was behind the wheel and fiddling with the ignition. Once the engine fired he opened the passenger door. Eddie climbed on board with reluctance.

"What are you doing?" He hissed, adding that Claudia told them to search the upper floors.

"Yeah, but she didn't say we had to walk," Marcus smiled, releasing the handbrake. The priceless car rolled off the platform and its tyres squeaked as it wrestled for traction on the immaculately polished floor. Even at fifteen miles per hour, Eddie was perturbed by how quickly the clothing racks and decorative stands of produce went flashing past.

"This is what I call shopping," Marcus nodded smugly. Before long, they were out of business attire and screeching through casual slacks. Eddie's heart then skipped a beat as they slithered through the racks of polo shirts before Marcus executed a perfect handbrake turn to launch them head-first into underwear. Once they'd negotiated socks and briefs, they arrived at the freight elevator.

"Going down," Marcus announced, as they rolled into the compartment and the doors closed. When they reopened, Marcus screeched backwards out of the lift and almost nailed a J-turn into home furnishings, but just clipped a ten-foot decorative tower of designer flower vases.

The noise was truly horrific.

"Bloody idiot," seethed Eddie.

"Relax, who's listening?" Marcus shrugged, flooring the accelerator in order to terrorise another department. They emerged from sporting goods unscathed, but left rather a mess in soft furnishings and the least said about their visit to the porcelain department the better. Marcus finally skidded to a halt beside the freight elevator.

"Done, and I'll bet we've finished before anyone else," he said.

"But we haven't found an exit, and that was the point," Eddie reminded him.

"Take it easy. Claudia will come up with something. She always does."

*　　　*　　　*

Claudia knew she had to come up with something. However, looking for an exit inside the basement had been fruitless. It wasn't helped by narrowing the search to the storage area. She felt it best to steer Doug away from the carnage in the parking lot, especially as she already knew its sole exit was blocked by a wrecked Mercedes. The storage area was her last hope, and that hope was fading.

"There's nothing here," Doug complained, kicking a discarded soda can along the ground. It came to rest in the far corner the basement, inside an alcove. It had the appearance of an extra room that hadn't been finished. Beside it were breeze blocks and cement, suggesting the builders had left the job until Monday to complete. Claudia wouldn't have looked at it twice, except that the soda can was drifting around on its bare floor, as if caught in a breeze.

The moment she stepped into the alcove, she detected something unexpected, which was fresh air. She looked up and saw three narrow ventilation shafts.

"Probably a new cold store," said Doug, adding that the shafts would expel gasses from the refrigeration units once they arrived.

"I guess all that Gorgonzola must be kept somewhere," Claudia smiled. "Could we climb up those shafts?"

"I doubt it," Doug conceded, patting his belly, which was much wider than the ventilation system. Claudia sighed as another idea turned to dust. Doug, on the other hand, was more upbeat. He grabbed a breeze block and started coating it with cement. Claudia asked what he was doing.

"I like to keep my skills up," he replied. "Give me ten minutes, I could finish this off."

"We're trying to get through a wall, not build one."

Doug nodded and backed away from the unfinished job, having added a solitary breeze block to the wall. Claudia led him away from the storage area, trying to decide how she'd break the news to her colleagues that they seemed to be trapped.

*   *   *

182

"There's no way out," Ian insisted, with a hint of self-righteousness as the Frisco Spiders compared notes in the Atrium café. None of the teams had found an exit; they were gathered around a suitcase bulging with money but no means of getting it, or themselves, to safety. Had the kidnap been planned in advance their escape would have been worked out to the last detail, but they were improvising. As a result, they were riding their luck, which was running out.

Eddie, keen to suggest anything that might help Claudia, asked if they could ram through the police lines with the Edsel.

"It's too slow," Marcus replied, adding they'd been fortunate to escape during the earlier car chase.

"And ramming the police lines might destroy the Edsel," Ian added.

"Maybe it's not such a bad plan," Marcus smiled.

"And us with it," Martina warned.

Silence descended on the café table. Claudia was on the verge of admitting defeat. Instead of providing a means of escape, she realised the Edsel was now a stone around their necks. It was vital evidence linking them to the ferry office job, and subsequently to the kidnap, so they couldn't leave it behind. Any chance of a clean getaway was diminishing by the second and Claudia knew time was running out to rescue the situation. At that point, she suddenly realised just how isolated they were. They were thousands of miles from home with very few allies. Had they been in Britain, it was likely the Black Widows would have leverage on a police chief or public figure who could help. The organisation had a network of corrupt officials coerced into service after accepting a small payment from an innocent-looking source only to learn to their horror it was a front for the Black Widows. Favours were then demanded in return for keeping their initial transgression quiet. Indeed, as the saying went in the Black Widows "once you've filled their pocket, they're in yours", but that network couldn't help Claudia now.

"Let's review the situation," she suggested. "We've got police to the front, solid walls to the rear, Mafia to the left, Triads to the right, news helicopters above and eight bodies in the basement. Now what?"

"Send out for pizza?" Marcus suggested. His attempt to lighten the mood fell flat.

"Could we shoot our way out?" Asked Doug, picking up his automatic for emphasis.

"Too risky. We could get killed," Ian replied.

"Yes, you might," Sophie observed, quietly slotting bullets into the Magnum's chamber.

"I'm with Ian," Marcus conceded. "A gunfight's too risky."

"Fine," Claudia sighed. "Anyone else with a bright idea?"

"Isn't that your job?" Martina smiled. "Maybe you're not so clever after all, sweetie."

Claudia's blood started to boil. Her eyes narrowed and it took every ounce of self-control not to make Ian's annoyingly beautiful girlfriend much less beautiful. However, Claudia knew if she lost her temper, she'd lose control of the Frisco Spiders.

"We can't allow everything to go up in flames," she announced, quietly and calmly.

"Really?" Ian asked. "Well I'd say it's already gone up in smoke."

"And there's no smoke without fire," Martina nodded, gripping her boyfriend's hand tightly.

"Fire," Claudia said to herself. Nobody else heard it, but it wasn't long before they'd noticed the smile on her lips.

"Right," she said. "Here's what we'll do."

Her colleagues listened as she outlined her plans. At first they reckoned she was mad, and even after she'd finished, some of them still did. It was certainly risky if not downright dangerous, but the situation was getting desperate. She knew the police, Mafia and Triads wouldn't wait outside forever. Time was running out, but Claudia knew that wasn't the only problem she faced. The second was getting rid of the Edsel; she wasn't sure how to do it, but that was a trivial issue compared with the last one. The third obstacle was potentially the biggest of all...and that problem was Martina.

*   *   *

The police chief was sick of problems. They never started out as his own, but inevitably became his responsibility. At work, it seemed every last crime and law enforcement blunder ended up being his fault. There was no respite at home either, with a continual diatribe of domestic dramas to defuse. It wasn't that he caused them, but had built a reputation at both work and home for resolving or at least limiting the damage when things went wrong. And things went wrong all the time, and what was his reward for dealing with those issues soundly and with little complaint? More problems.

Detecting there was a lull in the action, the chief removed his clown outfit, which he'd created earlier that day to solve one of the many problems he'd recently been handed. While lacking a uniform, he felt better placed to lead his officers in a shirt and slacks, and his deputy found him a spare hat and jacket. The two of them stared at the grand façade of the Mezzogiorno Warehouse in stony silence.

"It's too quiet," the chief muttered.

"Yeah, you took off your horn."

"I meant the warehouse. What's happening in there?"

His deputy could only shrug sympathetically. The police lines were rife with speculation, as was the media coverage, but hard facts were in short supply. All that was definite was the warehouse was locked down, the Mafia and Triads were probably involved and certainly watching every move, and the last time anyone tried going inside, every police vehicle within range became target practice for somebody who could clearly handle a

185

gun. Meanwhile, his officers were loitering around looking bored. He knew that was dangerous because if the shooting resumed, they wouldn't be ready. His officers needed to be on high alert. On that basis, he decided his next move.

"Tell the SWAT team to prepare to storm the building."

"Sir?" His deputy asked, with clear surprise.

"If you don't know what's happening, you must be ready for anything," the chief replied. His colleague nodded and asked when the operation would start. The chief checked his watch; it was eleven o'clock.

"In sixty minutes," he said.

"Twelve o'clock then."

"That's right," the chief confirmed. "High noon."

*   *   *

"Yes, high noon," Angelo confirmed to the van-full of Mafia gunman. He'd left the serenity of the air-conditioned Maserati outside the warehouse and walked three blocks in the increasingly hot sunshine to speak to, what was in effect, an overheating box of heavily armed masculinity. The oppressive air was thick with aftershave, gun oil and sweat. It was nothing short of a private army and was ready for battle. Quite probably, at that precise moment, if a bomb went off in that van, the bomb would lose.

"What's happening in the warehouse?" One of the gunmen asked.

"Hey, what do I look like, the chief of police?" Angelo replied. "The question isn't what's happening in the warehouse, but what's going to happen in the warehouse."

Angelo's smile was met with satisfied grunting and cackles from the gunmen, accompanied by the cranking of shotguns and the near-silent but deadly noise of safety catches being released. It led to Angelo's smile evaporating as he wondered if he'd gone too far in motivating the troops. The truth was, he had no idea what was happening in the warehouse, and no plan for its recapture. However, he was acutely aware that he'd assembled – or more accurately The Don had officially assembled – a private army that was growing increasingly restless. He had to keep them motivated and alert, which meant giving them a target.

"Our target is to storm the building in one hour," he announced. "High noon."

Six blocks away, on the opposite side of the Mezzogiorno Warehouse, Fong was giving a similar deadline to his personnel in the back of a van, and wishing they weren't quite so fond of garlic and tobacco.

*   *   *

"It won't be finished before noon," said Doug, coating a breeze block with cement. As part of her plan, Claudia had told him to finish the wall of the basement cold store. The pair of them were standing outside it, and Claudia was shaking her head.

"You said it would only take a few minutes," she reminded him. Doug stopped work, arched his back and expelled a sigh.

"Sorry love," he replied. "That's before I knew you wanted the space for the door bricking up too."

Claudia wasn't sure what made her angrier – the misleading quote regarding completion time from the the Frisco Spiders' only experienced builder, or being called "love". She was the leader of an armed gang which had seized control of a Mafia-owned warehouse and kidnapped one of its key members to extort more than fourteen million dollars. She was not a "love".

On the subject of the ransom cash, something had been troubling Claudia. While impressed the Mafia had delivered the exact sum on time, it must have been a nightmare to count and they'd probably been forced to do some of it on the way. If that was true, the Alfa Romeo would've left with more money on board than needed.

"I've been such a fool," sighed Claudia, slapping her forehead in frustration.

"Don't worry; most people can't estimate how long building jobs take," soothed Doug, still focused on their previous conversation.

"Yes, including builders," she muttered. "I was thinking about the ransom cash. I need to check something. Until then, get that wall finished, quick."

"What's the rush?" Doug sighed.

"By midday," Claudia insisted.

*   *   *

"High noon," The Seeker said to himself. His fourth coffee was no better than the previous three and the idea of another was less appealing than visiting the dentist. He was tired of waiting for something to happen at the warehouse, and fuelled by a mixture of boredom and too much caffeine, he was now thinking it was time to make something happen.

The café proprietor, the only other person sealed into the venue, was watching television coverage of the drama unfolding outside his establishment and ruing how little airtime his business was getting. By contrast, The Seeker was happy that news cameras weren't probing into the café. He usually preferred to keep a low profile, but wondered if the moment was approaching when he'd be forced to announce himself to whoever was still left alive in the warehouse. Sneaking inside would be risky, but he'd already decided this was his final job; whether a long and happy retirement followed remained to be seen.

The Seeker checked his watch. Fifty minutes remained until midday, which he'd now decided was the deadline where if nothing was heard from those inside the warehouse, they would be hearing from him.

"High noon," he reflected to himself, sipping a coffee that was becoming less satisfying by the second.

* * *

Claudia opened the Alfa Romeo's boot. Searching the dead Mafia gunmen for the keys was unpleasant but necessary. Within seconds of opening the lid, her suspicions were confirmed. There was a carrier bag stuffed with money. At first glance there was nearly a million dollars; it suggested the Mafia had left with fifteen million and removed the surplus bundles on the way to ensure they handed over the right amount.

There were many things Claudia could have done with nearly a million dollars, but while she was a crook, she was an honest crook. Claudia certainly didn't believe in ripping off her colleagues, which meant the surplus cash belonged with the rest of the ransom. For the time being, the large metal case had been moved from the atrium and locked in the Edsel's trunk, only a short distance from the wrecked Alfa. Claudia picked her way through the carnage of the parking lot and arrived at the getaway car. She opened the boot and spotted the empty rucksack from the failed job at the ferry office. The carrier bag with the surplus cash seemed flimsy, so Claudia opted to fill the rucksack. However, when she opened the bag, she had a shock.

"More money?" She asked herself. It wasn't a king's ransom and most of the notes were low in value. There was probably less than twenty thousand dollars. To most people it would be a nice bonus, but Claudia recognised it was a big problem. Given her time in the underworld, she was smart enough to realise that cash appearing from nowhere wasn't a blessing but a curse. Money always came from somewhere and almost everyone who lost it wanted it back.

Claudia cast her mind to the ferry office job. There was no cash in the safe, which she'd witnessed with her own eyes. However, she hadn't been watching when Eddie opened it, and the resulting alarm had been a huge distraction. She tried to remember what happened next – Eddie had curled into an apologetic ball. As ever, Sophie had kept her head while everyone else was losing theirs. It had also been Sophie who'd announced there was no cash, and yet the rucksack was now filled with crumpled green backs

"Oh no," Claudia sighed to herself.

It appeared Sophie had some explaining to do. Claudia dearly hoped there was an innocent explanation but it was just another problem in addition to handling their escape, dealing with Martina and losing the Edsel. In fact, there was another vital issue to resolve, which Ian had told Claudia about much earlier that morning, but which had totally slipped her mind.

Somewhere in the warehouse, having still not been accounted for, was another security guard.

*　　　*　　　*

"We were told to dispose of a car, not steal one," Eddie reminded Marcus. The two of them had returned to the upper floors of the warehouse where they'd left the Lamborghini.

"I'm not stealing it," Marcus replied, climbing behind the wheel. "I've nicked it once, so it's just reclaiming what's already mine."

"Are you keeping it?"

"Wish I could," he sighed, fiddling with the ignition, "but I'll settle for making sure it's safe."

Eddie wasn't convinced that racing a priceless car around a department store was the best way to keep it safe, and said so while climbing aboard.

"Chill out, we only need to drive into the lift," Marcus soothed, adding he'd swap it with the Edsel and bring the 1950s sedan back up in the freight elevator.

"What for?"

"Trust me," Marcus replied. "I can save the Lambo and get rid of that lousy Edsel at the same time."

The Lamborghini reversed into the freight elevator. It descended towards the basement after the doors closed. When they reopened, Marcus was sorely tempted to rev the V12 engine, but something made him stop. Claudia was standing right in front of them.

"What the hell's this?" She demanded.

"Lamborghini 350GT," Marcus smiled. "The company's first production car, three-point-five litre V12 engine, around 130 built between 1964 and 1967 and now virtually priceless."

"You did ask," Eddie muttered from the passenger seat, looking bored.

"I asked you to lose a car, not steal one," Claudia seethed.

"I told him that," Eddie replied obediently, elbowing Marcus in the ribs.

"Relax," he said. "It's all part of the plan. I'll swap this beauty with the Edsel and everything's fine."

Claudia stared icily at the getaway driver and wished she could believe him.

"Just stay out of the main car park when you make the swap," she advised. "It's not a pretty sight in there."

Marcus shrugged and span the Lamborghini into the quieter end of the car park next to the Edsel. Meanwhile, Claudia stepped into the lift. She was heading towards a confrontation she'd dearly hoped would never arise – she was about to quarrel with Sophie.

*   *   *

191

It was a wretched stairwell sinking into the most decrepit basement in San Francisco. It was dark, the air was stagnant, the floor was sticky, and lurking in the shadows, things scurried. Angelo hated the place. However, he knew what lay beyond the next door, and that the loathsome entrance was designed to deter passing trade. He knocked on the reinforced metal door. Above it, a security camera hidden amongst the blackened cobwebs noted his arrival. Thankfully for Angelo, he'd been invited.

The first thing that struck him when the door opened was the smoke. There weren't many places left in the developed world where cigarettes could be lit within the law, but the law didn't extend to this basement. The fact not everything being smoked was tobacco underlined the point. The hidden room was packed with tables encircled by gamblers who were mostly Oriental, mostly male, mostly old and mostly losing. However, it wasn't a casino, as there were no roulette wheels or cocktails. This was a gambling den, and you either played Mah-jong or took a hike.

Fong allowed Angelo a few seconds to fill his lungs with the foul atmosphere before making himself known.

"Thanks for coming," he said. "Meeting in public would be too risky."

Angelo could only reply by coughing, just as Fong had intended, for he wanted to speak first. He beckoned his guest into a quiet corner so their conversation wouldn't be heard.

"My men in your warehouse are missing."

"Then they shouldn't have entered it," Angelo replied. Fong smiled, correctly identifying the comment wasn't confrontational, but skilful sledging from a worthy rival.

"Yes," he agreed. "The decision wasn't mine, so I'm not responsible for this mess, merely clearing it up."

"It'll take a lot of cleaning," Angelo muttered, adding his team had also vanished.

"Which suggests another organisation is involved," nodded Fong.

"Along with the cops and the press, which makes it worse."

"Or better," Fong smiled. "You see, I didn't invite you here to ensure things ended well. I want them to end badly."

"Surprised you need my help," Angelo smiled.

"Problems are one thing," he replied. "But if you want a catastrophe, call the Mafia."

Now both men were grinning at each other. Neither wanted to be the first to change their expression, or even blink. Finally, it was Fong who relaxed his posture, chiefly because he needed something from Angelo, which was to back his plan.

"My reinforcements are restless. I imagine yours are too," ventured Fong.

"They need something to shoot at," Angelo confirmed.

"How about each other? You see, today isn't just a golden opportunity to rid ourselves of incompetent leaders, but useless functionaries."

"Clearing out the dead wood," Angelo nodded, "though a lot of guys will end up dead."

"Don't be sentimental. Nobody will die today who doesn't deserve it, and if the police get involved, the more bullets the better."

"So everyone goes into the warehouse, and nobody comes out."

Fong nodded, adding he would hold back his more competent gunmen to pick off anyone who tried fleeing the building.

"I'll do the same," Angelo agreed, adding they could eliminate the kidnappers if they hadn't already been killed in the crossfire.

"Very neat."

"Massacres usually are," Angelo smiled.

The men shook hands.

*   *   *

193

"We need to talk," said Claudia.

Sophie's eyes narrowed, partly through confusion, but mostly suspicion. She was on the second floor, monitoring Ian and Martina's futile search for a hidden exit. What Claudia had to discuss with her closest ally wasn't for their ears. She led Sophie to the nearby ladies' restroom, which proved to be a mistake. Confronting Sophie was risky, but what she'd overlooked was that it left Ian and Martina alone.

Claudia held the restroom door open. Rather than walking straight through, Sophie hovered on the threshold, eventually sidestepping to the right with her back to the wall. Few would have noticed the subtlety but she was determined to be nearest the door. She looked timid, in contrast to Claudia who hitched herself effortlessly onto the marble-topped line of sinks, crossed her legs in a flash and stared into the eyes of the accused.

"I've found some money," she revealed.

Sophie did not reply.

"It was inside the ferry office rucksack," Claudia added. Sophie's silence continued but Claudia knew her well enough to spot the fatal error – she retreated a further step towards the wall.

"Why did you do it?" Claudia asked.

"You need money," Sophie replied, without hesitation once she'd realised an explanation was unavoidable.

"You kept it for me?" Claudia asked. For the first time since striding into the room, there was doubt in her voice.

"Attending your father's funeral is costly," Sophie observed, adding that any surplus cash could be distributed amongst the gang.

"Like a rabbit from a hat," Claudia smiled, before asking the killer question. "How long have you been siphoning cash?"

At moments like this, Claudia wished her eyes were piercing blue, but they were grey like a February drizzle. All the same, they burned into Sophie's gaze. Her dead eyes didn't betray her, but a further step backwards gave her away. Yet even though

Claudia had exposed her, it was unclear what would happen next. If a fight ensued it would be spiteful and grievous. Sophie was stronger and far more dangerous than she looked. Claudia was smart, proud and resourceful. The opulent restroom was at serious risk of being smashed to pieces. Only Sophie had an easy escape, having positioned herself beside the door. At that moment, without warning, Ian barged through it and skidded across the polished floor. Claudia rolled her eyes.

"Yes, what is it?" She sighed.

"They've got Martina," he spluttered. Claudia knew Ian well enough to recognise he was worried; he often whined and complained, but rarely panicked. Now he was breathing hard and his eyes were bulging. Claudia dismounted the line of sinks.

"Who's got her?" She asked.

"An armed guard," he bleated, adding that Martina was searching for a hidden exit when the security man seized her.

"Then we'd better get her back," Claudia replied. She followed Ian out of the restroom, but paused for a moment as she passed Sophie, who'd pinned herself to the wall.

"We'll talk later," said Claudia.

Sophie said nothing.

*   *   *

The guard stank of drink. He was young, which was the problem. For him, Sunday morning is what followed the night before, and the night before had merged into the morning after in a haze of alcohol. He was now breathing it over Martina, leaving her deeply uncomfortable.

"Who are you?" He growled. She wasn't tied to the chair, but the way he towered over her made Martina feel like a prisoner. Instead of being rescued she felt captured. One moment she'd been seeking an exit, the next there was a gun in her back. Ian was searching elsewhere; it was unclear if he'd seen her being marched

195

away. All that was certain is that Martina now found herself trapped in decrepit chair in a dingy office facing a man with a loaded firearm.

"I said who are you?" He repeated, with increasing anger.

"I work here," Martina muttered, staring blankly at the guard.

"Then why are you shooting?" He barked. "I heard gunshots."

"Talk to the police. They're outside."

"But you're inside."

"Yes, I'm staff," Martina replied, raising her voice for the first time. The guard backed off, but his retreat was temporary. When he returned, he drew eyeball to eyeball with his captive, but lost the initiative when she broke the silence first.

"You've been drinking."

"No I haven't," he insisted, backing away to regroup. "Not on duty."

"And last night?"

"What does that matter?" He barked, waving his gun around petulantly. "I came here for a quiet shift and what happens? Gunfire in the lobby."

"Sorry if it worsened your hangover."

The guard wasn't smart enough to digest a well-directed insult. His right hand clenched into a fist. Yet he couldn't land the punch, partly because Martina was attractive, but mostly because she didn't even flinch when he drew towards her. There was no sign of fear; only contempt. He drew back once more to consider his next move. While doing so, it would've been wise to glance at the keyhole. Had he done so, the guard might have realised he was being watched.

*   *   *

"That's the dumbest thing I've ever seen," Eddie sighed, shaking his head. He was reading a sheet of paper. It had just been discharged from a printer which served the open-plan offices on the building's top floor. Marcus was sitting behind a desk, looking as well-suited to his surroundings as a commando in a crèche.

"Take it easy. I've never liked paperwork," he admitted.

"It's your idea that's the problem. It'll never work."

"We were told to lose the Edsel," Marcus reminded him, which was the first task for a while that he'd actually relished. His intention was to leave it on the Lamborghini's display stand.

"You can't pass it off as a classic car," Eddie muttered.

"It's old enough, and I've provided a back story."

"Which nobody will ever believe," Eddie frowned, before reading the paper aloud. "Marlon Brando's Ford Edsel."

"Sure. It was a gift from a film," Marcus replied.

"Which one?"

"*A Streetcar Named Despair*."

Eddie shook his head in disbelief.

"Is that the best you can do?"

"Don't worry. The car should be destroyed anyway, and sometimes if Plan A fails you just try something else."

"And what plan is this?" Eddie demanded, brandishing the paper.

"Let's see," Marcus reflected, leaning back in his chair. "Probably Z."

*   *   *

"What was your plan?" Snarled the guard.

"Me?" Martina asked, placing a hand across her chest. "I just want to get out of here."

Her words now rang truer than ever. She detested the interrogation in the dingy office, not because the guard was intimidating, but because he was repulsive. Every time he came close, she detected his foul hungover breath and the total lack of toothpaste or anything else that would mask his overindulgence the night before. Martina reckoned that the guard had every intention of hiding in the warehouse throughout his shift and recovering on the firm's time. However, on hearing shotgun blasts downstairs, even the laziest security men are forced out of hibernation.

"Why were you shooting?"

"I wasn't. I just work here."

"So do a lot of people," the guard frowned.

"Why are you questioning me? You should help me."

"All in good time," he replied. "Now tell me who else is in the building."

The two were eyeball to eyeball. At first Martina was silent, but then she began to talk.

"My boyfriend is…"

And that's as much as the guard heard. The next he knew, the locked door had been kicked in. He spun around to confront the intruder only to find nobody there. The next thing he noticed was a strange pain in his neck. He clasped it, and felt a tranquilliser dart just above his collar. He staggered to the floor and the last thing he saw before passing out was Martina shaking her head.

A few seconds later Sophie drifted into the room. She checked the guard was unconscious, totally ignoring Martina in the process. She was paid more attention by Claudia, who was next to appear.

"Feeling chatty?" She smiled.

"He had a gun," Martina replied, throwing a glance at the spread-eagled guard.

"With no bullets," Sophie revealed, checking his firearm.

Martina wasn't sure what was worse – being interrogated by the guard, or being trapped in a small room with the ever-conceited Claudia and her poisoned pixie of an enforcer. Somebody else then squeezed into the cramped office, but his arrival made Martina's heart soar.

"Thank heavens you're safe," gasped Ian, embracing Martina in her chair, adding he'd raised the alarm immediately after the guard seized her.

"And we were happy to help," Claudia added cheerfully.

"Nonsense," Martina scoffed. "You just didn't want me to talk."

"Not as dumb as she looks," Sophie muttered, but loud enough for everyone to hear.

"At least one of you is honest," said Martina, rising from the chair and staring daggers at Claudia before leaving with Ian. Claudia stayed behind for a moment, reflecting that Martina was now her biggest problem. The missing guard was neutralised, the Edsel was being dealt with and her escape plan was taking shape. However, Martina didn't figure in those plans.

If Martina left with the Frisco Spiders she'd be connected with them, which meant the police and rival organisations would have somebody to chase. A clean getaway was impossible if she was involved. Martina had to remain in the warehouse, and given that Romana's bodyguard had watched her being darted, ideally she had to be found unconscious. As a result, they'd have to turn a tranquilliser pistol on her, and this time for real. Claudia knew Ian would disapprove and Martina would be incensed. Perhaps it would be easier to fire the dart without warning.

Claudia stared at the unconscious guard and realised there was still a loose end. Romana's bodyguard had seen Martina being darted, yet two hours later she'd been abducted by the security man. Claudia had to hope he was sufficiently hungover not to register the time, but didn't like leaving it to chance. At that moment, a dangerous thought crossed her mind.

Claudia realised it would be far simpler if Martina was dead.

*   *   *

It wasn't easy deciding who should die. Angelo looked carefully around the sweaty gunmen in the back of the van. He wasn't just evaluating their usefulness, but their loyalty to The Don.

Six blocks away, Fong was facing the same dilemma. However, he was more robotic than his opposite number and it didn't take him long to choose. Zhou was trigger happy and an accident waiting to happen. The man beside him could barely shoot straight and was a liability. Wong was also volatile and a close relative of The Master who was likely to resent a takeover. Emotion only figured in Fong's final choice. Chang had bullied him at school, making his formative years a misery. Now it was payback time.

"The four of you will be the assault party," Fong announced. "The rest will provide support if needed."

All of the chosen quartet smiled; they felt honoured, especially those who reckoned they'd been selected because of fierce reputations. The others, who were more disciplined and wise, were also pleased, and smart enough not to show it. Fong checked his watch.

"In twenty minutes we go to war," he concluded.

*   *   *

"What bit of 'get rid of the Edsel' didn't you understand?" Sighed Claudia, rolling her eyes.

She'd arrived on the fourth floor to witness Marcus polishing its chrome-plated bodywork. It had pride of place on the raised platform, inheriting the privilege from the Lamborghini now hidden in the basement.

"You said yourself, the best disguises are always the most outrageous," Marcus replied, buffing the chrome. Eddie looked on, noting Claudia's expression changed from dismay to disbelief as she read the car's fraudulent history.

200

"Marlon Brando?" She asked, shaking her head.

"I didn't believe it either," Eddie muttered.

"Look, the car will probably be destroyed anyway," said Marcus, failing to conceal a smile.

"And if not?" Claudia inquired with suspicion.

"Then it needs to look its best," Marcus replied, rising to his full height after polishing the chrome.

"Whatever," Claudia sighed, adding that a more immediate concern was disposing of the security man who'd recently been tranquillised by Sophie.

"Another darted guard?" Marcus inquired innocently. "Are we collecting them?"

"Just leave the Edsel and put him with the others," Claudia instructed, rapidly losing her patience, which was underlined by the way she seized Eddie's shoulder when he tried following the getaway driver. Far from being affronted, Eddie was stimulated by the physical contact.

"What is it?" He croaked, with his reply bouncing around the octaves like a troll whose voice hadn't broken.

"Food," Claudia barked. She ordered him to fetch some rations with a similar deadline to the one she'd given Doug to finish the wall.

"Yes, by twelve," Eddie nodded submissively.

For the first time since arriving on the fourth floor, Claudia allowed herself a smile. Eddie didn't get everything right – few people did – but he was mostly competent and his loyalty was without question, or so it appeared. They were now alone and Claudia realised her hand was still gripping his left shoulder. She also recognised a difficult conversation with the poor lovestruck wretch, which had been long overdue, was now unavoidable.

"Eddie we have to talk," she conceded, releasing her grip. "I've known for some time you have feelings for me."

Bashful to the last, Eddie almost tried to deny it, before nodding awkwardly.

201

"Okay, that's fine," she replied cheerfully. "Here's what we'll do. I don't really want to date anyone in the gang, and I'm afraid that includes you, but there can be a happy ending."

"Which is?" Eddie inquired, with an equal dose of suspicion and desolation. Claudia noticed his lower lip was quivering. She gripped his shoulders firmly.

"Eddie, you'll be a great catch for someone, and when we get out of here, you'll be a multi-millionaire."

"What use is that?" He replied, on the verge of tears.

"I'll be honest, you'll never get me," Claudia replied, with a mischievous grin Eddie would never forget. "But I'm not the only girl in the world, and somewhere there's another who looks and might even sound like me."

"And?"

"Buy her diamonds and a Ferrari, because you can," said Claudia, releasing her grip on his shoulders and using her left hand to caress his cheek. "Then you can marry her and everyone's happy."

"Including you?"

"Definitely," Claudia nodded. "I don't even mind if you fantasise that she's me with the lights off. Just don't call my name in the bedroom."

Claudia stopped caressing Eddie's cheek and grabbed his chin playfully.

"I guess that could work," he conceded sheepishly.

"It will," she smiled. "Glad we had this little chat."

Eddie nodded obediently and went to fetch the food.

*   *   *

The Seeker was pondering whether to order lunch. Much of the fourth coffee had been drained. If needed, he could make it last until noon when he planned to leave the café and infiltrate the warehouse. He was a seasoned observer of police operations and recognised the officers outside were preparing to storm the building, and probably working to the same twelve o'clock deadline. When the SWAT team made its move, he'd abandon the café and follow them, capitalising on the inevitable chaos to slip into the warehouse undetected. What he'd uncover inside wasn't a prospect that filled him with enthusiasm.

As The Seeker stared glumly across the road, he reflected that few people had witnessed as much death and violence as him. It gave him a jaundiced view of the world and a cynical attitude towards humanity. As the years passed, and increasingly few remained, he'd developed a greater appreciation of the natural world rather than the one created by his own kind, which he now treated as a scar on the landscape. People were generally greedy, unpleasant, selfish and prone to spite and aggression when they didn't get their way. At least, that was his view of society, which was actually helpful in his line of business. He had no room for sentiment; people either needed dealing with, or not, and those that did rarely lived long. As the saying went, 'keep you friends close and your enemies closer', but in The Seeker's case, he'd surrounded himself with so many enemies that his friends were no longer visible.

The minutes ticked by, and the prospect of entering the warehouse, and the likely scene he'd encounter, wasn't appetising in the least. The Seeker decided against lunch and began to mentally prepare for the task ahead. He knew police were poised to strike and the Mafia and Triads were waiting in the wings. If any of the Falmer Spiders left the building alive it would be a miracle, but they'd surprised him before. Their survival was all the more remarkable given that one of them was a traitor. He wondered when they'd choose to stab the others in the back, or if they were already undermining the operation from within while keeping their true identity secret. If, and more likely when the shooting started, it would be interesting to see which side the traitor would choose.

*   *   *

The choice was bewildering. Eddie's nose was pressed against the glass of the vending machine. It appeared to sell everything so long as it wasn't nutritious. Countless columns and rows of prettily-packaged junk food stared back at him. The problem was emptying the stuff from the machine. His Black Widows skeleton key had opened the neighbouring cold drinks cabinet and he'd filled a bag with sodas, but the confectionery and crisps were harder nuts to crack. The only option was using coins salvaged from the drinks machine to buy the items legitimately, or as legitimately as you could with stolen cash.

Eddie jabbed A1 on the keypad for the seventh time. Another bag of tortilla chips dived mournfully off the top shelf and landed in the collection tray. Eddie put the crisps in his bag and repeated the exercise. It was agonisingly slow, and also monotonous; he was pondering whether to order a candy bar from D3 for variety. However, Black Widows operatives were trained to be disciplined. He'd persist with the crisps, and was so engrossed with his task he hadn't noticed someone was creeping up on him. He was also unaware they were armed.

The first Eddie realised he wasn't alone was when the vending machine's glass window shattered with a deafening crash. It was so loud, it muffled the sound of the handgun that inflicted the damage. Eddie's life flashed before his eyes and he felt rooted to the spot. Finally, he found the courage to turn around to confront the gunman.

Only it wasn't a man, but a woman.

Five storeys below, Claudia was sitting in the atrium café, facing another serious problem. She had to do something about Martina. Claudia was alone, with her shotgun resting faithfully at her side. She'd already decided that if Martina had to die, pulling the trigger was her responsibility. Asking Sophie to do it was cowardly and unfair. The question that now remained was whether the fatal shot had to be fired.

Claudia recognised Martina was a risk. She knew too much, and the second security guard had seen her when she was already meant to be unconscious. At the very least, she'd have to be darted again, but even if everything went to plan, the police would ask her every question imaginable. She'd have to give an Oscar-winning performance to ensure a clean getaway. Claudia didn't feel comfortable putting so much trust in her. It would be simpler if she was dead.

Meanwhile, back on the fifth floor, Eddie was staring at the woman with the gun. Sophie rarely smiled, but looked even more unimpressed than usual. Stepping around her colleague, she reached into the vending machine and retrieved three bars of chocolate, placing them slowly and deliberately in Eddie's bag. She then flicked her head towards the remaining contents. After an awkward moment, Eddie understood what was required and reached into the machine. Sophie nodded briefly before slipping away towards the lift.

Back in the atrium café, Claudia was staring into her shotgun. Inside each barrel was a blackened void that could deliver death in a heartbeat. However, she hadn't joined the Black Widows to kill people. She'd followed her father into the family business to stay close to him. Now that no longer mattered, and her next move was unclear.

Claudia knew eliminating Martina was the only logical thing to do. However, she wasn't a heartless bitch. The only time she'd taken a life was to avenge her father's death. She didn't intend to kill again unless it was unavoidable.

The shotgun was placed on the floor. It hadn't escaped Claudia's attention that if Martina died, Ian would retaliate. What shape his vengeance would take was unclear, but he loved her, and his response would reflect that; it would be savage. Of course there was a solution, but it left a foul taste in Claudia's mouth. It meant killing not just once, but twice.

With Ian and Martina dead, a clean getaway was possible, but Claudia knew there would be blood on her hands. The prospect filled her with dread; she wasn't a cold-blooded killer. The only other option was to trust Ian, and riskier still, to place everyone's fate in Martina's hands.

Claudia stared at the shotgun resting on the floor. She was reluctant to use it, but had to make a decision. At that moment, her thoughts returned to her father. She'd promised herself that something good had to come from his death. With that in mind, she took a deep breath and dialled Ian's number on her phone. The call was answered.

"We need to talk," she said.

"Can't it wait?" Ian replied.

"No, and bring Martina," Claudia insisted. "It's a matter of life or death."

*   *   *

The police chief hated sending officers on missions where they could die. San Francisco could be a rough town, he knew that, but it didn't make things easier.

The chief knew storming the warehouse was risky, in fact, it was suicidal. He didn't have enough intelligence about what was happening inside. A lone gunman could've fired the shots that destroyed the sirens earlier. On the other hand, they could be part of an army of ruthless killers. It was also unclear how many gangs were roaming the building. The Mafia and Triads were certainly keeping watch, and if anything went wrong, the assembled media would catch it all on camera. For all of these reasons, the chief was not about to launch a full assault on the warehouse. He had a better idea.

The SWAT team continued to prepare; they looked restless. At high noon, the chief would order a small number of them towards the main entrance to fire warning shots. They would then take cover in case anyone retaliated. While that unfolding, a trio of police marksmen would sneak into the emergency exit fifteen yards away, using the warning shots as a diversion. Their orders weren't to seize the warehouse but infiltrate it and report back. Once the chief had reliable information, he could decide whether to storm the warehouse with all guns blazing.

The chief examined his watch. Ten minutes remained until noon.

*   *   *

"I'll be done in ten minutes," said Doug, coating another breeze block in cement. He was working in the basement on the incomplete cold store, but Marcus and Eddie weren't convinced he'd meet the deadline.

"Several blocks are missing," wheezed Eddie, straining with the hefty bag filled with the plunder from the top floor vending machines. He dropped it awkwardly beside the wall.

"Careful, don't crush the crisps," said Marcus, who'd just finished dragging the second security man down to the basement.

"It's the drinks that weigh a ton," Eddie sighed, before passing a note to Marcus. "Here's the rest of the stuff we need."

"Thick blankets, toilet paper, two buckets," he recited.

"Oh, not slopping out again," Doug sighed, who was the only member of the gang who knew just how poorly a prison cell would score in the *Michelin Guide*. Eddie told Marcus he might find the necessary items in the cleaning storeroom.

"Is that beside where I parked the Lamborghini?" Marcus inquired.

"Yes," Eddie replied, "and don't even think about going for a spin around the car park."

"As if I would," the getaway driver smiled.

"You'd better not, or we'll set Sophie on you," Doug warned, lowering another breeze block into place.

"She's not so bad," Marcus shrugged. "Sophie never shoots anyone unless she's hacked off."

"But she's always hacked off," Doug reminded him.

"Oh, yes," Marcus conceded. "That would explain her kill count."

"No kidding," Eddie replied. "I've just watched her murder a vending machine."

His comment led him to glance at the bag of supplies salvaged from the top floor. With a sigh, he hauled it off the ground and fed it through the gap in the unfinished wall.

"That's why several blocks are missing," said Doug. "I can't finish the job until everything's inside."

Eddie checked his watch. Only a few minutes remained until noon, and he still had another job to do, which was far more dangerous than looting vending machines. He'd need a quiet place, just the right mix of chemicals and a very steady hand.

*   *   *

Ian knew Claudia well enough to realise something was wrong. When he reached the atrium café, he saw the look in her eyes – they were dead, just like Sophie's, which wasn't normal. She was sitting at a table, staring into space, and didn't even acknowledge Ian or Martina when they arrived. The table was bare except for the customised shotgun, and beside it, two cartridges.

"Who are those for?" Ian asked gravely.

"Take a seat," Claudia muttered.

"I'd rather stand," said Martina. Ian remained at her side. Claudia picked up one of the cartridges and started rolling it between her fingers.

"A job never works without a clean getaway," she sighed, "and that means no loose ends."

"We're not loose ends," Ian insisted. "We're part of the team."

"Grudgingly," added Martina.

"That's the problem," Claudia replied coldly, looking her straight in the eye. "I don't know if I can trust you."

Silence hung in the air. Claudia finished rolling the shotgun cartridge between her fingers and slotted it carefully into the firearm.

"Let's start with you, Ian," she said, without lifting her gaze from the gun. "Witnesses have seen you here and police will look for you."

"They won't find me," he assured her, adding that even if detectives tracked him down, he would say he'd left the warehouse before the kidnapping.

"Will they believe a member of the Black Widows?" Claudia sighed.

"Former member," Ian corrected her, "and Romana's bodyguard would confirm the story. He threw me out, remember?"

"And nobody saw him return," his girlfriend added.

Claudia nodded. She then picked up the second cartridge and turned her gaze to Martina.

"And what about you?" She sighed. "You can't escape with us."

"I don't wish to," Martina replied. "All I've wanted since this whole thing began was to get out alive."

"If only it were that simple," said Claudia, with a rueful smile. "I guess you haven't found a hidden exit or you wouldn't be here."

Martina nodded. She then looked with suspicion at Claudia's right hand, which was loading the second cartridge into the shotgun.

"So that's your solution is it? More killing?" Martina asked. Claudia looked up from the firearm. Her expression was mournful.

"I really wish I could trust you," she sighed.

"You can," Martina nodded. "And do you know why?"

"Because you'd lose your share of the ransom?" Claudia ventured.

"Keep your blood money," Martina scoffed. "I don't give a damn what happens to you, or your followers, but I care about Ian, and would say nothing that puts him in danger."

"Which means the rest of you are covered," Ian added.

Claudia's right hand moved away from the shotgun and onto her right knee as she crossed her legs and reclined in the café chair. There was almost a smile on her face. She glanced towards Ian.

"You've made an impression on this girl," she observed.

Martina didn't like being called a girl. It was almost as bad as "sweetie", but she held her tongue.

"She's the only reason I stayed in 'Frisco," Ian replied.

"Indeed, but if you want to leave it, there's only two ways out of here," said Claudia, running her hand over the barrel of the shotgun, "and this is one of them."

"What's the other?" Ian asked.

"Sophie," Claudia muttered. Within the blink of an eye, Sophie emerged silently from the background. In her favoured left hand was the tranquilliser pistol. She placed it beside the shotgun. Claudia gestured to the weapons.

"Choose," said Claudia, staring at Martina.

"Oh, you can't be serious," she seethed. "Not again."

"You can't escape with us," Claudia reminded her, adding that the only way she wouldn't be linked to the gang would be if she was found unconscious with Romana's bodyguard and the other two security men.

"Will she be safe?" Ian asked, clearly worried.

"As safe as she can be," Claudia replied, "and it's almost midday, so this must be done now."

Martina's heart sank, but she wasn't about to show any weakness. Doing so would be an admission that Claudia had won, and she wasn't going to let that happen. She strode forward and gripped the pistol.

"Good choice," Claudia smiled.

"Hopefully," Sophie added coldly, who attempted to take the gun from Martina, but found she was clinging to it tightly.

"You're not shooting me again," she muttered icily. "I'll do it myself."

"And do you know how that gun works?" Claudia inquired, adding that the dart must be fired into exactly the same spot as before. "You can't have two entry wounds."

Martina had already raised the pistol to her neck, but hesitated as she realised, to her disgust, that Claudia was right. She could certainly feel the wound, but it wasn't visible without a mirror, and she'd never fired a gun in her life. She looked towards Ian and the first hint of tears began to form in her eyes.

"You do it," she said softly.

Ian took the pistol. He frowned at the weapon. While his expertise lay in medicine and surgery, he'd received firearms training and knew how the gun worked.

"It'll be safer if you lie down," he advised, adding that he didn't want her to fall heavily on the ground. Martina nodded and rested on her side on the marble floor. Ian removed his jacket, rolling it into a pillow to place beneath her head. He then reclined beside her, holding the pistol just above the wound.

"I'm sorry," he whispered.

"It's not your fault," she said bravely. "Stay alive for me."

"You do the same."

"Just try to stop me," she smiled.

A moment later, Martina felt the dart enter her neck, and closed her eyes. She fell asleep in her boyfriend's arms, praying this would not be the last time it happened.

*   *   *

Bombs were not Eddie's forte, so he kept it simple. There would be no electronics, moving parts, timers or anything subtle. It also wouldn't win any design awards, given that it comprised a

211

battered metal bucket filled with vile liquid. However, if any skill was involved, it was the recipe for the cocktail of chemicals that turned an unglamorous pail of slop into a weapon of mass destruction.

Eddie might have admired his creation, were it not for the fact that it smelt foul. In fact, it stank. So bad was the odour, Eddie would've tied a handkerchief around his face if only he'd owned one. Instead, he'd resorted to removing his socks and tying them around his nose. They smelt less than enticing, but it was like walking from Satan's sewage farm into an enchanted rose garden by comparison.

Having added the last ingredient, Eddie tiptoed around the bucket. He'd placed it beside the perfume counter on the ground floor, the very spot where Ian first laid eyes on Martina. Eddie then tore up some newspapers and laid them carefully around the makeshift bomb to serve as a fuse. He wished he could produce something more sophisticated, but one morning of explosives training with the Black Widows didn't make him a nuclear scientist. However, so long as the newspaper caught light, and the flaming pages licked the surface of his wretched concoction, everything would be fine...unless of course you were standing beside the perfume counter, in which case you'd be blown to pieces.

Just two minutes remained before midday. Claudia had sent everyone to the basement, except Eddie, and she'd come to monitor his progress. However, she was barely within ten yards of the bucket when its stench reported for duty. Moments later, when she was directly in its firing line, she wasn't sure what to ask Eddie first, being torn between "what's that smell" and "why have you tied socks around your nose"? In the end, she asked neither, surmising the issues were linked. Instead, she pinched her nose and asked a third question.

"Is it ready?"

"Once I light the papers, we'll have a couple of minutes," he replied.

Claudia nodded. She gazed around the stylish and opulent interior of the Mezzogiorno Warehouse with its fine fashions and designer goods, and the grand atrium stretching towards the heavens. Everything about the view was grand, which meant her next instruction wasn't given lightly.

"Start the fire."

Eddie hesitated before nodding warily. He lit a match and within moments, the first sheet of newspaper was alight. Claudia then rushed to the basement with Eddie. They both realised there was no turning back now, and they'd have to trust their colleagues and their luck if they were to emerge alive from the warehouse. The point of no return had been crossed.

*   *   *

It was high noon. As the papers encircling the bucket started to burn, there was extensive activity outside the warehouse. In Stockton Street, the police chief gave the signal for the SWAT team to begin its operation. Six armed officers rushed towards the main entrance and discharged several rounds of ammunition towards the building. Within a heartbeat they vanished into hiding, while four of their colleagues slipped into one of the emergency exits. The police chief allowed himself a smile – they were inside the building, but now he was worried about what they'd find.

The Seeker was also apprehensive about what lay inside the warehouse. He was about to find out, as the police chief had been too busy congratulating himself on getting three officers into the building to notice that four people in uniform had sneaked through the emergency exit. In that regard, The Seeker had proved that the chief wasn't the only man who could lay his hands on a police jacket if he knew where to look. The Seeker had spotted it draped over the bonnet of a squad car while waiting in the café, and it had taken a matter of seconds to distract the café owner with a sizeable tip, slip outside into the police lines, acquire the jacket, and slipstream the trio of officers into the building. Once inside, he swiftly detached himself from the other three.

Meanwhile, Triads were gathering on the south side of the building in Pacific Avenue, just round the corner from the other emergency exit in Stockton Street. They'd used the distraction of the SWAT team firing at the main entrance to make their move. Fong sent four men into the building. He didn't expect them to return, and given the way he'd chosen his scout party, wasn't upset to see the back of them.

The Mafia would've sneaked into the building were it not for the fact that police had chosen the emergency exit Angelo intended to use. He'd found it harder to pick a suicide squad, hence was secretly pleased he didn't have to send four men to their likely death, or at least not yet.

It was one minute past midday. Four Triads were in the warehouse along with three police officers and The Seeker. Eight people were dead in the car park while five others lay unconscious in the alcove nearby, including Martina, who had Bianco, Romana's bodyguard and two security men for company. Ian rested Martina there gently with tears in his eyes, praying she'd be safe. Claudia assured him she'd be fine, but he didn't trust her. However, Ian had little choice, and no matter how hard he'd tried to leave, fate kept reuniting him with the Falmer Spiders.

At two minutes past twelve all hell broke loose. First, the quartet of Triads stormed into the warehouse's atrium. Second, the trio of armed police did the same thing from the opposite direction. Both sides stopped in their tracks when they saw their rivals. They were ten metres apart, and for a moment, it seemed time had stood still with neither side prepared to make the first move. It would only take one bullet, or a sudden move to unleash an apocalyptic gun battle. The tension was unbearable, and as the opposing sides stared at each other, nobody had spotted the makeshift bomb next to the perfume counter, surrounded by burning newspapers.

Meanwhile The Seeker slipped into the basement. What he found was utterly depressing. He paced mournfully on the cold concrete as he counted the bodies. Seven were visible, rising to eight when he came across the woman he'd seen exiting the limousine three hours earlier. It was a shocking scene; while The Seeker was no stranger to death, the scale of violence in the basement was chilling. It also pointed to a furious battle which had been unplanned. From his experience, if the likes of Section Eight were involved, it was rare to find bodies at the scene. Instead, they would reappear soon after in the car boot of a rival gang leader or public figure who'd refused bribes, or taken them and refused to cooperate. The Black Widows knew a well-placed corpse was a perfect way to leave enemies in serious trouble. As the saying went, 'never waste a body'.

Nearby, in an alcove, The Seeker found another pile of corpses. He sighed; more lives had been cut short and he was growing tired of the grim spectacle. However, he then noticed one of them was breathing. On closer examination, all five of them were. By their appearance, two were security men, one was a bodyguard, the next was a wounded Mafia gunman and the final one was a shop assistant. The last one was the most intriguing; while the others had been dumped without a hint of subtlety, she'd been laid to rest with the elegance of a fairy tale princess.

The Seeker reviewed the evidence; eight were dead in the basement, five were tranquillised and two cars were wrecked. By whatever miracle, the classic Lamborghini in the corner was unscathed, but that was the least of his concerns. What intrigued him most wasn't what he'd found in the basement, but what was missing. None of the Falmer Spiders were amongst the dead.

"Where are you?" He muttered to himself.

They were not far away. In fact, they were virtually under his nose.

Meanwhile, the police and Triads were still in the atrium, with guns aimed at their adversaries. None dared to blink, staring at their rivals through the cross hairs, until finally the first move was made. However, it wasn't the Triads who opened fire, nor the police. Instead, it was a deafening blast from beside the perfume counter. The shock wave ripped through the warehouse's lower floor without warning like a devastating hurricane, destroying everything in its path. All the police and Triads were thrown off their feet, landing heavily on the marble floor and sliding along until crashing into objects heavy enough to withstand the fallout. Those who then tried struggling to their feet soon became aware that the explosions hadn't ended. While the bucket of chemicals had caused the initial blast, a series of smaller shock waves kept reverberating around the atrium. Each one was a bottle of fragrance exploding in the heat of the fire caused by the makeshift bomb; Eddie had not left it beside the perfume counter by chance. The continual shower of ornate glass shrapnel forced the police and Triads to take cover behind whatever they could find, and all the time they cowered behind tables and chairs, the fire at the perfume counter continued to rage…and was spreading.

In the basement, Eddie was spreading cement over the final breeze block. Despite being a safe distance from the blast, he'd clearly heard it and certainly felt it, but wasn't scared. In fact he was relieved; his bomb was incredibly basic, but it had worked. Better still, the smaller explosions that followed suggested the perfume counter was helpfully coming into play. As a result, he was grinning when he passed the block to Doug, but his colleague didn't smile in return.

"Why did you do that, you pillock?" He barked.

"You told me to coat it with cement."

"A tiny amount," Doug reminded him, "not smear the damn thing to death."

The former builder began scraping angrily at the excess cement. Gazing on were Claudia, Sophie, Marcus and Ian, who all winced at the noise of the trowel grinding along the block's abrasive sides. However, with the series of blasts upstairs, nobody else could hear the wretched noise. In fact, it would have been completely inaudible to anyone just around the corner in the basement car park, and that's exactly where The Seeker found himself. He was gazing at the ceiling, frowning at the dust that came down after each explosion like a cynic watching the grim November drizzle. It took more than a few explosions to scare him away, but he was seasoned enough to know when things started going 'bang', it was wise to walk the other way. He strolled, unhurriedly, around the corner into the storage area of the basement.

The Seeker looked around. Discarded building supplies were on the floor, but aside that, he was staring at four bare walls. One looked newer than the rest. He went to examine it, smiled, and walked away.

In the atrium, the trio of police scrambled from their refuge behind a café table and crawled along the floor like petrified worms. One of the Triads had a clear shot at them, but mercifully for the officers, it was Chang, the only member of the quartet who hadn't been chosen for being too trigger happy. He chose to let them leave, after all, they were seeking a multi-million dollar ransom, not a pitched battle with armed police.

Thirty seconds later, the officers dragged themselves through the same emergency exit which minutes earlier had led them into the stand-off which could so easily have killed them. Their colleagues gave covering fire as they hauled their exhausted and lacerated bodies to the safety of the police lines. None were seriously hurt, but all were too emotionally and physically spent to provide a clear account of the operation. All the police chief could understand from their traumatised babbling was that several bombs had exploded, armed Triads were inside the warehouse, and it was now on fire.

"Fire," the chief muttered to himself, gazing around the police lines. Paramedics were on standby but the emergency service he needed the most was nowhere to be seen. He sighed and shook his head.

"Call the fire department," he groaned to his deputy.

Moments later, the first flames were visible and smoke was drifting out of the grand façade. Beyond the police lines, Angelo watched the drama unfolding, and while he maintained a poker face, inside he was smiling like a schoolboy on the last day of term. The operation sanctioned by The Don hadn't just gone badly, it had ended in total catastrophe. He swaggered back to the van containing his assault party and stood them down, then strolled to the waiting Maserati Quattroporte. The driver expected him to occupy the passenger seat, but Angelo assumed the more comfortable and spacious rear seating.

"Boss sits there," the driver grunted.

"Yes," Angelo smiled. "He does."

The Maserati glided away from the kerb, leaving the burning warehouse in its wake.

Inside the building, the quartet of Triads struggled to their feet but were now choking on the acrid smoke flooding the lower floor and spreading uncontrollably upstairs. All the fragrance bottles were destroyed, but now millions of dollars' worth of designer fashions were alight, and a renewed barrage of explosions was inevitable once the flames reached the countless bottles of Sambuca on the second floor. In many regards the warehouse was a tinderbox and once a serious fire took hold, it would be impossible to stop. For that reason, sprinklers had been fitted throughout the building…which Eddie had disconnected.

Chang, as the most senior of the Triad quartet, realised it was his responsibility to decide whether to continue or abort the mission. There was no sign of the ransom money, they'd encountered armed police and more could be hidden around the building, and more to the point, the whole damn place was on fire. The other thing Chang couldn't overlook is that Fong had ordered him into this death-trap, and they'd always hated each other.

"Let's get out here," he shouted, and led his men towards the nearest emergency exit. They were almost coughing themselves to a standstill when they finally tasted fresh air. Thankfully for them, such was the confusion amongst the police lines with officers being treated for trauma and frantic instructions being radioed to the fire department, nobody noticed them leaving the building. They slipped around the corner into Pacific Avenue where Fong was waiting for them nonchalantly. He tried not to smile when he noticed their clothes were singed.

"No money?" He asked lightly.

"What do you think?" Chang snapped. "The entire place is on fire!"

Fong nodded sympathetically and ushered them towards the nearby van. Once the quartet was inside, Fong shut the doors, slapped the side of the vehicle and it departed. Fong then returned to his Mercedes S-Class and awaiting driver. Not a word was exchanged as he assumed the rear seats and the car left the scene. He felt slightly guilty he'd condemned four men to death, but only slightly. As it happened, they'd all emerged alive. Thankfully for everyone concerned, their survival wasn't a catastrophe, it was merely unplanned.

"Maybe they didn't deserve to die," Fong reflected to himself.

The Mercedes headed towards the heart of Chinatown. Its journey, along with the remaining tenure of The Master, would be short.

As Fong was driven southbound along Stockton Street, three fire trucks with sirens screaming charged in the opposite direction. Within moments of them reaching the police lines, a scarlet Shelby Mustang 500GT screeched to a halt in their wake. From the driver's seat emerged the fire chief, who sidled across to their opposite number in the police department. The fire chief was approaching fifty, hard as nails, and tired of people remarking that she was a woman. She didn't bother shaking her opposite number's hand, or even acknowledging his presence, but simply stared at the flames and smoke billowing up the grand façade of the Mezzogiorno Warehouse.

"What the hell did you do?" She grumbled.

"Me?" The police chief complained. "My boys did nothing."

"No change there," she sighed. "Fire looks bad. What happened to the sprinklers?"

"Sprinklers?" The police chief replied. "What do I look like, a gardener?"

"No, a clown."

The deputy police chief coughed to attract her attention.

"Actually, he removed that outfit," he announced, trying to be helpful. His superior jabbed him in the ribs.

"Just get your part-time army out of here and let the professionals take over," the fire chief ordered. With a click of her fingers, hose reels were unfurled and within seconds, thousands of gallons of water were discharged into the fiery heart of the relentless blaze. However, much as she hated to admit it, the fire chief recognised the building was a lost cause before they'd even been summoned.

Inside the warehouse, department after department was reduced to ashes. Clothes, furniture, designer goods and soft furnishings were systematically destroyed. The atrium was a raging inferno with flames leaping from the lower floors to those above until even the offices on the top floor were gutted by the blaze. Desks caught light while any discarded papers on their surface only helped to fuel the inferno. Soon after, the door to the computer suite was breached and the banks of circuit boards and telecoms were melted beyond repair. In fact, nothing was spared in the wake of the remorseless blaze as it spread from floor to floor, with one exception, which was around five and half metres long and protected by a security device none of the building's occupants even knew existed.

Outside the warehouse, the fire chief watched her officers wage a losing battle against flames that were destroying everything within sight. She'd ordered the adjoining office building to be cleared, but nobody was inside, and the walls were thick enough to prevent the blaze spreading. The Mezzogiorno Warehouse, however, would be gutted from floor to ceiling, and the fire chief knew there was nothing they could do. However, properties could be repaired or rebuilt; what she couldn't replace was people. By now, she was aware the establishment was closed due to "a death in the family" but obtaining a list of personnel inside the building was impossible. She glared at the fire which had dared to occur on her watch and shook her head.

"There better not be anyone inside," she muttered.

In answer to her question, aside the five people unconscious in the basement, six more were yet to leave the warehouse.

$$* \qquad * \qquad *$$

The Mezzogiorno Warehouse burned.

And burned.

It continued to burn throughout the afternoon and all the firefighters could do was douse the building with water until the flames gave way to smoke and finally to ash. When the steam and haze cleared, it was apparent everything from street level to the roof had been gutted. Not a single gown, suit or fragrance would have survived. Everything in the store was destroyed. However, the warehouse was still standing; it had been built to last, which was crucial in a city ravaged and scarred by earthquakes.

Once the flames were out, rescue workers started the perilous task of looking for survivors, which all too often turned into the grim undertaking of salvaging bodies. There were no signs of either in what had once been the main entrance and atrium. The search moved to the basement, the only part of the building which hadn't been destroyed by the blaze as it rose from its source to the roof, gutting everything in its path. What the rescuers found sent shock waves across the city.

Even before their grisly discovery, police knew some kind of battle between rival gangs had unfolded at the warehouse. Triads were seen when officers entered the building, while the Mafia was almost certainly involved, given the property's ownership. The eight bodies in the basement confirmed those suspicions, with four deaths on each side. Seven were gunmen, but the eighth was a woman, and once police identified her, it became clear what triggered the carnage between the city's most feared criminal organisations.

Police soon realised San Francisco could be on the brink of the most destructive gang war it had ever seen. The murder of a Mafia boss's daughter was the spark that could trigger a wildfire of violence. However, in the hours that followed, the city was strangely quiet. Instead of Mafia and Triad gunmen terrorising the streets, both organisations retreated into their shells. As it turned out, the battles in the aftermath of the warehouse massacre were internal, and didn't involve bullets but politics. Once the dust had settled, there were two notable casualties.

On the subject of casualties, along with retrieving eight bodies from the basement, rescuers also found five survivors. All had been tranquillised and they woke at various intervals after being carried from the scene. One, who appeared to be a Mafia gunman, found himself in hospital under guard when he regained consciousness. He was recovering from a bullet wound, which intriguingly had already been treated when rescuers found him. Hospital doctors confirmed it probably saved him from bleeding to death, and the level of expertise shown in the surgery raised some eyebrows. It could only have been performed by someone who really knew their profession. However, police weren't as interested in the mystery medic's identity compared to what the wounded Mafia gunman might tell them about the mob, especially if it meant avoiding eight counts of murder.

From his hospital bed, Bianco faced a hideous dilemma. Out of loyalty, he could stay silent, but recognised he'd never walk the streets as a free man again. The alternative was betraying the Mafia and hoping the relocation and new identity which followed would be enough to buy him a few years, and maybe more.

While Bianco contemplated his fate, the other four survivors found themselves in custody, having woken in separate police stations. Romana's bodyguard was the first on his feet, by which point it was early evening. He was particularly unhelpful when detectives sought his account of that morning's events. He clearly derived perverse pleasure from frustrating their inquiries and taunting them with the fact he was under no obligation to stay unless they arrested him.

So they arrested him.

Romana's bodyguard then said nothing, at least until a disagreeably slick lawyer arrived, who advised him to say even less. Detectives recognised it would take a while to break him down, but the longer he was silent, the greater the risk he would be charged with the same eight murders that were also hanging over Bianco. Either one of them could stand trial, or maybe neither, as they both held useful information about the mob which could lead to more convictions, and just possibly, avoid further killings in the future.

While Romana's bodyguard and Bianco were potential goldmines of information, once they woke, the two security men found alongside them didn't appear so interesting. Neither had obvious Mafia connections, aside working in one of their buildings, and were employed through an agency. Both were home before breakfast the next morning. The guard who'd been darted in the computer suite was genuinely unable to provide anything of value. The other's account was hazy to say the least. He reckoned the building was under attack, but had no idea who was behind it, and the only person he'd come across was a lowly store assistant who appeared to know even less. While asking her questions, he recalled being darted, and then nothing more.

The store assistant also woke in custody, and was the last to do so. In the aftermath of the Mezzogiorno Warehouse massacre, it was inevitable mistakes would be made as police wrestled with such a complex and major incident. However, their greatest error was believing the store assistant was the least interesting of the five survivors. It was easy to see how the mistake was made; she had no position of authority, an unremarkable background and no criminal record or links. Her visa was valid, along with her passport...once police had found somebody who knew what a valid Slovenian passport looked like. However, the main reason she appeared above suspicion was her interview, which was nothing short of flawless.

Her account from opening the store to being darted in front of Romana and her bodyguard was detailed and convincing. She said they were ambushed by three intruders wearing white overalls and masks, making them impossible to identify. None spoke, and the smallest shot her with the tranquilliser pistol. The only thing she omitted from her account was that the dart was a blank, while the only thing she changed was the time she met the second guard, ensuring it was earlier that morning. Luckily, the guard's account was so flaky that her more lucid version seemed the only reliable one. However, before she could leave the police station, she still faced a major problem. Somehow, she had to explain what happened to Ian.

"So Romana's bodyguard threw him out," the detective confirmed. "Where is he now?"

"I don't know," she replied quietly.

"Has he tried to call?"

Martina paused and looked the kindly-faced policeman right in the eye.

"If you'd just learned your girlfriend was mixed up in the Mafia, would you see her again?"

The detective nodded sympathetically, for he already knew the answer. They had Martina's phone and nobody had rung except her sister and mother.

"You've no idea where he is?" The policeman asked, one final time.

"No," she replied, shaking her head. "I wish I did."

In that respect, she was telling the absolute truth. She desperately wanted to see him again but couldn't be certain where Ian was, if he was safe, or even if he was still alive.

*   *   *

After two days of chaos and turmoil, the Mezzogiorno Warehouse finally fell silent. It was the early hours of Tuesday and virtually all the emergency services had been withdrawn. Before that, they'd been swarming around frantically like bees in a hive. Without a list of who was inside the building, the search for survivors and fatalities continued throughout Sunday, into the night and into Monday morning. However, not a trace was found aside those recovered from the basement.

Detectives knew the warehouse was a crime scene. Eight people were confirmed dead and all the evidence pointed to a gang war that only ended when the building went up in flames. How the blaze began was a vital question that fire investigators had to answer. It was suspicious on three counts; first, how it started, second, why it spread so quickly, and third, why the building's safety measures failed to work. The answer to the final question was somebody had disconnected not only the main water supply to the sprinklers, but the auxiliary system. It had spread quickly due to the combustible nature of the store's products, especially the fragrances, liquors and ample supply of clothes. How it began was a large explosion timed shortly after midday by police at the scene. It all pointed to one inescapable conclusion; it was a blatant act of premeditated arson. With that conclusion, it was clear another crime had been committed, and police had even more work to do.

By Monday the search operation was being scaled down and a forensic examination of the charred remains on each floor was underway. Only the basement, which had been cleared of everything including the wrecked cars, was not crawling with personnel in white overalls, as their work there was already done with countless photographs taken and evidence logged. Everything pointed to a gun battle which claimed eight lives, but how the five unconscious survivors came to be in the alcove around the corner was a mystery. It was obvious other people had been involved, but it was unclear who they were. The police scout party had seen four armed Triads but identifying them from partial sightings either side of an explosion was impossible. Detectives already knew, with grim resignation, that suspects had fled the building without being caught. It was now their job to find them and it wouldn't be easy, hence they needed every last clue that could be salvaged from the smouldering ashes of the devastated building.

Police recognised more personnel were required to investigate the Mezzogiorno Warehouse massacre, not only at the scene, but elsewhere. Officers were swarming around Chinatown looking for the Triads seen inside the building. As was usually the case when organised crime was involved, finding anyone willing to talk was impossible.

The amount of staff required to deal with the investigation also had a side effect. Less serious crimes that would normally have attracted a reasonable amount of attention received very little at all. For example, thousands of dollars were stolen from various handbags on a tour bus at Twin Peaks, but negligible action was taken. Also, just before the warehouse massacre began, the Alcatraz ferry office was burgled. Two inexperienced officers were sent as it didn't seem a crucial case. The only description of the raiders was that they wore track suits and left in a Ford Edsel. Neither of the officers recognised the significance of the car. However, with time, detectives would fit the jigsaw pieces together and realise the same vehicle had been chased across the city and vanished in Chinatown...suspiciously near the Mezzogiorno Warehouse.

Back at the crime scene, by Monday afternoon, investigators reached the fourth floor where Marcus had left the getaway car. Amongst the debris they found something surprising. It was metallic, six metres long and three metres wide and left them baffled. However, they'd have to wait until the next day to uncover exactly what it was. By Monday evening the initial adrenaline that fuelled the emergency crews in the crucial hours following the massacre was draining away. Empty stomachs had to be filled, neglected families craved attention and tired eyes needed sleep. The evidence bags and magnifying glasses were stowed, the white overalls were hung up and the investigators went home, leaving the scene in the overnight care of two policemen who reckoned their biggest challenge would be staying awake through the boredom.

Now it was Tuesday morning – very early on Tuesday morning – and all was quiet, except one thing. Someone, somewhere, deep in the warehouse, was beating a wall with a hammer, as if trying to escape. The building was not so empty as police had suspected.

*   *   *

As the muffled hammering continued deep inside the warehouse, three miles away in her tiny flat, Martina couldn't sleep. It was a sultry night where the heat of the day was stubbornly refusing to leave. Yet it wasn't the temperature that kept her awake, nor was it the prospect of more police interviews. She wasn't a suspect but was a valuable witness. Testifying, if it came to that, would be tough, but that wasn't why she couldn't sleep. She was still awake because she was thinking about Ian.

Martina shuffled restlessly on her covers. Beside her bed, a phone rested on a table. She picked it up; the burst of light from its screen dazzled her eyes. Once they'd focused, she found Ian's number. Crucially, it wasn't listed in his name, but Mi Amore, which didn't interest police much when they trawled through her contacts.

Martina's index finger hovered over the screen. Should she call? It was four in the morning, so she decided against it, and instead sent a message. She then put the phone on the table and it went to sleep. She did not.

Much nearer the warehouse, in his hotel room at the Ritz-Carlton, The Seeker was also awake. His curious profession required unusual working hours and he only slept if he was tired. It meant his body clock was less reliable than a shoddy rail company.

He was sitting quietly at a desk, compiling his final report, but didn't believe what he was writing.

It was blissfully simple for The Seeker to list the Falmer Spiders as missing presumed dead. They'd entered a building, so had rival gangs, it had burned to the ground and they hadn't come out. He'd even gone to the bother of sneaking back into the ruins. When everyone else was dressed in white overalls and masks, it wasn't hard for a seasoned pro to blend into their ranks. Yet sifting through the debris, he'd found as much of interest as the police, which was nothing.

The Seeker reclined in the elegant chair beside the antique writing desk. He knew something was wrong. Declaring the Falmer Spiders dead would be easy and neat. Death normally brought grief and anguish to most, but to The Seeker, it was often a useful means of tidying things up. It wasn't a glowing end to his final job, but it was simple, and that's what concerned him. Life, from his experience, was never simple.

The Seeker was restless. He rose from the chair, put on his jacket, left his hotel room and walked into the night.

*   *   *

The hammering continued. Every couple of seconds, a fresh blow rang out through the warehouse's gutted remains. They were coming from the basement, but even someone standing inside it would struggle to identify the source.

More hammer blows echoed through the ghostly calm of the basement. They weren't quite audible outside the building, which meant the two policemen sulkily guarding what remained of the main entrance heard nothing. Finally, the hammering was accompanied by the sound of cracking cement. Dust was falling from one of the walls, specifically, the one in the storage area newer than the rest. Several breeze blocks were on the verge of giving way, until finally, half a dozen tumbled noisily to the ground.

Outside the warehouse, the policemen looked at each other and shrugged. Even at night, San Francisco was never quiet, which meant a muffled bang from an unknown source was unlikely to arouse their interest much.

In the basement, the dust cleared from the broken wall. A face appeared. It belonging to a thing with dreadlocks, gratefully filling its lungs with fresh air.

"That's better," Marcus sighed contentedly. "What the hell did you eat, Doug?"

"Crisps and chocolate," came the gruff reply behind him. "Same as you for the past two days."

With difficulty, but obvious relief, Marcus, and his cement-dusted dreadlocks, emerged from the cramped hideout behind the temporary wall. Sophie was next, and would've been first with pistols raised if there'd been any sign of trouble. However, all was quiet, except the groaning and coarse mutterings of Doug as he forced his ample frame through the hole in the wall. It was easier for Eddie, who came next, but he found to his displeasure that his hair was full of cement dust.

"That's why I said only put a tiny amount on the blocks," Doug reminded him.

"Any more and we'd have been hammering until dawn," Ian added, slotting himself through the gap and keeping his suit remarkably clean. Through the hole, he took delivery of rubbish sacks and two buckets whose contents were best left unmentioned. They were handed out by the final person to leave, who'd also been last into the hideout. They climbed through the gap and emerged with a suitcase. It contained fifteen million dollars.

"Let's get out of here," Claudia smiled.

Marcus, however, was frowning, which was unusual. What displeased him wasn't related to anything in the basement, but in fact, what was missing. Detectives had removed the bodies, both

229

wrecked cars and rescued all five survivors. They'd also taken something else.

"The cops have nicked my Lamborghini," he complained bitterly.

"It wasn't yours," Eddie reminded him.

"Possession is nine tenths of the law," Marcus replied, "and I stole it fair and square."

On the subject of cars, Claudia had to ensure the Edsel had been destroyed in the blaze. It had done them proud, she'd freely admit, but it linked them to the ferry office job and was a liability. She handed the job to Eddie and Marcus. The latter headed to the lifts and jabbed the button. Eddie shook his head and reminded his colleague there was no power. Indeed, if it wasn't for the torches on their phones, they wouldn't be able to see a thing, and if it wasn't for the Black Widows procedure of ensuring phones were fully charged before a job, they'd have run out of battery long ago.

"Brilliant," Marcus sighed. "Four flights of stairs."

He trudged towards the steps with Eddie in tow. Claudia then asked Sophie to check if the main entrance was clear and she vanished into the shadows. Ian was asked to dispose of the rubbish.

"What about me?" Doug asked, having not been assigned a task. Claudia didn't reply and simply threw a glance towards the two buckets from the hideout.

"Oh, not slopping out again," he groaned.

"You're the only one with past experience," Claudia smiled sweetly. The Welshman trudged off with his two pails of wretchedness, cursing under his breath. As he did so, four floors above, Eddie and Marcus had picked their way through the debris to where they'd left the Edsel. They were in for a surprise. Instead of a vehicle gutted beyond recognition, they found something metallic which was six metres long and three metres wide. It was basically a giant steel box which had been lowered from the ceiling. The panels were light and it seemed likely they could be folded to reduce the storage space required.

"Who put this here?" Marcus inquired, staring at the box in bewilderment. Eddie glanced at the chains above it, hanging from the ceiling.

"It must be a safety measure," he diagnosed, adding that if fire broke out, it would be lowered by sensors to protect the Lamborghini. He trudged through the ash towards the nearest wall and found a control panel.

"Here it is," he announced, adding that Marcus hadn't needed to rescue the Lamborghini as it would have been protected.

"Typical," Marcus sighed. "I could've still driven it away; it would have been fine here."

"So if we didn't rescue the sports car..." Eddie muttered, before his sentence tailed off. He stared at the getaway driver, who rolled his eyes in disbelief.

"Oh no," he groaned. "Will I never get rid of it?"

Eddie couldn't help smiling. He found an auxiliary power supply, flicked a switch, and slowly the box was raised. Quietly, inch by inch, it retreated towards the ceiling. It unveiled a pristine and completely undamaged Ford Edsel.

"Bollocks," said Marcus.

Back in the basement, Ian had rejoined Claudia while Doug waddled into view with two empty buckets.

"I'm not doing that again," he complained, putting them in the cleaning storeroom.

"I blame that wretched food," said Ian.

"That's all Eddie could find in the vending machines," Claudia replied.

"Vending machines," Ian muttered. "We're in the remains of a warehouse that sold the finest Italian food and wines and it didn't cross your mind to fill the hideout with those instead?"

Claudia's eyes narrowed and a frown crossed her face.

"Damn," she said to herself. However, she didn't have long to rue the mistake. Something caught her eye and immediately triggered a surge of adrenaline. The display above the freight elevator had sparked into life. First the number four was lit, then three, then two; the lift was heading their way. Sophie and her pistols were nowhere to be seen. Claudia looked around for her shotgun and realised to her horror it was propped beside their temporary wall and the lift would arrive before she could get there. She waved Ian and Doug against the nearest wall, then joined them, and braced herself for what would emerge from the lift.

When the answer came, she couldn't help laughing, to relieve the tension if nothing else. Marcus drove the Edsel out of the freight elevator with Eddie seated in the rear.

"How did it survive?" Ian asked.

"There was a metal box," Eddie replied, before explaining what else happened, including that he'd found a reserve power supply for the lifts.

"Just as well. We could hardly leave the car here," Ian observed.

"No," Marcus sighed. "We couldn't, could we?"

Claudia put the ransom and her shotgun in the Edsel's trunk. She asked Ian and Doug to guard the car park shutters and raise them when she gave the signal. However, she couldn't risk leaving the warehouse until she knew what was outside. She'd asked Sophie to check if the coast was clear but heard nothing from her, which meant she'd have to investigate.

Claudia climbed the stairs. The first thing she noticed was the ash, which hadn't been present in the basement. Arriving on the main shop floor, she realised just how much destruction had been caused. Everything was gutted and the scene was unrecognisable. It was hard to get her bearings, especially in the dark, with only the faint torch on her phone available. She pondered ringing Sophie to ask where she was, and if she was okay. However, Claudia had total faith in her, and knew if Sophie was lying in wait or creeping up on someone, she wouldn't appreciate a phone call. Instead, Claudia picked her way towards the main entrance. It seemed there wasn't a soul in the world anywhere near her, but then she felt the hand. It came from nowhere and was wrapped around her mouth, stifling any attempt to scream. The other arm was clamped around

232

her waist to prevent her escaping. Claudia turned with dread to see the face of her captor.

"Boo," Sophie whispered. Once she was satisfied Claudia wouldn't react, she released her grip, then placed a finger to her lips. Claudia knew better than to ask Sophie to explain herself and remained silent. Sophie crept towards the main entrance, which was a few steps away, and crouched on the floor. The distant glare from the street lights outside briefly flickered on the metal of the tranquilliser pistol. Claudia held her breath. Sophie took forever to pull the trigger, but knew when you had the element of surprise, it was vital to be accurate. Finally, a pair of darts were fired in quick succession. Outside the main entrance, the faint sound of groaning was followed by two thuds as the policemen on guard slumped to the sidewalk. Sophie then climbed off the floor and walked a few paces until standing on the threshold. She turned back to Claudia.

"You can come out now," said Sophie.

Claudia wasted no time in leaving the warehouse and ran down the street towards the car park shutters. She gave the Frisco Spiders' secret knock. Within moments, the shutters were raised, then lowered once the Edsel emerged from the basement, its paintwork sparkling under the street lights. Claudia and Sophie climbed aboard and the car vanished into the night.

Watching the spectacle, hidden in the shadows opposite the warehouse, The Seeker shook his head in disbelief. With a warm grin, he returned to his hotel, then went to sleep.

*   *   *

Dawn was breaking over the Golden Gate Bridge. The six lanes across it were quiet ahead of the morning rush that would soon follow. In light traffic, the Edsel slipped quietly across the mile-long structure. Inside the car it was quieter still. There was no sense of jubilation, just fatigue mixed with relief. The most obvious smile was displayed by Ian; he'd received Martina's phone message, which made his heart soar. He'd felt uneasy finding no trace of her after leaving the hideout, but then again, if everything had gone to plan, Martina would no longer be in the warehouse. The message confirmed she was safe and Ian couldn't wait to see her. Hopefully they'd go wine tasting, just as he'd planned before his former colleagues accepted his invitation for breakfast...and stayed for two days, triggered a gang massacre, extorted fifteen million dollars and reduced a building to ashes. In that respect, Ian was hopeful lightning wouldn't strike twice, but you never knew with the Frisco Spiders. After the wine tasting a romantic meal would follow, and if the mood was right, he might suggest nightcaps at the Ritz-Carlton. After all, his booking only lasted one more night, and it would be a shame to waste such a sumptuous double room.

As for the rest of gang, they still had much to do, but after nearly two days sealed in their hideout, it was nice to taste fresh air. They'd been kept alive by the air drifting down the ventilation shaft designed to expel gasses from the fridges that hadn't yet been installed. The shaft was too narrow to climb, but wide enough to keep them breathing. It also allowed the noise of the sirens and the chaos of the blaze above them to penetrate down to their ears. It had been terrifying, but nobody wanted to be the first to crack. Claudia reckoned if one of them broke down, others would follow. Hence, they shared the food and played games on their phones to distract themselves. They also slept as best they could, which became easier as fatigue finally overwhelmed them. As a result their sleeping patterns were shot to pieces, but that mattered little to Claudia, who later that day would catch a transatlantic flight that would leave her jet-lagged anyway. In twenty-four hours, she'd be home. That made her feel nearly as good as the fifteen million dollars in the Edsel's trunk.

The 1950s sedan pulled off the road as the Golden Gate Bridge gave way to the greenery of Marin County, across the bay from San Francisco. The car eased to a halt in a quiet corner of the H. Dana Bower Rest Area at Vista Point. Eddie, Sophie, Ian and

Doug stretched their legs before assuming a nearby picnic bench. Marcus leaned on the driver's door while Claudia hitched herself onto the vehicle's hood and drank in the dawn. The red cables of the iconic bridge were catching the first rays of sunshine. The sea was becoming a deeper blue with every moment, while the orange glow in the eastern sky was spreading further west. It was a beautiful scene.

"Maybe 'Frisco wasn't such a bad idea," Ian conceded.

"It's what you make of it," Claudia replied.

"That's the American way," added Marcus. "America helps those who help themselves."

"And we've helped ourselves to fifteen million bucks," Eddie observed.

"Result," Doug smiled, "and once I get my share, I'm sticking my arse on a beach."

"That'll leave quite a mark," Sophie observed.

Claudia would've happily watched the sun rising over the Golden Gate Bridge until the rush hour had been and gone, but there was work to do. Fifteen million dollars was sitting in the Edsel, along with firearms. To spread the risk, she'd ride with Marcus to the secret armoury to return the weapons. Meanwhile, Eddie, Sophie and Doug would catch the first bus of the morning and deliver their loot to The Maid. Given the sum involved, Claudia reckoned he wouldn't mind being woken early. She also trusted her colleagues with the ransom; despite explaining the facts of life to Eddie before the blaze, Claudia reckoned his loyalty was still beyond doubt. As for Doug, he would surely overpower anyone who tried snatching their highly valuable luggage, and if he was stupid enough to make off with it himself, she had every faith Sophie would shoot him. One way or the other, the cash would reach The Maid. The Frisco Spiders – minus Ian who'd make his own way to the Ritz-Carlton – would then meet at their motel, pack their bags and leave. Soon after, they'd check into another hotel to throw potential pursuers off the scent, but they had no reason to believe anyone was watching them.

After all, until that point, The Seeker had kept himself in the shadows, often literally.

It was agreed that Eddie, Sophie, Marcus and Doug would stay in town until the money laundering was complete. Claudia would fly home later that day and would be driven to the airport by Marcus, who planned to leave the Edsel roughly where he'd found it. Given that its parking was valid for three more days, he figured if he restored the original paintwork and registration, there was a good chance its owner would collect it and be none the wiser about the car's recent adventures.

The sun was now climbing in the sky. All of the Frisco Spiders had something to do, which also applied during their unscheduled trip to the warehouse. Claudia recognised everyone played their part; Eddie's technical knowledge saved them on several occasions. Sophie was a vital member of the team, which had been proved many times. Ian, albeit reluctantly, had provided invaluable help and probably saved the life of the wounded Mafia gunman. As for Doug, they couldn't have built the temporary wall without him, rendering their escape impossible. Then again, it was only thanks to Marcus and his driving skill that they reached the warehouse at all. As for her own contribution, Claudia reckoned destroying the police sirens with her skilful shooting bought just enough time to devise an escape plan, which had worked.

"We all did our share," she reflected out loud.

"That's what good teams do," Eddie agreed.

"Not bad, given there's only six of us," added Doug.

"Eight," Claudia corrected him.

"Eight?" Ian replied, looking baffled. He assumed Martina was the seventh member, but as for the eighth, he was clueless.

"Isn't it obvious?" Claudia asked. "It's the car."

"Oh, the car," Marcus sighed, leaning against it with grudging affection. "How could I forget the car?"

"And we came out alive," said Claudia. At that point, her thoughts inevitably turned to her father, who hadn't been so fortunate when they'd been cornered in the barn. She'd promised herself something good had to come from his death, and in the Californian sunshine with fifteen million dollars secured, she knew it had been achieved. However, something else had resolutely refused to leave her mind, which had been there long before losing her father. Claudia wasn't accurate enough to compete at the Olympics and wasn't quite stunning enough to be an actress or model. She'd been searching for something at which she was truly world class, and with a sudden feeling of unease, she realised what it was.

Claudia was remarkably good at being bad.

*   *   *

"And that's how it happened," The Seeker concluded.

The Maid had listened avidly to his account; it helped to explain why he'd taken delivery of fifteen million dollars. The two men, dressed impeccably, occupied the secluded corner booth at Always Maxed Out. The Maid had arrived as soon as the venue opened that morning; he had work to do. He hadn't appreciated being woken by the Frisco Spiders ringing his doorbell, but forgave them after looking inside their case.

"It's a remarkable story," he reflected. "It seems you can't underestimate Claudia."

"A dangerous woman," The Seeker warned. An uneasy silence drifted across the table. It was finally broken when The Maid offered his guest another cup of Earl Grey.

"What will you do about her gang?"

"Officially they're missing presumed dead," The Seeker replied.

"You're prepared to leave it that way?"

"Depends if they're likely to do more harm."

Silence returned as The Seeker stirred his tea with elegant precision.

"I'm not concerned about the four young gentlemen," he continued. "I'd expect them to join the Black Widows' amnesty and drift into obscurity."

"Who wouldn't with a share of fifteen million dollars?"

"Quite, especially if you're presumed dead."

"What about the two ladies?"

The Seeker was poised to taste his tea, but hesitated on hearing the question. He carefully set the cup back on its saucer.

"Neither will join the amnesty," he sighed, adding that he understood Claudia was poised to slip back into Britain to attend her father's funeral.

"She's smart enough not to get caught," said The Maid. "I guess the question is what she'll do next."

"Indeed. I hope she doesn't drift back into crime, especially as she's alarmingly good at it," The Seeker reflected. The two men looked at each other gravely, but soon began to smile.

"Would you like breakfast?" The Maid inquired.

"That would be lovely."

"It's my treat," smiled The Maid. "I've just come into some money."

"How nice for you."

Both men ordered scrambled eggs on toast with salmon. They'd just started buttering the toast when The Seeker returned to events at the warehouse.

"What's truly remarkable is the gang pulled this off with a double agent in their ranks."

"So you said," nodded The Maid.

"Many try to infiltrate the Black Widows. Only the best succeed," observed The Seeker. He added security services needed moles inside the organisation, not so much to secure convictions, but to raise the alarm if something really damaging was looming. Awkwardly, to avoid detection, double agents often participated in criminal activity. However, if they maintained their cover they could provide useful intelligence, especially if they rose into the organisation's senior ranks.

"Do you think the rest of the gang knew anything?" The Maid asked. His companion shook his head.

"I doubt if the others have the slightest clue Sophie's working for MI5."

The End

About the author:

Warwick Payne spent a decade in newspapers and is former chief reporter of the *Hampshire Chronicle*. Winning regional and national awards, he cut his teeth writing university, pub and hotel guides.

His debut book, *The Portland Contract*, was released by Olympia Publishers in 2013. This was followed by *Always Maxed Out* on Amazon Kindle Direct and Create Space in 2015. His third book, *The Frisco Spiders*, came out in 2017.

He left newspapers in 2012 on being offered a role in Southampton City Council's cabinet and has served as its deputy leader.

His interests include local live music, cycling, golf, real ale, classic cars and, of course, writing. He lives in Woolston, Southampton, with his wife, Louise - who is also a former news and music journalist - and their daughter, Tabitha.

By the same author:

The Portland Contract

Oliver Dart wanted a quiet life in the West Country. He isn't going to get it...

An author of children's books, his past as a national crime reporter catches up with him when a former colleague is murdered and he inherits a story that could be the scoop of the decade. He also acquires something else... her eleven-year-old son, Kieran, who believes that Oliver is his father.

Despite being a children's author he has no idea how youngsters 'work' and his life is turned upside down. Kieran is determined to find his mother's killer and urges Oliver to come out of retirement to finish the story. So begins a frantic chase around the West Country to crack the conspiracy.

Plunged into car chases and pursued by guards while charging towards iconic landmarks such as the Tamar Bridge, the unlikely duo has no time for formal introductions. Instead, Oliver and Kieran must learn to trust each other in the face of constant danger. This will not be easy, especially as they're still not sure if they're father and son.

What is clear is that neither will be safe until they unravel The Portland Contract.

Always Maxed Out

If you had a credit card with no limit, what would you buy?

Maxine Bridger lives in fear of her bank statement. She is addicted to coffee, magazines, cigarettes and Italian dresses. Her working day is spent in a dowdy shoe shop, far from the career she craves in fashion design.

She shares a Brighton flat with two women. One of them, Cat, would be a music star if only she could only play the guitar, and a model if she could only stay off the bacon sandwiches. The property's owner, Heather, is a financial wizard. Yet when she loses her job, her life is plunged into turmoil.

Heather's former employer, Moneymax Credit International, is on the verge of launching its new service for millionaire clients. The Infinity Card, as it is known, has one major selling point...limitless credit.

Naturally, it really shouldn't fall into the hands of wage slaves and their unemployed landlord. To make matters worse, if these women chanced upon an Infinity Card, they'd have very different ideas on how it should be used.

If you could have anything you ever wanted, what would you have? Maxine may have to ask this question, and decide if she can afford the price.

Printed in Great Britain
by Amazon